SHADOW

SHADOW

Jenny Moss

SCHOLASTIC PRESS / NEW YORK

Library of Congress Cataloging-in-Publication Data

Moss, Jenny
Shadow / by Jenny Moss. — 1st ed.
p. cm.
Summary: When Shadow, whose job all her life has been to stay close to the young queen
and prevent her prophesied death at the age of sixteen, fails in her task and the castle is
thrown into chaos, she escapes along with a young knight, embarking upon a journey that
eventually reveals her true identity.
ISBN: 978-0-545-03641-2
[1. Fairy tales.   2. Imposters and imposture — Fiction.   3. Kings, queens, rulers,
etc. — Fiction.]   I. Title.
PZ7.M8533Sh 2010
[Fic] — dc22
2009014209

10   9   8   7   6   5   4   3   2   1   10   11   12   13   14

Printed in the U.S.A.   23
Reinforced Binding for Library Use
First edition, April 2010

The text type was set in Granjon Roman.
The display type was set in Captain Kidd.
Book design by Lillie Mear

For The Table at St. Agnes Academy

Chapter One

I stood at the queen's tall arched window. A blast of cold wind chilled my face, but I kept looking. I wanted to be out there, not just in the green grass of the queen's gardens, but out farther, beyond gray and stone, out into a land I had never set foot upon. We were up so high in our untouchable castle on the hill that the dark green treetops looked like branches strewn about the ground.

Behind me, the ladies-in-waiting dressed the young queen in rustling blue silk and brushed her long blond hair. I glanced back at their tight circle, wondering what it felt like to be a part of their shared secrets and whispered words.

But they looked at me with suspicion even now as they giggled and gossiped. *Traitor, traitor, traitor*, they seemed to say, eyes on me. Or perhaps, *witch, witch, witch*.

"Close the window, Shadow," the queen scolded me from her warm place by the fire. If there was a witch amongst us, it would be she. She was the one with the strange visions, which she had learned to hide from the others. But I knew when one filled her mind. Fear always flashed in her eyes for just a moment, enough time to be noticed by one who watched for it. And how could I help but see it, when I was forced to stay by her side, always.

One of her hands encircled her neck as she gazed in the glass Lady Fay held before her. Her eyes said what her lips did not. She was perfect: wide slanting eyes, with just a touch of blue, like a clear sky at the peak of day, and cheeks naturally pink and plump, and skin like a white pearl.

I did not act as the queen bade me, savoring the moment of my disobedience. But I knew the rebuke would soon come.

I had lived out my almost-sixteen years in the queen's room. A large room, but too small to be one's whole world. We were not allowed out *there* often. For the queen's life was in danger.

My head jerked back, and I felt a quick stab of pain at my scalp. Ingrid, the most gentle of the gentle ladies, was yanking my black hair. "Go rub Her Highness's tender feet, you lazy girl." She pushed me out of the way and shut the shutters against the cold, plunging us into an eerie dark, with the only light from flickering candles and the roaring fire.

The queen kicked off her shoe. It flew into the air and bumped against a tapestry covering the drab wall.

I did as I was ordered, sitting where I was told, on the rushes covering the cold, gritty stone. I was too close to the fire. The heat seared my back, and I began to sweat in my coarse red dress despite the coldness of the room. The smoke caught in my throat and made my eyes water.

I picked up the queen's dainty white foot. I watched her looking at herself in the glass. She rested her fingers on her forehead and then swept back her hair. In that moment, she was oblivious to all of us. If I were she, I would detest all the hands fussing over me all the time, soaping up arms and hooking hooks and cleaning out ears.

She presented a hand to Hilda, the youngest lady, as if it were a gift. Hilda glanced at me as she used a silver file to clean the queen's nails. "Stop staring," she said, kicking me in the back.

I looked up to Queen Audrey's smirk.

"She's always staring at everyone, Your Majesty," said Hilda. "It will not do."

The other ladies laughed while the queen put down her jewel-encrusted mirror and fingered her blue silk dress.

Fay, the slyest of the ladies, brushed out the royal hair with a gleam in her eye. She was the one you had to watch out for. She tricked you into confidences and then whispered them to the other ladies behind your back. Of course, she didn't trick me. Not anymore. I was rarely spoken to, except when I was told what to do.

I was the queen's shadow. I could not remember a day when I was not at her side. The three old men in gray hooded capes, which strangled their wrinkled necks and flowed down to the floor, ordered me to stay with her at all times. I knew they hoped a flaming arrow flying her way would pierce and burn me, not her. As if I would not move aside to save myself instead.

My role was not completely clear to me, nor to anyone. It was established long ago and no one dared question it now. I wasn't a servant, really. I had no list of daily chores. I was not lady, cook, maid, laundress, nor spinster.

But why try to riddle out my place here? I had long ago given that up. Who knew the aims of three old men?

They wanted me to be afraid of them, but I was not. They would watch me as if they didn't trust me, especially the oldest one. Eldred was the one who told the others what to do. He was the one who would occasionally speak to me.

It was a lonely life, but I accepted it. I might not be a queen or a gentle lady or even a saucy servant girl who had a real cot to sleep on, but I knew none of that mattered.

So I would empty chamber pots, dig out grunge from under dirty toenails, and endure slapped cheeks and sharp words — but I knew what I wanted. I lived for a hope: One day I would leave the queen's dreary castle and venture out into the world. Unlike before, I would successfully escape. Only, it was impossible at present. *Especially* now.

The wooden door swung open as if it were a leaf blown by the wind. The burly knight who guarded the queen's room every morning tapped his spear and announced the arrival of a visitor. It was the boy knight. He lived at the castle and visited her daily.

On that particular day, he was dressed in sea green, from tunic to toe. He stared at her with eyes the color of morning. He looked more like her brother than one who wished to marry her.

There, he was foolish. She would never be allowed to marry one below the rank of prince. And although Sir Kenway was the son of a once powerful lord, he was not royalty. *He is barely a knight*, I thought, smiling to myself. Usually, a squire doesn't become a knight until the age of twenty-one. Sir Kenway was only sixteen.

Queen Audrey stood quickly, pushing us all away. I fell backward, dangerously close to the fire. My foot caught on the hem of Hilda's gold gown, and she tumbled with me, her legs and arms flying. She pushed herself up and whacked me on the head with a fat hand, saying, "Stupid girl!"

I looked up into the eyes of Sir Kenway. His hand was out for me to take. I wanted to refuse it, for I did not like help, but I had a strong desire to feel his touch, my hand in his. I hid these feelings, or so I thought.

The queen fussed, "Kenway!"

He turned his head. I stood on my own.

When he looked back at me, I raised my chin. *Let him go run to her.*

The queen smiled at him. He took her small hands into his. The ladies bustled around, trying not to look.

But I looked. I watched their shadowy forms. He reached

forward for a strand of her hair and twisted it in his fingers. Their eyes locked.

I felt the sting of the *slap* on my cheek. Pain shot through my neck.

"Ingrid!" scolded Sir Kenway. He was beside me now, his hand gripping Ingrid's wrist.

I stared into her furious eyes. *I do not fear you. You cannot hurt me.* And she stared right back at me.

"Not necessary to treat her so," Sir Kenway said.

"It is just Shadow," Ingrid said, tossing a confused look his way before glaring back at me.

"Yes," he said, nodding. "But she's done no harm."

Just Shadow, he had agreed. He so easily dismissed those not of his rank. I leaned in and said very quietly so only he could hear, "But am I a witch, sir?"

His face paled. I had heard Sir Kenway was afraid of nothing — except for witches and spirits. I believed in neither, despite the whispers that a witch lived in the castle years ago. Sometimes I did feel as if something was watching me, something not seen. But if I could not see it, why worry? For what could be done?

"Kenway." The queen's pretty face was flushed red. "Why do you bother with my shadow?"

"The girl is as conniving and sneaky as a spy," said Ingrid, her jaw set. "She cannot be trusted."

And with those words, all concern slid from Sir Kenway's face and doubt took its place. He too suspected me. And this brought me a pain I didn't want to feel. Thus, I buried it.

Ingrid began pushing me out of the room.

The guard blocked our way. He said nothing and, indeed, wouldn't even look at Ingrid, but he would not let me leave. She scrunched her eyes at him. Her huge chest moved up and down as she took a breath, but she acquiesced, as I knew she would. She clapped her hands, and all the ladies bustled out the door after her.

I was left with the queen and Sir Kenway. I went to the window and cracked open a shutter. But I couldn't keep my eyes off of them, off of him.

The queen took her seat on her velvet-cushioned chair by the fire, and with a wave of her hand, gestured for Sir Kenway to sit opposite her. He sat on the backless bench, leaning forward with his elbows balanced on his knees and his hands clasped together. Such grace in his movements, tenderness in his eyes.

He treated her with a certain gentleness I didn't understand. I attributed it to her beauty, which I conceded was . . . there.

Her hair was so smooth it was like the finest silk. I touched my own thick mass, trying to slide my fingers through it, only to find tangles and knots.

Was it only beauty they saw in each other? The perfection of their skin, the easy blueness of their eyes, the hair entwining his finger a moment ago the color of his own? Were they in love with beauty itself, or each other's beauty, or even their own beauty, perhaps?

And me? Why would my eyes not leave them?

I knew their beauty might bind them to each other, but no beauty would bind me. Nothing could hold me in place.

The door burst open. Sir Kenway shot up as if he had been doing something wrong.

It was the oldest of the three old men. Eldred. The queen's guard glanced at Sir Kenway, so I knew he'd reported that the two of them were alone. No one thought of me as a chaperone. I was just a shoe that always had to be on her foot.

Eldred was a formidable figure, tall and gaunt. He had

served Queen Audrey's father. He took in the room quickly: me by the window, the queen and Sir Kenway by the fire. He jerked his head. Sir Kenway left. The queen dropped her gaze. She always lost her haughtiness around Eldred.

The guard closed the door as Eldred left, leaving the queen and me alone. She smiled a little and turned a circle, sending her blue gown billowing out like a flower.

I peered through the cracked shutters of the side window and watched until Sir Kenway appeared below.

He glanced up, his eyes seeking . . . seeking . . . I stepped back into the shadows. It couldn't be me he sought, and I wouldn't let him see me looking.

The ladies flew back through the door, surrounding the queen and giggling with her.

"Old Eldred threw him out again," said the queen.

"He is only concerned for your safety," said Fay, with a strange smile. "Your birthday is soon, Your Majesty."

"Oh," said the queen, waving her hand to dismiss the idea. "We won't speak of that, Fay."

Fay nodded, but her eyes showed she was thinking of it still.

It was prophesied the queen would die before her sixteenth birthday. Twenty days away.

Chapter Two

I slipped by the guard. He opened one eye and nodded. Crafty Sennick was rarely on duty because of his age, but Eldred allowed him to watch the queen's door once every other full moon. More guards were posted farther down the hall and at the various entrances and exits, so Queen Audrey was quite safe. She actually liked the old guard, mostly because he looked the other way when Sir Kenway visited.

Sennick and I had a pact: He would, at times, let me pass and I would not reveal he dozed on duty. Of course, when he slept, I left without his permission.

But I could not go far. The private stairs to the left led to a secluded garden perched on a high cliff. My sole escape was over the edge, so not one I would ever use. But when the unkindness of those in the castle bore down too greatly upon me, I'd found that being outside, particularly if I was alone, lessened the pressure in my chest. I was grateful for my rare interludes in the night air.

The queen was afraid of heights and so never visited the small garden. And its unreachable position meant no guards were needed between her chamber and the outside door. Down the steps I went, eager to be out of the stuffy castle.

The garden was cold and quiet. I snuggled my cheek against the warmth of the fur-lined collar of the queen's cape. It was a risk taking it from her wardrobe. The last time I had done so, she had worn the garment the next day. When her ladies had slipped the luxurious cloth over her royal shoulders, the queen had caught the scent of "some wild animal." She'd flung it away from her, not realizing it was my unwashed smell from the night before still clinging to the fabric.

I breathed in the night, taking the air deep into my lungs. When I was a child, I'd pretend the air was healing magic. I would capture it with one big gulp and take it back in with me to the queen's crowded chamber. That air trapped inside me would melt any cruel words before they reached me. That pretense helped me through many dark and lonely evenings.

I was strong, but others wearied me, *especially* the queen, with her changing moods and tantrums. I knew, probably more than anyone, the damage done to her by the visions haunting her day and night. I wondered what she saw that disturbed her so; the images seemed to be pushing her toward madness. Being closed up in the castle only worsened her condition, I thought.

Queen Audrey did not wander out much. An occasional festival or tournament was held, but those were infrequent. More common were her small picnics, held on the green yard inside the castle walls. I would lie on the grass with no blanket between me and the Earth, absorbing its peaceful spirit, and shut out the royal gaiety, which didn't include me anyway.

I sat down on the stone rim of a large fountain in the garden. Very little water dwelled in its circular basin. I looked up at the statue in the middle, wondering, as I always did, who she was. Perhaps she was just the artist's muse. He had been in love with her, I thought. That reverence could be seen in the graceful hands, the delicate arms, the beauty of the cold dress, its drapes lovingly etched out of stone.

Alas, she no longer wore a head. But her long thick hair still rippled down her gray back.

I had always thought it curious she was facing the valley, not the castle.

Her arms were out, palms up, cupped, as if she were collecting the rain from the sky. An odd need swept my heart: I wanted to wrap my fingers around hers. I stood on the fountain's edge and reached up. I felt a little shock at the ice-cold of the water pooled in the lady's stone hand.

I stumbled and fell back. I knew not why it felt like such a loss.

I turned my back on the headless lady, looking out onto the moonlit valley. *Ah, if I could only go out there. Or even just return to the garden whenever I wished.*

Such a little thing, to be able to step outside to see the moon or the sun when one wanted. But I did not have that little thing, so it seemed very great.

Chapter Three

It was the afternoon. We sat at the window, with welcome sunlight pouring in upon us. I closed my eyes, feeling the warmth seep into me. I could not explain it, but I thought of my mother and began to write.

The tutor — a gangly man with small elflike ears and a giant's nose — peered over the queen's shoulder. Her page was marred by ugly ink blots.

I looked down at my own perfect letters. I enjoyed writing. Perhaps it was because I hardly heard the sound of my own voice. My written words were my voice, speaking, singing, living a life beyond thick stone walls and forced duty. I was there on the page.

I sprinkled powder across the parchment to dry the ink and then shook the paper.

A cool breeze picked up the powder and blew it into the queen's pert little nose. Out came a dainty sneeze.

Queen Audrey grabbed the paper from my hand, crumpled it up, and threw it out the window.

The tutor gave me a grave look. After all, I had provoked Her Majesty by writing so well when she could not. I knew better. Still, I was disappointed. The words flying out the window were about my mother. It didn't matter. I would find the paper later when — if — we were allowed out for a walk.

I had never known my mother. Her soul flew to the heavens the moment I fluttered my eyes open for the first time. The gentle ladies tittered to the queen that my mother's breath had left her at the sight of me. With my eyes a strange blue and my hair as black as a pagan's robes, they whispered I was touched by something not of this earthly world.

What silliness these women engaged in when all they had to occupy themselves with were hair and clothes and boy knights. But sometimes, I wondered if they were right. I, too, felt I was different from them. I tried to ignore the feeling, though, for why should I fret about something I could not know or change?

They also gossiped about my father. Not known, they said. A mystery. Hilda even taunted me that he was one of the three old men.

Could it be Larcwide — the plump, silver-tongued one? Or sour-faced Raeden? Surely not Eldred himself?

Not possible, I thought. *How can I be the queen's shadow if my father is one of her advisers?*

The queen jumped at the loud knock on the door.

It was Fyren and his servant — the only ones I liked in the castle.

Fyren was a great man, the regent of our kingdom, Deor, acting as ruler for the queen until she was old enough herself to do so. And that she would be on her sixteenth birthday. He was the dead king's own cousin, the king's only living relative besides the queen, his daughter.

The ladies said evil things about the regent's interest in me, but none of them were true. He was almost twenty years older than I, and never overly familiar.

I liked to watch him, ordering around the brave knights. He could even silence old Eldred, who would stare at the regent with cold, colorless eyes, but always do as he was told. Fyren never yelled. He was just obeyed.

He had a servant boy, Piers, who attended him. The boy

had no one to care for him, to watch over him. He was thin and had a scared look to him, his gray eyes darting about as if no one were to be trusted.

But I cared for the boy, as if he were a younger brother.

I thought of the night I found him ill. It was last year, after Sir Kenway had been knighted. A few hours before light, I sneaked out of the queen's chamber, past the slumbering guard, with only my rolled-up wool blanket in my arms. It had been deliciously easy and freeing to slip out while the inhabitants of the castle slept off their loud and long celebrating from the night before.

I stopped to tell Piers good-bye. As I watched him toss and turn feverishly on his cot, I knew I couldn't leave him in such a state. So I took a chance and made my way to the kitchen. The cook was in a foul temper, even more so than usual. While the castle slept, she still cleaned.

The next day's soup simmered over the fire. I begged her for a bowl, lying that it was for the queen.

She eyed me as if she knew the truth and pinched my arm to see if I would give it up. When I did not, she slopped some of the clear bubbling liquid into a wooden bowl and thrust it into my hands.

After I spooned the hot soup into Piers's mouth and covered him up with my only blanket, I left him. The temptation was too great. I had myself to think of.

I had been quickly caught. I did not even reach the outer wall that time. I was punished, of course, but the punishment was forgettable. Only guilt over leaving Piers lingered, as well as the sad knowledge I would do it again.

Off to Fyren's side, Piers stared at me. I smiled. He rewarded me with a quick nod. He knew me for what I was. I was a friend, but for myself first. I guessed he was the same.

Out of the pocket of Fyren's cape popped the reddest apple I had ever seen. The queen burst out of her seat in happiness. But Fyren presented the apple to me with a flourish.

"Go ahead. Eat," he said, his eyes pulling me in. He gave me a quick, mischievous smile.

I felt drawn to Fyren. He was consistent in his manner, not fickle, never concerned with pleasing anyone. And he had a playful spirit, which both Piers and I enjoyed.

The queen glared at him now. Fyren bowed slightly.

He was the queen's only blood relative. They detested each other.

"What is it that you want, Fyren?" she asked, her voice quivering with anger.

The apple was so sweet. I took small bites, trying to make it last. I had not eaten an apple since last year, when Fyren had given me one from the first harvest. The royal gardens still overflowed with pears and plums, and cauliflower and cabbage, while the rest of the fields in the kingdom slowly died. No one understood why this was so.

This apple was also fresh. It tasted of rich soil and sweet rain. And of the delicate coos of the doves nested in the tree, and of the laughter of the workers in the grove, and of the sun shining down on all of them.

No one would believe these things. I would not share them anyway. These were my feelings, my connection to the Earth and sky.

I called Piers over. We munched on the apple together.

"Lord Llewyn desires an audience with you, my queen," Fyren said. He watched her as carefully as I watched him.

He was a vain man, with dark wavy hair and a lovely nose. His chin was prominent and bearded. He loved his capes. I recognized the one he wore: soft black wool lined with ermine. He must be having a good day. It was his favorite.

The queen rolled her eyes. "Not another lord. What does this one want with me?" Then she turned on Piers. "Would you stop smacking there, boy? Fyren, why do you bring the filthy thing in here?"

I drew up, ready to defend, but Piers's hand was on my arm. "Don't, Shadow," he whispered. "You'll get slapped."

I bit my tongue for his sake, for Piers did not like to see me punished. But I seethed inside. I could not explain the anger that came upon me when Piers was mistreated. I just knew I felt it most keenly.

Fyren's mouth twitched. He glanced at me.

"Do you not remember, Your Majesty?" he asked the queen, still looking at me. "What the lord wanted?"

She turned on him. "Are you talking to me or my shadow?"

I could not help but speak. "The lord's lands are in dispute."

The queen's eyes bore into mine, then widened with some malicious delight. She looked at Piers. A wave of panic rippled through me, for she knew my one weakness.

I stepped forward. "Are you so stupid you cannot remember the concerns of your own lords?"

Her mouth dropped open with shock. It *was* a bold thing to say to a queen, and made worse because it was true. Still, I was surprised at the fury distorting her face. She lunged at me and came up with her hands full of my black hair. The apple dropped and rolled.

Piers jumped toward me. "No, no," I told him, while trying to push her away.

Fyren pulled her off so quickly, she didn't get much of me. "Are you hurt?" he asked, smoothing down my hair. My scalp stung, but I had a thick mane. I could afford the loss.

"I hate you!" she raged at me.

I was breathing quickly, but a surge of life flowed through me. I was more than a shadow, I told her with my eyes.

I blinked. The room was filled with the queen's court, alerted by her screams. Ingrid and the gentle ladies rushed to her side and led her to the bed. There, they pulled my devilish hair from her white, angelic hands. The queen's guard hustled the tutor out.

Piers picked up the apple, wiping it on his shirt. He held it out to me.

"Thank you, Piers," I said, still breathing hard. "But it is yours."

The regent smiled at me. "You remember Lord Llewyn, Shadow?"

I nodded. "He's a large man." I raised my hands, flattening out my fingers. "With hands like paws."

He gave me a long look. "You are the doe I saw at dawn yesterday. Her eyes were wide and watching." Glancing at the queen being comforted by her ladies, he whispered, "She could take a lesson from you."

He pulled his cape around him in a grand gesture, leaving the room, with Piers trailing behind him.

Once the door closed, Queen Audrey flew at me. Her ladies tried to pull her back, but her rage was too great. I had never seen her like this.

I lifted my hands to protect myself from her claws ready to scratch. But she kept coming. I grabbed her wrists and held on tight, her nails hovering. I looked her in the eyes, and I swear I saw madness there. The ladies were all around us, slapping at my hands. I held on and squeezed her wrists.

"You're hurting me!" she screamed. The guard rushed

in and wrapped his arms around my waist. As he pulled me away, the queen's nails tore down my cheek. My hand went to the sting.

Ingrid started toward me. "How dare you provoke the queen!" Her hand went up, but I slapped it back.

"Perhaps she should be taught a lesson this time, Your Majesty," said Fay, standing off to the side.

The queen whipped around to her. "What?"

"Imprison her," Fay said, looking at me. "She's attacked her queen." I could see something in her eyes. Was it jealousy? How could that be? Why would she be jealous of me?

"Yes!" yelled the queen. "Guard, put her in a cell in my dungeon."

The guard shook his head at her. I wrenched myself from his grip.

"Now!" yelled the queen. "Take her now!"

The guard looked from her to me to her. I knew he had orders from Eldred to always keep me with the queen. I was not worried. But to my surprise, he grabbed my arm and pulled me toward the door.

"And keep her there!" yelled the queen.

The dungeon for me.

Chapter Four

The cell was small with neither bench nor pallet. I sat on the stone floor with my back against the damp wall, my fingers pressed to the scratch on my face. How it stung. The queen had dug deep.

The air stank of sweat and fear. Moans of some unfortunate soul came from the cell next to mine. It was a woman, her cries awful to hear. Eldred was behind it, I was sure, torturing her for news of plots against the queen. Had he always been so cruel? Or did fear for his kingdom make him that way?

I'd never been in the queen's dungeon before. It was dark and cold, the eerie quiet broken only by an unseen *drip, drip, drip.* Despair lived here. It tried to seep into my skin. I fought to keep it out.

I'd already been over every stone in the floor and in the walls, crawling on my hands and knees, scratching fingers on rough surfaces. There were no cracks, no secret doors. The only opening was a slit of a window high up the wall.

The old advisers hadn't rushed down to free me. Perhaps they'd found a new shadow. Larcwide, the most devious of the three, disliked me, I knew. He didn't give me the intense stares Eldred did. But I had the feeling he resented my presence, as if my being alive took something from him.

It made no sense to me, so I did not dwell on it.

I rubbed my arms, trying to get warm. I trembled either from the cold, or something else. I was glad no one was here to see my fear. I couldn't bear it if the queen did, if anyone did. The only way I coped with this life was with a sealed heart. I would not let their scorn inside of me. Indeed, I would keep even my own emotions from brooding there. It was the only way to survive.

The prisoner moaned again. At that dismal sound, I felt a sharp pang in my chest, as if her pain had lodged in me as well. I doubted she would make it through the night. I touched the thick wall separating us. "Hold on," I whispered. "You must not die."

I wondered what she had done to be put in this dismal place. The dungeon was rarely used; thieves were banished from the kingdom, murderers executed. It is true traitors were imprisoned here. Perhaps my companion was an assassin sent to murder the queen before the coronation. More likely she was an innocent accused of something she did not do.

Whoever she was, she was now quiet. I felt her in the emptiness.

And that emptiness deepened, extending out from her to me, flooding my soul with such despair. An odd sensation came over me, as if my very breath was being stolen. And I had the strange feeling she was in that breath, and her spirit was leaving her body, just as my breath was leaving mine.

I pulled air into my lungs, shaking out the demons in my head. I must have been too long in this place. Its shadows were filling my mind, as dark visions filled the queen's.

I longed for things green and fresh. Nature had always fed my soul, given me comfort. At least when I was locked up in the queen's room, I could look out her window.

I closed my eyes and imagined myself in the royal orchard. I could almost feel the peace of its shaded nooks, but it was just out of my reach. The desire for it was so intense, so strong . . . I only felt frustration.

My eyes flew open when I heard his voice. "Is that you, Shadow?"

I knew it was him before I saw his face. Sir Kenway looked in through the barred opening of the door, illuminated by the flickering light of a torch. My heart sped. I could pretend it was because I might be rescued or that I had someone to talk to in this lonely place, but it was not that.

Sir Kenway had come to see *me*.

"You're here to rescue me?" I asked, glad for the darkness that hid the delight that was surely on my face.

He said nothing for a moment. "You are imprisoned by the queen's command."

"Because I am such a threat?" I asked, standing.

"Her Majesty's life is in danger," said Sir Kenway. "Any attacks need to be handled quickly and forcefully."

"You believe I was trying to murder her? That I'm an assassin?" I was beside him now, the door still between us. "I make a very poor one." I stared through the bars at him.

He looked nervous. Could it be because I was so near? What a thing to hope.

He glanced down the torch-lit hallway and back at me. "The threat against the queen is serious. Deor is in a fragile state, vulnerable to attack from our enemies to the west."

"And our friends to the south," I said, knowing allies sometimes became enemies if the reward was high. "So you think I am in league with foreigners?"

"You dislike the queen," he said.

Yet, in that moment, when he stated it, I didn't believe it was true. It *should* have been true, after all she had done.

He leaned forward, looking into my eyes. I could feel his warm breath on my cold face. I tried not to shiver. I wouldn't let him see how he affected me.

"I cannot figure you out, Shadow," he said. "Are you loyal?"

"Your queen attacked *me*."

He looked skeptical. Was he really so innocent to her true nature? Did her beauty blind him? Did her power? "*My* queen?" he asked.

"Yours."

"She is yours as well," he said. "Have you no love for Deor and her queen? You should treat her with reverence."

"Because she is so far above me?"

"She is your queen, Shadow," he said. "And you are . . ."

"Yes? I am what?"

"Not her equal."

"And not yours, either?" I asked.

He hesitated.

I heard footsteps coming down the stairs, belonging to a different guard than the one who had locked me in this cell. I drew back a little, watching the man from the shadows. He was large, but looked to be all belly. "Please, sir," he said to Kenway. "The queen forbade the prisoner to have any visitors. I shouldn't have let you down here."

Sir Kenway nodded curtly. "I'm coming." But he kept looking at me, and I felt my heart flutter. What did he want? Why was he really here? Perhaps he was the queen's spy.

The guard hadn't moved. Sir Kenway glared at him. The guard bobbed his head and left.

"I'll speak on your behalf, Shadow," said Sir Kenway. "But it is late. The queen has retired. You must resign yourself to staying in this place for now."

I nodded.

He pushed a blanket through the bars. "I thought you might need this."

I stared at it, confused by this kindness.

"You don't want it?" he asked.

I took it and wrapped it around my shoulders.

"Good night," he said.

I leaned my face to the bars and watched him walk away from me. "I cannot figure you out, either," I whispered to the dark.

Chapter Five

The night was cold, and the floor was hard. I pulled Sir Kenway's blanket closer around me, pushing my nose into it. It smelled of him. Was this one from his very bed? Thick blankets, red apples, smiles from Piers . . . these were all gifts I treasured.

Sir Kenway's kindness stayed with me as I dreamed.

I woke to light streaming in from the lone window. The guard appeared at the door with one bowl. I looked at the cold mush and wondered what the queen was eating.

Perhaps she broke fast with fresh blackberries from the bush she'd had the royal gardeners plant for me during my eighth year. It had been a delightful surprise, and I had been touched by her kindness. How her face had glowed at my happiness. She'd linked her arm through mine and told me I was like a sister to her. Hadn't we always been together?

Eldred had not been pleased, fussing at her for giving me special attention. I didn't deserve such an honor, he'd said.

The queen had always been frightened of him, and yet, she defied him to give me a gift so perfect for me. I never loved her more than I did that day.

Must I always think of her? Here I was banished to the dungeon, far from her plush room in the tower, and yet my thoughts were on her. Whatever I had meant to her, it had long since faded in her mind. I doubted she could even remember the blackberries now.

My stomach growled.

I ate the mush.

I paced the cell, walking from wall to wall. I yelled up at the guard, who ignored me. I tried to speak to the other prisoner. But she'd been quiet since last night.

The day was long. I watched the shadows grow until I was overtaken by them. And closed my eyes. Sir Kenway had not returned.

I awoke to creaking. It was still night.

Fyren was there, torch in hand. The flame danced and crackled.

"Are you well, Shadow?" he asked, shutting the door behind him.

I sat up, very awake, and leaned against the wall.

His footsteps were loud in the quiet. He placed the torch in a holder and stood over me.

"Have you come to let me out, Regent?" I asked, trying to keep my voice steady. He was here alone, at night. Whatever he was up to, it was not something he wanted others to know about.

"Perhaps," he said quietly.

The silence stretched between us. I felt cold and pulled Kenway's blanket in close, trying to keep the concern from my face. *It is the regent*, I thought. *He will not harm me.*

"I want you to do something for me," he said. "I will trade you a favor for a favor."

Whatever he would ask for in the secret of the night, I would not like. Any value I had to him was due to my proximity to the queen. I didn't want to be involved in the quiet war that went on between the two of them.

Did I have a choice?

"You will get me released," I said, looking up at him.

"If I don't, you will be here a long time, Shadow."

Ooh, that chilled my heart. I had not been here two full nights yet and already the yearning to get out was great. "What is the favor?" I asked, standing. I kept my back to the wall.

"You must first agree to do my bidding," he said, tugging at his beard.

"Before I know?"

He nodded.

I studied him for a moment. Wouldn't I do what I wanted even if I promised him? But then, there would be consequences that I would not like.

I shook my head. "I don't want the trade." I could not harm the queen, no matter what she had done to me. And I was sure this was what he wanted.

"I can give you even more than your release." His voice was too soft to be trusted.

"What, then?"

"Knowledge."

I smiled. "I have the queen's tutors for that."

"Then they've told you about your mother?"

My head whipped up.

He laughed at me. "You are as transparent as the queen. I can see what you want most."

"You see freedom in my eyes, then."

"I see a child's desire."

I paused. What could he tell me about her? What could be worth whatever sinister deed he had in mind? I should not be so eager to discover small facts about a dead woman.

I watched his smirking face. There was something in him now I had not glimpsed before. I did not like it.

He put his face into mine, whispered, "Don't you want to know what she was?" I could smell the sweet wine upon his breath, which turned my stomach, but I could not move away. Because I did want to know, desperately.

"Perhaps," he said, pulling back a little, "she was like the woman in the cell beside you."

"In what way?" I asked quickly, looking into his eyes, still too close.

He patted my cheek with an icy hand. "I would like to tell you."

I slid down the wall and sat back down.

To my surprise, he joined me on the floor.

"The floor is damp, Your Grace." I wanted him gone.

"I see that," he said, irritated. He took off his cape, folded it, and then sat on it. "What I want you to do will be for Deor."

"Deor?" I scoffed. "I thought you knew me, Regent."

"You have no love" — his voice cold — "for your country?"

I shrugged.

"You have been with my cousin too long. A queen who thinks she rules a castle, not a kingdom. She will ruin us."

"She has no influence over me, Regent."

He smiled and nodded. "Deor is the only thing that matters, Shadow. It was my mother who taught me that," he said. "You see, *I* knew *my* mother." He looked at me meaningfully, trying to tempt me again with knowledge.

But I would not bite. "What was she like, Regent?"

"Your mother?" he asked.

"Yours."

He laughed a little, giving me an admiring look. He liked to banter, but most courtiers were too in awe of him to do so. Perhaps they had too much to lose, whereas I had little to begin with.

But then something passed over his eyes and he grew serious. "My mother was meant to be the ruler of Deor. You know that?"

"She was the eldest. But her father, your grandfather,

passed her over in favor of her dead brother's son, King Alfrid." I knew my Deorian history. "For she was a woman."

"Bah! A shrewd woman. And she loved this kingdom, knew its worth, and would have ruled it better than my uncle's son."

"How so?" I asked, curious. King Alfrid was remembered as gregarious and exuberant, but he was also considered to have been a frugal prince.

The regent flashed an irritated look my way. "You are impertinent."

I held my tongue.

"But so entertaining. You amuse me, Shadow, more than anyone else in this castle. If I were king, I would make you one of my advisers. That would kill old Eldred." He smiled. "So you will help me do what's best for Deor."

Saying no would be foolish, but I could not say yes. "Will you give me time to think on it, Your Grace?"

"Ah, Shadow." He stood and tapped me on the head. "I'll come again."

Chapter Six

I awoke to loud voices. Footsteps shuffled past my door. The visitors weren't here for me.

I looked out the bars. The door to the cell next to mine was open. I could see the grim faces of the guards in the bare morning light. The youngest one, perhaps the same age as Fyren, was the leader. He was in the doorway, motioning the older two into the cell. He was not so much tall as imposing, and his jaw had a cruel set to it.

The two guards pulled down a long board leaning against the wall. I now knew why I had not heard my companion since that first night.

I watched them take her out. It would not be right for her to leave this place without someone to mourn her. So I kept looking, though I didn't want to. No blanket covered her. She was on her back, clothed in a long, dark gown. The light of the torches on the wall gave the procession a rightly solemn feel.

I shivered. I couldn't get Fyren's earlier words out of my head. And so it seemed to me this might be my own mother they carried out.

Her eyes were closed as if she only slept, her face softened by that eternal sleep. Or perhaps I only imagined it for my own peace of mind. Her hair was gray and thin, and loose except for one narrow braid, longer than the rest. It hung down the side of the board, dragging on the dirty floor. I could see no bruises or welts upon the woman, but her collar was high and her sleeves long. She was old, the age of a grandmother.

"What is her name?" I yelled out to the guards as they passed me by.

One of them looked over his shoulder at me. "They called her Maren."

Maren. Not a common name, and not one a courtier would use due to its plainness. But I would not forget it. I would do her that honor. My name had long since been forgotten. I'd wished many times someone remembered it.

"What did they say she did to be put in this place?" I asked.

"Witch." The word slapped me in the face. No. Not like my mother.

I will remember you, Maren.

I had no stomach for my second morning of mush, but I forced myself to eat it.

Light seeped out of dawn. The prison no longer smelled rank. I was a part of its smell.

The quiet rang loud in my ears. I longed to hear something: the scuttling of mice, the shutting of a door, some sound of life or movement. I even missed Maren's painful cries, shameful as it was for me to think it.

Was there an end to all this? Fear gnawed away at my hope, and the walls pressed close upon me now.

I remembered another time when the queen had shut me up in darkness and I'd been afraid I would not get out. That child-felt terror came upon me again.

I had been but ten years old. The queen, my constant companion, had bid me watch a black spider weaving its web. It was at the bottom of an empty trunk about to be filled with her silk dresses, newly arrived from the rich fertile country across the green seas, the kingdom Fyren coveted.

The creature's back was red and black, matching the uniforms of the queen's guards. I smiled and looked back to point that out to her when she gave me a strong push. I fell into the oversized trunk, and I heard the queen giggle as she shut me in. My first feeling was shock, because the queen had been so kind to me until that moment.

The blackness and the close space made me feel as if I were in my tomb. It was instantly hot. I pushed at the lid, but it would not budge.

"You are locked in, Shadow!" she yelled. "I will not let you out until you promise to stop answering all the questions my tutor asks me! Do you hear me?"

"Yes, I promise!" I called out. Anything to be released.

"And if Fyren asks your opinion, you must not go on and on. You must say you do not know!"

"Yes, yes. Let me out."

"I think not yet!"

And then I heard nothing at all. "Your Grace? Your Grace?"

I kicked and screamed. *Would they ever find me?*

I'd never known such black fear, so great, perhaps, because it was the result of a betrayal. The world becomes a very dark place then.

My fear quickly turned to anger. I do believe it was rage that kept me from going mad in the trunk. Once Eldred released me, I ignored all my promises to the queen. I answered questions before she even had the chance and laughed outright with Fyren at her stupidity. Such antics only brought me more slaps from the ladies and more hatred from the queen. And more admiration from the regent.

I soon learned that my rage made me vulnerable. All emotions did. Eventually I learned to shield myself from the allure of the deeply felt feeling.

I would not let the queen make me afraid again.

I took a deep breath, fighting off the panic. I would get out of this dungeon. I would.

A noise at the door caught my attention. This was not a guard. I crept over, crawling on the floor. Something came from above me and hit me on the head. I grabbed the offending bag and leaped up. Through the bars I saw a little face grinning up at me.

"Piers?" I asked.

He glanced toward the stairs and put his finger to his lips.

"How did you get in here?" I whispered, worried for his safety.

His grin widened.

I laughed quietly. "I've missed you."

This pleased him, I could tell.

"Look, look in the bag," he said.

I poured seven nuts out into my hand. "Oh, Piers."

"Almonds," he said.

"How did you get them?"

He just laughed. He had an infectious laugh. It was a boy's giggle, filled with delight and mischief. Just hearing it always brought me a bit of joy. "Eat one," he told me.

"You take one."

"I already had my fill. These are for you."

I slipped one in my mouth and closed my eyes, savoring the deep rich flavor as I chewed. "So delicious," I murmured. One after the other I ate them while Piers watched me.

"You are a good friend to me, Piers, but you should not take such risks. You need to go before you are found out."

"We must look after each other, Shadow," he said, looking at me expectantly. "You are all I have now."

Something grasped at my heart. Similar words came to my lips, but I could not say them. I could not be bound to anyone. I thought he'd understood this. My silence weighed heavily upon me.

"I must go, Shadow," he said, a little sadness edging into his voice.

"Yes, yes," I said, "you must not get caught."

"Do not lose hope." And then he disappeared into the darkness, in the opposite direction of the stairs.

With seven almonds and a friend's hope in my belly, I was soon lost in sleep on my third night of imprisonment.

The door swung open. It was not Sir Kenway.

Early evening light strained in from the small, high window above. Before me stood four people: one small, two broad-shouldered, and one with a bright white cape.

"Hello, Shadow," said Fyren. He stood between two guards who held torches before him. Another torch was lower to the ground. I could see Piers's face in the shadows.

I only nodded.

Piers ran to me and put the torch close to my face.

"You'll set me on fire," I said, pulling back, wincing at the light and smoke.

He laughed. I smiled at him.

Another figure moved into the cell. "Get up," said Eldred, his voice sharp.

"I think not," I said.

He stepped toward me. "Get off the floor." He made a quick upward motion with his fingers.

I did not move. Let him force me.

Fyren laughed. "Angry, Shadow?"

I knew he didn't refer to his leaving me before. He wouldn't let Eldred know of that visit. "Why should I be angry?" I was cautious with my words. Would he still ask a favor, or had he released me out of pity?

"That little idiot of a queen," Fyren stated, "shouldn't have been allowed to put you in here."

The guards looked uncomfortable, glancing at each other.

Eldred was still and quiet. I would not look at him.

Piers sat cross-legged in front of me. "It's dreary in here. Were you scared?"

"I enjoyed the peace," I said, "my little loyal friend."

His eyes regarded me with such seriousness. I put my hand upon his cheek, feeling its child softness. But then I felt a twinge of something else, something not pleasant, as if a string were attached from his heart to mine and it had been yanked, hard. I dropped my hand.

He looked at me curiously. I smiled at him, guilty I had pulled back again. I was not what this boy needed, but he made *my* soul less black. Sometimes I thought my care for him was the only thing keeping me from a withered, dead heart.

"Come, Shadow," said Fyren, "let us get you out of this place. Piers is right. It is dreary."

I was glad to leave my cell. I curtsied to the guard with the cruel face, Sir Kenway's blanket sliding from my shoulders. Eldred grabbed it off the floor and gave it to the guard. I longed to grab it back, but stilled my hand. I would not let Eldred see me disappointed. Instead, I flashed him a wide smile. The old man's expression was unreadable.

We stopped in the great hall, which was large and almost empty of people. The expansive room was mostly dark except for an occasional torch along the wall, but one table held hundreds of bright candles. Several of Fyren's most loyal men, all sons of rich lords, were dining there. Their laughter could be heard from where we stood across the hall.

As we approached, the smell of spiced meat wafted our way and made my mouth water.

"Have you left me anything to eat?" Fyren asked,

slapping one of them on the back. The man laughed. It was Lord Oswald. He was blandly handsome, easily insulted, and betrothed to Lady Hilda. I could not help but revel in the lady's unhappiness with the match. Neither liked the other, but their families had arranged it.

I didn't notice Eldred was not with us until he yelled for me. "Shadow!" He gestured for me to follow. Then he headed toward the exit, his long cape billowing out around him. But I stayed in place, watching Fyren settle down at the head of the table.

"Eldred!" yelled Fyren. "You are not dismissed."

The old man stiffened and stopped walking. He turned slowly toward us and looked. Would Eldred disobey the regent?

"Come!" Fyren commanded in a booming voice.

Eldred hesitated for just a moment and then began the long walk across the hall. I was eager to hear what Fyren would say to him.

The regent was still as he waited for the old adviser.

"Yes?" asked Eldred.

Fyren picked up a succulent piece of turkey and stuck it in his mouth. I put a hand to my rumbling stomach. Oh, I was so hungry. Piers gave me a sympathetic smile.

Lord Aiken, sitting on Fyren's right, leered at me. I did not like him and did not like the way he looked at me. "You're not at your best, Shadow." He was a large man with thick muscular arms, the oldest of the sycophants surrounding Fyren.

"My cell was not clean."

He laughed. "So Sir Kenway was right. You were in the dungeon."

That news hurt a little. The knight had not bothered to get me released and had gossiped about me as Fay would have. Had he laughed at me to the queen? Had he only been spying on me after all?

"Sir Kenway," repeated Fyren. "The queen's own knight." He looked at Eldred. "How did a traitor's son get so close to our queen?"

Eldred did not answer, just stared at the regent quite boldly. The story about Sir Kenway's father, Lord Leofwine, was well-known. The once great man now hid in his castle to the west and was never seen at court.

"So, Shadow," asked Aiken, "why were you in the dungeon?"

My hand went to the healing scratch across my cheek. "The queen was not pleased with me."

His eyes laughed. "What did you do?"

"Defended myself, Your Grace."

Aiken guffawed, as did Fyren and the other men at the table. The queen was not held in high regard by these lords. They played a dangerous game. Fyren was their only protection. Perhaps mine and Piers's as well.

Piers grabbed my sleeve and held on. I looked down at him. He said nothing, just gave me a cautioning look. I knew he thought I spoke too freely. I smiled at him, trying to reassure him. I would be good. I'd had enough of punishment for a bit.

But standing here beside these well-fed lords with their riches and power made me worry about my friend. He was small in size, with thin shoulders, and eyes vulnerable and kind.

I could not bear it if they ever hurt him, if they treated him with the same cruelty the ladies showed me. I must remember to tell him not to take any more risks. He should make sure he was not noticed. He needed to learn to care for himself because I would not always be here, I hoped.

"Do you have any further need of us, Regent?" asked Eldred. He didn't mask his distaste for this company very well. He usually made more effort.

Fyren took a slow sip from his cup. I myself was parched. He leaned back in his chair. "Where were you yesterday, Eldred?" His eyes were narrow, his face cold.

Eldred did not hesitate. "At Lord Callus's castle, Regent."

This would not be welcome news to Fyren. Lord Callus was an influential member of the nobility. His castle was not far from us, just to the north. He was an irascible old man, firmly stuck in the past, people said, but with many followers amongst those who longed for the days of King Alfrid. Now that I thought about it, he and ancient Eldred were well-suited as allies.

"I know that, Eldred," Fyren said with a meaning-ful look.

The adviser's eyes flickered in Lord Oswald's direction. "Your spy lagged behind. You should replace him with one not so inept."

Lord Oswald began to stand, his mouth open, his hand to his dagger, but Fyren gestured for him to sit. The young lord had a violent temper. His immaturity made me smile. He caught it and glared at me, his hand still on his knife, squeezing it. *Did he think I was afraid of him?* I glared right back until his face splotched red.

I saw Fyren looking at me and smiling. But then his mouth grew thin and angry. He turned his attention back to Eldred. "What business did you have with Lord Callus?"

"Two old friends visiting, Regent. That was all."

"No news of Erce?" Fyren asked.

I looked at him, puzzled. *Erce.* I'd not heard the name before.

Eldred paused, clearly startled. But then the emotion left his face. "I have not heard any."

Fyren waved his hand dismissively, not even looking Eldred's way. The old man gave him a quick nod. I followed him out.

I glanced back at Fyren. His eyes were fixed on us. I wondered what their conversation meant. And I wondered what the regent would ask of me now that he had had me released.

Halfway up the stairs, Eldred turned and stared coldly at me. "You are filthy."

"I have been in the dungeon."

"She won't let you in her chamber smelling as you do. And there is a banquet tonight."

I smiled. I would get a bath.

Chapter Seven

Eldred had allowed them to sit side by side. His eyes were on them as he drank from the wooden goblet he always used, the one with the E carved on the side. *Awful man*, I thought. He'd dangled the hope of a hot bath in front of me, and then had given me a rag and a bowl of cold dirty water. I had done my best, but dungeon grime still clung to my skin.

Queen Audrey flicked her long lashes at Sir Kenway and let out a shallow laugh. She was not herself.

Another dark vision had visited her, while she was being dressed by her ladies. I had seen the look. Ingrid had, too, for she reprimanded me with her eyes when she saw me watching the queen. The servants gossiped that the queen was cursed and the curse would fulfill the prophecy by destroying her mind.

"What are you staring at?" whispered Piers, elbowing me in the ribs.

He and I sat behind them, cross-legged on the floor, with a splintery board balanced on our knees. We shared a stale bread trencher, which on this night held a sweet chicken and rice paste. But I could eat little. I breathed in the stink of the many tallow candles and the tension in the air. No matter, Piers was ravenous.

Although we were on the queen's raised dais, we could see little on the lower floor. Too many feet and skirts in our way. But I didn't need to see the faces of the fifty lords and ladies gathered here to know the mood. Only whispers and black smoke drifted up into the vaulted ceiling of the great hall.

"You're always looking at them," he said, nodding toward the queen and her knight. Gripping his wooden spoon as if it might be snatched from him, he shoveled a large helping of the chicken into his mouth.

"And Eldred is always looking at me," I told him, pushing the trencher toward him. I fought the urge to lean forward and pinch Queen Audrey's long white neck to see what Eldred might do. My eager fingers twitched.

Eldred had told me to watch over the queen, always. Was evil lurking near her person? Was someone by her soup with a vial of poison? Did I see a blade drawn close to her? Ridiculous.

He had pulled me aside before the banquet. "No one notices you, Shadow."

How many times had he said that to me?

Sensing my insolence, I was sure, he became impatient. "Except when you make yourself known," he said. "As you did when you were imprisoned. You should be at Her Majesty's side."

As if that were my fault.

"Be invisible," he snapped. I had never seen him so agitated.

It was because we moved closer to the day. The queen's birthday. If she was murdered, would I be blamed for not protecting her or even for being complicit in the plot?

Fyren stood, his long cape touching the floor. His vanity sought fashionable clothes, which he wore well.

The lady Fay sat in one of the coveted seats next to Fyren. I would not forget she was the one who had told the queen to put me in the dungeon. Fay's father, Lord Westing, lived in a small manor house on the eastern coast. He'd been quite fortunate to place his wily country daughter as one of the queen's ladies.

Out of the corner of my eye, I saw her looking at Fyren with undisguised longing. That explained some things. Turning slightly, Fay gave me a sharp look. I returned her gaze.

Fyren lifted his gold goblet, and everyone did the same. Piers pushed ours my way, but I left it on the board.

"Let us remember our . . . *great* King Alfrid, and this day, the anniversary of his marriage to . . . *sweet* Queen Anne."

I delighted in the look of irritation that crossed Eldred's wrinkled face. Fyren's speech dripped with sarcasm. Only he would dispute that King Alfrid had been a great king, but no one remembered Queen Anne as sweet. She'd been from a foreign land, and reserved and cautious, although all had known how much she'd loved the king.

Sir Kenway stood, throwing a quick look in Fyren's direction. The regent smiled and nodded.

I knew all eyes were upon the knight, especially those of the ladies. He had a natural confidence. His form was long and lean, but his shoulders wide.

"To brave King Alfrid and devoted Queen Anne," Sir Kenway said in a strong, clear voice. He raised his cup in Queen Audrey's direction. "The father and mother of our young queen."

Everyone stood. The cries went up. "To Queen Audrey! Our Audrey!"

Piers and I stayed on the floor. No one noticed, so eager were they to toast the queen. She was the hope of Deor, the hope for prosperity, which was sorely needed. We were a country slowly dying. Our winters had turned long and bitter cold, and our soil was no longer fertile. We lived in an almost barren land.

Queen Audrey was destined to marry some wealthy prince, anyone who could bring us the necessary riches. That was not Sir Kenway. I hoped a fat, ugly king would whisk her away and allow Fyren to govern in her absence. But what was it to me? I would be gone soon. It must be soon.

After taking a sip of the too-sweet wine, I set the cup down. Piers had drunk all but the dregs. The board was unstable on our knees and the goblet began to slide. Piers tried to grab it, but missed. It thudded on the wooden floor, red liquid dribbling from it.

Sir Kenway turned. I felt his eyes on me. My stomach twisted with a thrill of pleasure at the sight of his face. At the same time, though, I felt a rush of anger. Hadn't he left me in that cell and not returned? *Fyren* had freed me, not Kenway. Because Sir Kenway would not dare disobey his queen.

The queen said something to him. His face was to me, not to her, and I saw a quick look of impatience cross his eyes. But he turned to her, and she didn't seem to notice his slight hesitation. An odd sensation came over me and I felt as if he still looked at me, as if his heart . . . I shook my head. What nonsense! I would not trust what I could not see. But then, I didn't even trust what I *could* see.

Piers's gray eyes studied me.

"Yes?" I asked him, raising my eyebrows.

Using the rushes off the floor, he sopped up the bit of spilled wine.

"You are not good company tonight, Piers," I said. The queen was admiring a gold ring Sir Kenway always wore, lingering over it, her gold hair sweeping his shoulder. Kenway looked uncomfortable. "Much too serious . . . and hungry," I continued.

Piers belched and patted his stomach. The queen tossed us a disgusted face and pinched her nose. But she was no longer stroking Sir Kenway's hand. When she turned away, Piers gave me a wicked grin.

Here it was — this other Piers. The one he showed me little of. Most of the time he was docile and quiet, but every now and then, an impish side appeared. I could not help but smile.

He yawned.

"Do I bore you?" I asked. "But how can that be, sir?" I patted my thick unruly hair. "You dine with such a fine lady."

He turned his small face to me. His eyes were large and serious, but his nose was tiny and his lips were those of a child. He claimed not to know his age, but I doubted that was true. Surely he was no more than ten.

"You like him?" he asked. He said it rather loudly. I felt the heat rise into my cheeks. I knew of whom he was speaking. The queen shot us a glance and Sir Kenway shifted in his chair.

I raised the empty goblet to my lips, feeling a little off balance. I did not like the feeling.

Piers grabbed my hand, holding it firmly. He turned it over, tracing the creases in my palm. "My mother said these lines mean something."

I jerked my hand out of his grip. Sometimes I could endure his affection, but other times it rattled me. I was used to slaps and pushes, not this. Physical touch felt to me like someone was reaching through my skin and brushing my heart. I could see I'd hurt his feelings.

"What was her name?" I asked softly, trying to make it up to him.

He ignored me. I chewed the inside of my mouth, unnerved at how vulnerable this small boy could make me feel. He came too close.

I could not gnaw the guilt out of my mouth. Reluctantly, I laid my palm in his small hands.

He let it sit there for a moment, but then took it. A sudden sense of loneliness rushed into my fingers. I was confused, but fought the urge to pull my hand away.

Piers traced the lines on my palm again, his touch like ice that burned. "You have troubles ahead of you, Shadow."

I could tell the words flowed out of his imagination, but I let him continue, silently willing him to hurry. Coldness crept into my wrist.

"But it will turn out in the end."

He smiled at me. He folded my hand over and pushed it toward me. Relief swept over me.

"And will you be there with me?" I asked.

It was the wrong thing to say. I had left him before. He *must* know I would again.

"Why don't you like to be touched?" he asked, disarming me.

Sir Kenway put down his wine and leaned back in his chair toward us. Suddenly I felt the whole room was too close. I said nothing.

"I miss my mother's touch," Piers said. "I can still feel her, though."

I studied his pale face. "How do you mean?"

He patted his chest. "In here." He leaned forward and whispered, "It's like magic. I feel her spirit, hear her laugh." He poked his finger at me. "Don't you feel your mother there?"

I slapped his hand away. "No."

"She's there. You don't try to find her."

"I have no shared feeling."

"We're all connected, Shadow. My mother — and others — taught me that. We're all connected to . . ."

"To what?" I asked.

But he shook his head and would not speak. I looked up to find Fyren's eyes on us. He turned back, and I wondered why he was so interested in the sad words of a servant boy. I was also amused. Here they all sat together, the rich and powerful. And yet, they were intrigued by the servants dining on the floor.

Later, with the queen's white face finally pressed against her pillow, I stood by the side window, looking out onto the moonlit yard. I had lied to Piers. I, too, felt a connection with others at times. I did not understand nor like it. For whatever it was, it took from me and gave little in return. Or at least that was how it felt, as if I were being sapped of my very spirit. So my desire to escape was great.

There was one I wished to know, and I reached for her. But my mother did not come, for she was long dead.

Chapter Eight

The queen cried out. I jumped up, expecting to see an intruder with a dagger. But there was only the two of us.

She was asleep but restless. I looked down at her slumbering in her silk sheets, her head jerking from side to side. She moaned, then whispered, "No." Still, she did not wake.

In the past I would rouse her when she was trapped in these nightmares. But as I looked at her perfect face I remembered my nights on the hard dungeon floor. I lay back down on my pallet.

I woke to the queen's stillness. The room was a little dark, a little hazy with morning light straining to peek through the slats in the shutters. I lay on the stone floor, feeling its hardness beneath my straw pallet, knowing something was amiss. There was no movement in her bed.

Slowly, I got to my knees, looking around for a sign of someone. But the queen and I were alone. I pulled myself up, peered over the edge of the bed. She lay still as stone. Her lips, silent. Her eyes, closed. Her face, so perfect, like a white marble effigy for a tomb.

I gave a little cry and reached out to touch her. I never felt such coldness.

I must have screamed because the guards, the gentle ladies, the old men were all around me.

"She is dead!" screamed Hilda. The others broke into sobs. Ingrid looked at me with fierce eyes as if I had done this terrible thing.

Eldred grabbed me roughly by the arm and pulled me through the arched doorway that led from the queen's chamber to his. His nails bit into my skin. I jerked away.

He thrust my drab red dress and cloak in my face and gestured for me to put them on over my wool shift. I slipped my dress over my head, thinking how quick he was for remembering to get my clothes. I belted my waist with my only sash and pushed my wide feet into leather shoes.

Into his chamber floated the remaining two old men

and Sir Kenway. Sir Kenway's face had collapsed into grief. They took him to the other side of the room and whispered to him. I do not think he heard a word they said. He seemed in another place, dark and small.

I noticed the looks my way. Larcwide gestured to me and shook Sir Kenway by the shoulder. He was roused from his shock and stared right at me, taking me in.

Did they think I had killed her? I felt panic rising in my chest, remembering my nights in the dungeon. I could not go back there.

Outside the wooden door that led into the passageway, I heard many voices, but one rising above the others. It was Fyren.

I relaxed a little.

Sir Kenway pulled me into a small back room, which was cluttered with leather-bound books and wooden bowls and long glass tubes. He put his finger to his lips and whispered for me to listen. His eyes were red, and he suddenly looked older.

I listened.

Voices coming from the crowded room were difficult to distinguish from one another, but they all asked the same question: Who had done this?

Eldred's deep voice rose above the others. "Everyone must leave. The regent and I must talk together."

I heard loud footsteps and the shutting of the heavy door.

I couldn't make out their words for they spoke in low voices. I cracked the door. It made not a sound, but Sir Kenway was beside me quickly. He gave my sleeve a sharp tug. I ignored him.

The regent's back was to me. Beside him was one of the queen's guards, Geoff, who had disobeyed Eldred's orders. He had remained when he had been told to leave. His broad shoulders were stiff. His short dagger was out of its sheath and in his hand. His fingers gripped the handle, tightening and repositioning the weapon.

I could see Eldred's face, and he might have seen me looking in at him. Some emotion flashed in his eyes, but I couldn't read it.

And then it happened.

Geoff lunged toward Eldred, grabbing his arm and thrusting the dagger into his stomach. My mind wouldn't accept what I was seeing. I tried to make it turn out right, like the queen's adviser was only sick and in need of help.

But Eldred collapsed onto the floor, a jagged spot of red widening on his gray cape.

Sir Kenway grabbed me from behind and quietly shut the door. All was confusion with the screams of the old men and the yelling of the knights in the passageway.

I was pulled toward the back wall of the small room. I leaned against the stone, cold even through my shift and dress and cloak, smelling the terror in the air. Sir Kenway snatched a lit torch from its iron holder. He pulled the ring and pushed his right hip into the rough stone beside me. The wall moved easily, making an opening not higher than my head.

I knew magic when I saw it, but I didn't speak. I couldn't still the thoughts running inside my head. Was Fyren behind all this? Our enemies the Torsans, could they be in the castle? Geoff, one of their spies?

Sir Kenway yanked me through the opening, shoving the wall back into place. It was not thick stone at all, but a door of wood with a false front. Not magic after all.

"Come," he said.

He took my hand — surprisingly, his felt cool and sure — and we rushed down a tight twisting staircase that dropped into the pit of the Earth. The light from his torch flashed here and there on the steps below. The rapid scuffle of our shoes on stone echoed in the dark.

After many circles around and down, my nostrils filled with the full smell of moist soil and the bare one of wet stone. We reached the bottom of the stairs, and I felt flat earth beneath my shoes.

We walked in the tunnel beneath the castle for a long time, neither of us speaking. What was there to say? The queen was dead. All of the advisers might be dead. After fifteen years among them, I had not known friend from foe.

I still did not.

Chapter Nine

The stone tunnel became a dripping, musty cave. No human skulls lay under our feet, but bats squeaked above us, their lit-up eyes like stars in a black sky.

At the end of the cave, a pile of rubble greeted us. Sir Kenway stood still for a moment, the torch high in his hand, looking at the piled-up mess before us. His face was lost in shadows and smoke, but I saw the pain there plain enough. He was thinking of her, not the rubble. I felt a pang in my heart at his sorrow.

But I was desperate to throw off the stones and get out of the cave. I was so close, closer than I had ever been to freedom, even though a wall of rock stood in my way. I waited for Sir Kenway to speak.

He pushed the end of the torch into the wet ground and began to move the rocks. I helped him. Silently we worked.

We cleared an opening large enough for us to squeeze through, for we were both thin and long. He went before me, feet first. When only his head was poking through, I was reminded of Eldred, clothed in gray and always watching me.

I went as Sir Kenway did, feet first, and slid down jagged rocks to a soft forest floor. I forgot my cares because I was *free*.

Sir Kenway was already walking through a grove of tall trees. Looking up, I knew they were pines. I had smelled their sharp pungency when I was enclosed inside the walls. I touched the rough bark and peeled off a piece and put it to my nose and sniffed. I put it in my mouth and bit. I rubbed it on my cheek.

Sir Kenway stared at me. "We have no time for this." He turned and walked away.

I don't have to follow, I thought, thrilled by that hope.

I tossed my head back and looked up at the blue morning sky, peeking back at me through tree branches. My thick hair flowed down my back. I spun in circles, feeling dizzy and light. Free air had a different smell, so fresh and sweet.

Sir Kenway grabbed my arm. I whipped my head down and jerked out of his grip.

"You must come with me," he snarled with a vicious face. I was stunned by the change in him.

"Why?" I asked, moving away from him.

"The regent will be looking for us. He'll murder us, too. We are —" His voice cracked. "We were the queen's." I felt pity for him. He was so distraught. "Or at least I was. You will come with me now!"

"What have I done to provoke this anger in you?"

I backed up as he walked toward me quickly. "I know what you did."

"I don't know what you mean —"

"Come with me now!" he yelled. "I will drag you if I must."

I could tell he would do it. I nodded and followed him into the thick woods, wondering what he thought I did. If he thought I'd murdered the queen, why would he take me with him?

I shook my head, angry. He had no *right* to accuse me.

I felt so foolish. All it took was a gift of a blanket and I had seen him as kind. Perhaps his visit to the dungeon had been for the queen's sake, because he thought me a traitor and hoped to find that out, and not because he held any real affection for me.

I was not yet free.

I looked around, seeing only trees and more trees. Sir Kenway knew these woods and I did not. If I did escape, I would be lost or even found by those in the castle who would take me back. So I fought the urge to run. I'd wait and watch for my chance.

We walked on and on. The sky was free of clouds. The sun, strong, warmed us.

The queen lay dead in her bed. I hadn't known a day without her. I could not help but think of how she'd loved me when we were children. So long ago, and yet I could still taste the memory.

I had ignored her cries the night before. Had she been dying then? This thought made me feel as if I'd been punched. I shook my head. It was not my fault she died. And anyway, I had no feeling for her. She didn't deserve my love. I needed to leave her behind, along with the look in Eldred's eyes as he was stabbed. Their deaths were too heavy to carry.

But . . . I could not escape the horror of the scene. Had Geoff murdered all of the old men? I closed my eyes. Their screams were not easy to forget.

Oh, none of it mattered. What did any of them matter to me? They had never treated me kindly. Why should I care so?

Except for Piers, sweet Piers, whose friendship had kept me from seeing all people as selfish and cruel. He had risked coming to the dungeon just to bring me almonds he'd stolen from the kitchen, and I'd deserted him.

I'd had to leave him. There had been no time, no choice.

There had not been.

I stared at Sir Kenway's stiff back. Why did he take me with him? I was glad to be out of the castle, but there was some reason he had taken me. I was but a lowly girl to them all, less than a servant. What could he want of me? *A favor for a favor*, Fyren had said to me. Did the knight want the same thing as Fyren had?

I heard the sound of a gurgling stream to the right of us and caught the scent of wild blackberries in the air. The fruit I most desired and that the queen had grown to detest. How could it be? It was too cold for blackberries.

"We must stop and rest," I said, anxious for the delicious fruit.

Sir Kenway kept walking.

I said what I thought would convince him. "The regent will be searching the castle for us before he starts on his horses. We have time for a drink. We must have water."

He turned and gave me a weary look. His face was different from yesterday. It looked as it did when he first came to the castle four years ago. Like that of a wild boy raised by wolves.

"We must continue on, Shad —"

"Do not call me that, boy knight!" I yelled, my fists clenched at my sides.

His head jerked up.

"Not out here," I said. "I'm not that anymore. I'm no one's shadow." I turned off the narrow path and dove into the woods, following the sound of water splashing on rocks. Branches scratched my arms as I struggled through thick bushes and tight spaces, but soon I was at the stream.

It was the loveliest place I had ever seen.

I sat in the cool earth of the bank and dipped my hands into the water. I poured it into my parched mouth and let it run down my hot neck.

Sir Kenway was at my side. He crouched down and took several drinks, then flicked the water off his hand. "I am no boy knight," he said. I looked at him directly, and his eyes held mine. I remembered the stories the ladies told about him. How bravely he had fought when the Torsans attacked a western port of Deor last spring. "We can rest here for a few moments," he said, standing. "No more."

I gathered blackberries from a nearby bush, carrying them in the front of my scooped-up dress. Purple-black stains deepened into the coarse cloth.

"It's strange," said Sir Kenway. "How did they survive the cold?"

They're here for me. Grown for me. The thought excited me because I knew it was true. Someone was providing for me. I couldn't explain my feeling, and I knew not the origin of it, but I was certain.

I sat on the bank and ate the blackberries one by one, letting the juice dwell on my tongue. For the first time, I was choosing what I wanted to eat, not eating only what the queen selected.

Sir Kenway stood by a willow tree whose branches wept to the ground.

He watched me as the old man used to do. With an outstretched arm, I offered him a blackberry. He did not take it.

"What is your name, then, if it's not Shadow?"

"I don't know," I said, shrugging, "but I know my mother didn't name me that."

"That's why you never call anyone else by name," he said, as if it were fact. I said nothing. He sat by me in the dirt.

I finished the blackberries — heaven! — and rinsed my hands in the cold stream, watching the water flow from my hands to lily pads and algae-covered rocks.

"You hardly spoke to anyone at all," he said.

"I spoke to you."

"The regent was your only friend." His eyes were fierce, like those of Ingrid, when she thought I had murdered the queen.

"It was not I who killed her," I said.

"You did not like her," he accused. "You admitted it."

I said nothing.

"You eat blackberries and play with your fingers in the water. Where's your loyalty?" His words were tight with rage. His eyes were red, and he didn't look like himself. He had loved her. And I didn't know what that felt like.

"The queen treated me like her puppy. I am as loyal as any dog."

He flung dirt into my face and stood over me. "You are lowly born. You were a dog beneath her feet. She deserves your grief." How had I ever thought him kind?

I turned my face from his pain. I spat the dirt out of my mouth and wiped it off my tongue. His grief would make him careless. Ah, yes, I would slip away in the dark while he slept.

With a strong grip on my arm, he jerked me to my feet. "Your rest is at an end, Shadow."

For now, boy knight.

Chapter Ten

"Hurry," he said to me again and again. *Hurry, hurry, hurry.*

We walked quickly through the trees. The air grew warm as we moved toward mid-afternoon. I threw my cloak over my arm.

"We'll arrive by nightfall," said Sir Kenway, calling back over his shoulder.

My calves ached, and the soles of my feet were sore, but I cared not. Each step took me farther from the castle and its high walls.

"What is our destination?" I asked.

He looked back at me. His blond hair stuck to his sweaty face. "My home," he said, with a touch of his old pride back in his voice.

Yes. The home of his father, Lord Leofwine, the traitor. I had thought as much.

"Sir Kenway?" I asked to his back.

He didn't reply.

I was patient.

"Sir Kenway?" I finally asked again.

"What is it?" he snapped.

"Why are you taking me with you?"

He stopped. I stumbled into him, gripping the front of his tunic to keep from falling. He put his hands over mine and tried to set me on my feet. His grip was warm, soft, firm — sending a sweet, sharp ache to my heart, like pain and longing together. I wanted to let go, and to hold on.

Our eyes met. I saw distrust there. But then that faded and something else, something like curiosity sparked. This unsettled me and I forgot my question. We quickly separated.

He walked on. I followed, feeling a bit foolish. Confusing feelings had swept through me so suddenly I didn't have time to hide them. Sir Kenway must have seen.

Kenway brought us out of the trees onto a wide road. To my surprise, he kept us on it. I didn't see or hear horses, but I listened. I guessed he was listening, too, but I worried he was being careless. I didn't want to go back to that place, my cage.

"We shouldn't be on the road," I said.

He didn't answer.

The woods on the other side were thick and full. We couldn't make our way through that thicket. Perhaps it thinned out farther down the road.

"If Fyren is after us," I said, "and I do doubt that, but if he is, his troops might come this way." More likely, they'd come across us while looking for someone more important and still take us back.

"He will seek us," Sir Kenway claimed.

I disagreed, but said nothing. I thought Sir Kenway's arrogance made him elevate his worth.

"But he'll move on another first," he added.

I thought on that. "You believe he'll move on Lord Callus."

"I don't believe. I know. . . ."

A few paces ahead, a boy rested against a silver birch tree.

"You are not to speak," Sir Kenway said in a harsh whisper.

The boy's sunken cheeks and hungry mouth begged for us to stop. I put my hand to my own gut, suddenly feeling his hunger there, a hollow throbbing. This new sensitivity I had to the pain of others gnawed at me. I was becoming as weak as the queen had been.

As we passed him, the boy followed me with eyes that seemed to have lost all color, the sky with its blue washed out. I thought of Piers and felt a sharp pang.

I knelt beside him.

"Shadow!" yelled Sir Kenway.

"Where's your mother?" I asked.

"Dead," he said. His voice was already that of a man's. I had thought him younger.

Sir Kenway stood over me. Any moment I expected him to yank me up. I spoke quickly. "There will be a path to your right as you pass a fallen tree trunk along one side of the road. You'll see it."

He looked confused.

"Take the path and follow it until you hear a stream. Follow its gurgling and you'll find a bend in the brook that almost meets the path. There is cool fresh water and more blackberries than you could ever eat."

Sir Kenway dragged me to my feet.

"Can you get up?" I asked the boy.

Sir Kenway pushed me. "I said not to stop."

I followed him, walking backward to see what the boy would do. He rose slowly. He waved, but did not see me wave in return.

We plunged into the woods on a narrow path.

"It's the regent's doing, you know," said Sir Kenway after a time.

"What is?" I asked, confused.

"In the days of King Alfrid, the people had plenty to eat. The poor were always taken care of by their villages."

I knew what he was about to say. The tutor had carefully divulged it in whispers and meaningful looks, which the queen no doubt did not detect.

"Now," Sir Kenway continued, "no one can even feed his own. The villagers can't worry about orphans. Especially orphans as old as that boy."

I studied his fine tunic with its gold trim. "You did not take pity on the orphan," I said to his back.

He snorted. "And where is your pity for Piers, that servant boy you coddle? I don't see you anxious to go back for him."

I bit my lip, angry. He was no different from his Audrey, trying to hurt me where I was most vulnerable. I wouldn't think about Piers. I couldn't.

As we continued through the forest, I planned my escape, while the sun slid slowly across the sky, like rich butter across the queen's china plate.

After a time, Sir Kenway stepped off the path. We made our way through biting branches and stinging bushes. Everywhere I looked was sameness, but Sir Kenway knew these woods well.

The sun was low and the forest in shadow when he plopped down against a gnarled oak tree. I sat down on fallen leaves and watched him. He said nothing.

"You're waiting for the darkness," I said.

He gave me a curt nod. He didn't trust me. He was wise not to, for I would be gone by morning. I'd disappear tonight, while he slept.

"Do you think the regent has spies in your father's castle?" I asked, trying to draw him out.

"He is evil, Shadow." I could not see his eyes well, but I knew they were on me. "He's depleted the treasury of our great dead king. There's nothing left. If he continues to rule, the people of Deor will die." Such *disdain* in his voice, all kindness gone. It was clear what he thought of me. He truly thought I'd killed her.

The injustice of that riled me. "And you spoke to

our queen about this? Pray, what did she say to do about it?"

He said nothing.

"It is no matter because it's the land that has died," I said, stating what everyone knew. "That's not the regent's fault."

"But why does he still take that barren land? Why does he tax the richer lords? He steals from all of us!"

"Fyren has a legitimate claim to the throne, Sir Kenway," I said, wanting him to admit that truth at least. "His mother was the rightful heir, pushed aside because she was a woman. She taught him to love Deor, and he does love it."

"He doesn't love the *people* of Deor! Don't you see he's starving our kingdom?"

His accusations wearied me. "It is not my kingdom. I have never seen it." I closed my eyes, leaning my head back against the tree. I was ready for silence.

Something hit me on the head. He had thrown it, but I couldn't tell what it was. "Do you care for nothing but yourself?"

Me? I thought, rubbing the sore spot on my head.

Once, I was walking behind the queen and Sir Kenway. Their fingers touched briefly as they strolled along the green. Neither noticed that she dropped her white handkerchief. I picked it up and held it against my cheek. Distracted by the linen's softness, I tripped and fell into black mud.

The queen laughed. Her little foot tapped me on the back — one, two, three. I looked up and saw Sir Kenway staring at the queen with a look of disbelief. His hand reached out to me, but the queen had grabbed it.

His voice came at me now, tight and angry. "Who are you, Shadow? Are you not what you seem?"

"I am no one at all," I said, pulling my cloak around my shoulders.

"I was told to watch over you. Why?"

Watch over me? An icy terror gripped my heart. I knew the old men would use me for their purposes, without a thought to my well-being. But why me? I had no riches, no power, no knowledge beyond what the tutors and Fyren had told me.

I thought of those moments alone with Fyren in the dungeon. I was certain he had told me nothing that could be of use. Maybe Eldred had known of the visit and thought I knew something I didn't.

Sir Kenway clucked his tongue in disgust. "Why do you have any value then?"

Why, for myself, I thought. *I have value for myself.*

Chapter Eleven

It was dark. Sir Kenway told me to stay close. We moved out of the trees into a wide moonlit clearing that encircled the walls of a town. Torchlight blazed in buildings towering over the wall. The town was small, not nearly as large as the castle grounds.

So this was his home. The gentle ladies had whispered about Sir Kenway's father, a fine rich lord. Eldred claimed Lord Leofwine had been one of King Alfrid's closest allies. A man of great dignity, and a fierce, loyal subject of the queen, despite the dim view the realm held of him now.

I only half-believed Sir Kenway was from such stock. Four years ago, he arrived at the castle gates with his father's men accompanying him. He'd said little that day. He had looked as if he might reach out and strike anyone who spoke to him.

The knights had beaten him many times before he was tamed. They were allowed to treat him roughly because of his father's fall from favor. Standing in the shadows then, I watched him and admired his defiance. But how could such a wild child come from anything but a hole in the ground?

Sir Kenway pulled at a large stone in the wall. He gestured for me to help. It was a struggle for us to move it, but we did at last.

We slipped through an opening, arriving behind a house built close to the wall. Sir Kenway moved into a back alley.

My heart was beating fast, from the exertion, and also excitement. Our nighttime prowling reminded me of my attempts at escape. I'd found it exhilarating to move about in the dark while those with casual liberty were in their beds.

The alley spilled out onto a narrow road. Buildings, mostly made of wood and weed, lined the street on each side. Some hung over our heads. With the moon's help, we made our way. The town slept.

We moved around and around in a spiral, circling up and up until we arrived at another high wall. Between two lit torches, Sir Kenway clambered up the side, stepping on uneven stones as if they were the rungs of a ladder.

I was close behind him. As I climbed higher, a cool wind whipped my cloak and my hair around me. The height and the darkness were thrilling.

At the top, Sir Kenway sauntered along a six-inch-wide ridge. He glanced back. His look seemed to challenge me. The ground on the outside wall fell farther away, but that on the inside wall drew up to meet us. When we jumped, it was but a three-foot drop.

The stone courtyard was empty, but lit by torches. Large open windows looked down on us, so we darted in and out of the shadows. We slipped in a side window that had no covering cloth and through small rooms that fell one into the other. Not like the queen's castle, where everything was large and open.

Loud voices came through an open door. I smelled broiled fish and freshly baked bread. I followed Sir Kenway into a large room. A sea of faces looked back at me.

"Kenway?" asked one.

"What is wrong?" shouted another.

He quieted them.

I was introduced as Shadow.

Chapter Twelve

"Father, have you seen anyone from the castle?" Sir Kenway asked. "Any of the queen's men?"

He leaned forward over one end of the long trestle table, his hands pressing against the rough wood. I stood behind him. His father, Lord Leofwine, sat in a large wooden chair at the other end.

The room was long and narrow, with no windows. Smoking torches lined the walls. Platters with spiced fish and roast swan covered the table, along with numerous burning candles. My stomach rumbled.

"We have seen no one from the castle," said Lord Leofwine, pushing his thick silver hair off his forehead. He was a large man, with broad shoulders that belied his age. But the edges of his watery eyes bore the creases of time.

Saliva, carrying a bitter taste, filled my mouth. I felt a rage in him, rooted deep. It was the strangest sensation, to feel it *in* me, and to know it was his feeling. Thankfully, the moment passed quickly. I dismissed it as my imagination. What else could it be?

The servants — an angular-faced girl and a sour-mouthed man — turned to leave, but Sir Kenway gestured for them to stop. "I don't recognize these servants, Father."

Lord Leofwine waved them out of the room. "They are loyal and tight-lipped."

Four people, other than Lord Leofwine, remained: a pretty woman not yet thirty, a young man who was a slightly older version of Sir Kenway, and two young girls.

The fire behind Lord Leofwine crackled and sputtered. The room smelled of smoke, and of the perfume reeking from its inhabitants.

The young man stood, his silk clothes swishing as he moved. "My brother, why are you here? What has happened?"

"The queen is dead, Darwin," said Sir Kenway. His voice cracked, lost and desperate, as if he was seeking comfort now that he was home.

His father's face darkened.

Sir Kenway hung his head. "I'm sorry, Father."

The lord's eyes were on his son, but he seemed to be looking into himself. "The past clings to us."

All began talking, words spilling on top of one another. Sir Kenway straightened. I heard him take a breath. "You must listen."

They were still, and he related the events of the morning.

This family's fate was tied to the queen's. I sensed their fear — dark, rising, reaching for me, too. I fought a feeling of dread. They were not safe.

The woman leaped up, her eyes and hands in a panic. "My husband, what will happen to our daughters?"

Sir Kenway's brother glanced her way, disgust clear on his face. I could not tell to whom she spoke: the brother or the father. She was too young to be Sir Kenway's mother.

"Be quiet!" ordered Lord Leofwine, his deep voice booming.

She fell back into the seat, slumping over. The two girls huddled to her. The older one, her own lip trembling, patted her mother's arm.

"It is odd you haven't heard this yet," I said. They stared at me then. "The castle is close by horseback."

Lord Leofwine gave me a cold look. I knew he thought me insolent. But it was pure joy to give voice to my thoughts without the queen shrieking at me to be quiet.

"My lord," I continued, "you were not meant to know it. Yet."

Sir Kenway's eyes were on me, hot as the fire. "It's not your place to speak here, Shadow." His voice was low, threatening.

He was wrong. The queen's death had freed me, and no one could take that from me now.

"It was the regent who murdered Queen Audrey," he said. "In her sleep." He looked at me when he said it, his belief of my guilt still in his eyes.

Lord Leofwine gripped the edge of the table and leaned forward. "Do you have proof?"

Sir Kenway hesitated. "I didn't see him do it, but I believe it was Fyren. The advisers were afraid it might be so."

What he said was most likely true. It must be Fyren, or else Lord Leofwine would have heard the news from men loyal to him. Only Fyren had the power to conceal the truth this long.

"Either Fyren killed her or he himself is dead," I said.

"He did it," Kenway said, warning me with his eyes.

"The devil himself," Lord Leofwine muttered.

The woman grabbed his hand, her face wet with tears. "We must leave, my husband. We must."

But Lord Leofwine shook her off, and she crumpled back into her daughters. With their dimpled cheeks and chestnut hair, they resembled their mother. The older girl stared at me with pensive blue eyes, though very unlike her mother's small brown ones. She tucked her younger sister closer to her.

"We are loyal to the queen," said Lord Leofwine, his eyes clouding over. He seemed . . . ashamed.

"She's dead!" yelled his wife, grabbing his hand again. "What good will our loyalty serve us now?"

He wrenched out of her grip. "We stay with our town."

"Shadow and I must leave before the sun breaks," said Sir Kenway. "I'll need horses." He flushed. "And a new sword. . . . Everything happened so quickly . . . I had to leave mine behind."

"You idiot," spat his father.

Darwin glanced away. Their reaction irritated me. It might be embarrassing for a knight to lose his sword, but it did not mean he was inept.

Sir Kenway's cheek twitched. "Fyren's troops will be here soon. Our lands, our town is too valuable. He'll try to take it. And soon."

"How do you know he's not on your heels?" Darwin asked.

"He'll move on Lord Callus first. I am most certain he has already done this. If he takes that town, he'll be here, I know it."

"I think you know little for certain, Kenway," said Lord Leofwine.

Kenway ignored this. "You must leave, Father."

"Is that all you can think of? Running? Fyren will be our kingdom's undoing if he's not stopped."

I felt sorry for Sir Kenway, the way he stood there, so shaken by his father's vehemence, but resolute. He leaned forward. "Father. If you leave, we can regroup. Retreat to Lord Heaton's castle. It is farther from Fyren, and easier to defend. Send word out to Redway and Winbolt to meet you. We can rally there."

I saw the wisdom in his plan.

His father rose. "We stay, even if you desert us."

"The advisers gave me a task to do." Sir Kenway looked at me. "We must do it."

And why must I do it if you were given the task? I thought.

Lord Leofwine scowled. "Elene!" he bellowed. He looked soberly at his son. "We must talk."

The bread and yellow cheese on the table were within my reach. My stomach rumbled again loudly.

"Take it," said Sir Kenway, waving his hand. I did.

The angular-faced girl appeared, holding a thick, burning candle.

"Find the girl a place with the servants," Lord Leofwine said, gesturing at me.

"No," said Sir Kenway. He closed his eyes, shaking his head a little. "Elene, take her to the bedchamber next to mine."

The old man gave out a knowing laugh, and his wife eyed me with a disgusted look. My face felt hot. I was suddenly awkward, as silly as the queen's ladies. Even Sir Kenway seemed ill at ease, which made me blush more.

Elene led me down a long passage, lit by torches, which ended at a flight of stairs. All the while, I gobbled up the bread and cheese. At the top of the steps, we passed through a thick wooden door.

The chamber was small, but everything in it was rich

and fine. The servant lit a fire while I looked about. One large window overlooked the town and beyond it. I stuck my head out and breathed in the cold air. I could see only what the moon would allow, but it was clear the drop was too far to the roof below. I could not escape through the window.

The four-poster bed was raised high off the floor. Deep blue blankets were piled on top of the mattress. Not the queen's luxury, but close to it. I felt a smile twitching at my lips. This chamber was delightful.

Elene closed the window, shutting out the cold. She curtsied before turning toward the door.

"Why do you curtsy?" I asked her. "Surely you know I'm not a lady, especially in these coarse and dirty clothes?"

Her face was in the fire's shadows. "You hold yourself like a lady. And speak like one."

"But I am not one." I looked around me. "Is this where I sleep?"

"Is it not to your liking?" she asked.

I laughed. I had never slept in a bed. "Leave me, if you will. I'm settled here now."

I was anxious and wanted to be alone.

When she'd gone, I buried my hands deep in the chill of the covers. What softness. I laid my head against a pillow and sank into the down feather mattress. I could feel the tension leave my legs and arms, my back, my neck. The rich should never be cross or cruel. They had such comforts.

There was a tap on the door. It was one of Sir Kenway's sisters, who could not be more than nine or ten. She looked at me in her brother's earnest way. "May I come in?"

"Yes," I said, eyeing her. But I doubted she could be much trouble. And her serious nature appealed to me.

But with my nod, she dashed across the floor in her silk shoes, slipping on the rushes. She threw herself upon the soft bed.

"Will you marry Kenway?" she asked, peeking out of the covers at me with shining eyes.

Startled by this sudden change in her, I did not answer, but pulled the heavy blankets around me. The large fire crackled, but its warmth had not reached us yet.

She dropped the covers, showing her sweet face. "You don't want to marry him?"

"Your brother's a knight. I am less than common. There will be no wedding for the two of us."

She crinkled her nose. "You are filthy."

I sighed. "It's true," I agreed, thinking of the bath I almost had the day before.

"But you have lovely eyes," she said quickly. "They *are* a little odd, but lovely. Like the sky right before nightfall. A deep blue, like that." She kept looking. "But not exactly like that. But they are beautiful, your best feature."

She was less like her brother than I'd thought. She knew more words than he, or at least she used them more. And I knew Sir Kenway did not find any part of me beautiful and would never say it if he did.

"How long have you known my brother?" she asked.

"Since he came to the queen four years ago."

"Father sent him there," she said, lying on her stomach and cupping her little face with her hands. "He didn't want to, even if Kenway was always in trouble." She knocked her slippered feet together as she spoke. "My brother would never listen or do what he was told."

"I remember when he was like that," I said. "He changed."

"Yes, he is different than he was."

"Always doing what he is told now, I think."

"He does what he thinks is right! He's a loyal knight to the queen." She hesitated. "But now she is dead."

She looked a little worried, but I didn't know what to say to her. "Tell me, why didn't your father want to send your brother to the castle?"

A few wispy strands of hair fell into her eyes as she moved about. "Because the regent is there."

"Ah. Then why did the lord, your father, send him there at all?" I leaned toward her to brush those locks away.

As I came close, she turned up her nose, then pinched it. "To redeem our honor," she said in a nasal voice.

I laughed. "Do I smell?" I sniffed my clothes. "Do I?"

"You need a bath," she said, looking so full of sorrow I laughed again.

"I think you are right," I said. "If only I could."

"I'll find Elene." She ran out of the chamber, yelling for the servant girl.

The two returned. The servant's face was pinched in irritation. But she did as her young mistress bade her, making me a hot bath, with water hauled up from the kitchen and heated over the fire. The little girl put candles all around the floor before she left for her own bedchamber for the night.

As Elene poured in the last steaming bucket, I noticed a wooden medallion hanging from a piece of twine about her neck. The carving was intricate and detailed, but difficult to see in only candlelight. I thought I saw a woman's face upon it.

"What is that?" I asked. "It's beautiful."

She gave me a weary smile. "Why, it's the mother of us all."

I didn't know what she meant, but it was clear she thought I should. "Where did you get it?"

"From my father. He lived in the mountains to the north and made it for me many years ago. It is a treasure. Not many exist." She studied my face for a moment, and I wondered at her thoughts. But then she just shook her head and mumbled to herself. I reached for the medallion, but she tucked it into her dress. "Come on. Let's get you clean," she said, not unkindly. She was tired, I was sure, and had had enough of me.

I had never had a bath.

Water dripped from the wooden tub. I stepped in carefully, feeling the delicious heat pull at my toe, then foot, then ankle, then calf. Finally, I stood with both feet in, and then dropped down, bottom to the tub floor. My body sank into bliss. I closed my eyes and sighed as my sore muscles relaxed.

The girl scrubbed my scalp and cleaned my teeth. She brushed out my hair, each stroke upon my head a scratchy pleasure, and dried it in the heat from the fire.

She settled me into my sheets and covers, and blew out the candles. Even her quiet shutting of the door added to my feeling of peace.

I listened to her retreating footsteps, humming a little to myself. I had never been so comfortable, so clean, and surrounded by such softness. Then I remembered, the thought jarring me: I should be planning my escape. Soon all would be sleeping, and I must leave.

I must.

I closed my eyes. The sheets smelled so fresh. I smelled so fresh. I didn't drift into sleep, though; my body seemed to be on edge, as if it was waiting. But for what? A sign that the house was quiet? That all were in bed?

In the distance, I heard footsteps, a door shut close by. Noise drifted in through the connecting door. I heard a cough and knew it was Sir Kenway. Quiet again.

I dreamed of baths, dry fountains, headless statues, medallions . . . and Piers, his gray eyes accusing me.

Chapter Thirteen

I awoke to shouting.

It was dark, not yet dawn. I pushed Piers from my thoughts, as well as my memory of the grim morning before when I'd found the queen.

I sat up, listening.

Quiet.

Had we been discovered? So soon? Were we so valuable? I cursed. I'd been foolish. I should have fled during the night.

I got up and crossed the chamber, stepping into the passageway. The torches were low, so I could see little. I peered through the open doorway of Sir Kenway's large bedchamber to my left. The fire still burned strong, but his room was empty. A large tub of water stood in front of the fireplace.

I hesitated, shivering in my white shift. It was time to leave this place. I headed back to my own chamber to find my clothes. But then I heard shouting again. I put on the thick dressing gown lying at the foot of the bed. Grabbing a torch, I lit it in the fire, welcoming the rush of heat on my face.

Then I plunged back into the cold, drafty passageway.

Shadows flitted up and down the stone walls. All the other doors were shut. Did no one else hear this shouting?

Carefully, I took the stairs. This could not be Fyren's men. The shouting was sporadic and brief, breaking open the quiet for just a moment before retreating again.

I placed the torch in an empty iron brace at the foot of the stairs. Agitated voices came out of the great hall the family dined in. I pressed my back to the hard wall and listened.

"How could you do this, Kenway? How could you let this happen?"

"I could do nothing to stop it, sir."

"You have failed me, then! And you'll be judged by that failure."

"Judged by whom? By you?"

"By yourself."

The fire crackled in the quiet. But then Kenway's low voice could be heard. "I'll not waste my life away as —"

"What? As I have?"

Silence again.

"And who is this mysterious girl you've brought with you? You . . ." The rest was so low I missed it. I crept closer to the doorway.

Oh so quietly, I peeked in. Lord Leofwine, such a large man, looked down on his tall son. Sir Kenway wore a loose white shirt and no tunic. His hair was wet as if he had just gotten out of the bath.

"I cannot say," he told his father.

"You keep secrets from me? You and that old man? There was a time I knew all of Deor's secrets."

"Those days are past."

The smack came loud on Sir Kenway's face, jerking his head to the side. I almost gasped. He snapped it back and met his father's angry glare. I saw him clench and unclench his fist and noticed I was doing the same to mine.

"*I* was the king's closest friend!" yelled Lord Leofwine.

He turned. I ducked back.

Silence, except for Kenway's quick breaths. I looked back in.

"You were always a coward, Kenway. I remember how you hid when your mother died."

He was wrong. Kenway was no coward.

"You mean when I was *five*, Father."

"Cowardice always emerges at an early age," said Lord Leofwine, sneering. "Still seeing ghosts?"

Sir Kenway flinched.

"I should have sent your brother to the castle instead of you."

"But you could not part with him, my lord, so that wasn't a path you would have ever taken."

"You are no longer welcome here."

"Father," Sir Kenway said. "I must speak to you about your plans."

"You will be gone before I wake."

"You must reconsider your decision to remain. I don't believe it's the wisest —"

"Leave me."

"The girls, Father —"

"Leave me!"

I hid in the shadows while Kenway strode past. In the wild light of his torch, his face looked like the lost boy I had first seen so many years ago. My stomach lurched. I swear I felt my own cheek pound in pain.

I must have made some noise because he turned to look.

"What are you doing there?" he demanded, coming toward me.

I said nothing. I should have been more careful.

He pulled me farther into the shadows. "Eavesdropping?"

I could not deny it.

"And did you hear what you came to hear?" he asked in an angry hush, looking back toward the great hall.

I glanced that way as well, seeing nothing. Was his father listening to us now? "I heard voices. I thought we'd been found."

He stepped closer, his eyes on mine, his voice low. "You are always where you should not be." He studied me as if he were just now seeing me, and all I could do was look back. "Why did Eldred trust you, Shadow?"

"I'm not sure he did."

"He told me to keep you safe, at all costs. Why would the queen's closest adviser give me such a command?"

I shook my head. "I am as confused as you."

"And you expect me to believe you?"

"As you say, *Eldred* must have trusted me." But as I said the words, even I could not believe them.

"I do not," he said, but softly, as if he didn't own the words. He was so near, looking at me in a way I was not accustomed to. I dropped my eyes and found myself staring at the bare neck above his collar. I could not help myself. I wanted to feel his skin just there. I raised my hand; it was shaking. I could see his heart beating.

But he wrapped his fingers around mine, stilling my hand. "Did you kill her? *Did* you?"

"No," I said quickly. "I didn't." I looked up, and there were his eyes.

"Swear it."

"I do swear. I did not harm her."

We were both quiet as we looked at each other in this new, close way. We seemed fixed in this place.

"Who are you really?" he asked, in a different voice. "Are you not what you seem?" This softer tone drew me toward him. "Shadow," he said, his breathing fast. He put his hand on the side of my face, sending a spark through me. I knew what he was feeling. It was desire, curious and sweet. "Such eyes."

I leaned in, feeling his warm breath upon my mouth, wanting —

"I will speak with you!"

We broke apart. Lord Leofwine stood in the doorway, staring at me.

"What do you want with her, Father?" Kenway asked. He seemed remarkably unflustered, while I felt my face burn red.

"I told *you* to go," Lord Leofwine said, turning on his heel and going back into the room. "Come, girl!"

Sir Kenway took my arm. "I'll see to him." He jerked his head in the direction of the stairs. "Return to your chamber."

I pulled out of his grip, looking at him in surprise, wounded he would treat me so after such a moment.

He stared at me, his mouth set in that stubborn line. "Shadow," he said, his voice now softer.

"I'm not afraid of your father." I turned away before he could answer.

Lord Leofwine sat in his place, his back to the fire. The smoke of numerous fat candles drifted between our faces. I pulled my dressing gown tighter around me.

I stood at the end of the table, facing him. I couldn't see his features well. But he could see me, I knew, because torches blazed on the walls beside me. *Do not let him frighten you*, I thought. I had dealt with old men before. Still, my heart raced.

He drummed his fingers on the table. I waited.

"Tell me your name!" he demanded.

"I have no name, my lord."

"Don't play with me. What is your name?"

"It died with my mother, I guess."

"My son said you are called Shadow."

"If you knew my name, why did you ask me it?"

His chair skidded back as he sprang to his feet. "You insolent girl! I will turn you out." I could feel the violence in him, emerging from a soul boiling with bitterness and rage. It made me wonder what he was capable of doing, and what he might have done in his past. I held still.

He came toward me. "How did the queen die?"

"It must have been poison, my lord."

He pushed his face into mine. I caught my breath. He smelled of old sweat and stale beer. "You were in the bed-chamber with her?"

"Sleeping on the floor next to her, my lord."

"Did you murder her?"

"No."

"But you are not sorry she's dead," he said, startling me. A smile crept across his face. "You are more transparent than you think. Yes, I believe you are a hard-hearted girl."

This rich old man, who had never had to saddle his own horse or dump his own chamber pot, thought he could judge me. What did he know of the betrayal only the poor and powerless could feel? If my soul was filled with shadows, it was the queen who put that darkness there.

"What does Eldred want with you? What?"

"I don't know, my lord," I said.

He crept even closer, thrusting his face into mine, peering at my every feature. "You are familiar to me," he muttered.

He was half mad, I knew.

"Get out," he said, quiet now. "Out."

I backed away, wondering if he'd always been this way. Sir Kenway's life had not been the easy one I'd imagined.

Once in my chamber, I fell onto my bed, shaking. Despite his age, Lord Leofwine was a formidable man. An intense power emanated from him. He might now be in disgrace, but he was no traitor. His loyalty to the crown did not seem feigned.

But as much as these thoughts confused me, another pushed them away. Sir Kenway. He had almost kissed me, and I was giddy with delight, but that was coupled with a feeling of foolishness. I had observed this same silliness in the queen and silently mocked her for it. I admitted to myself, with reluctance, that I now understood her a little more.

I buried my hands into the down mattress, slipping into its softness, letting it soothe my anxious thoughts. Who knew the touch of a pillow could be so gentle, like a caress upon the cheek?

I should feel gratitude to old Eldred. If not for him, I would not be in this bed. Still, I could feel his icy dead hand upon my back, directing me this way and that. I was free, but he was here, too, pushing Sir Kenway and me to follow his orders from beyond the grave. What could he possibly want of me now that his queen was dead?

I never believed I was actually born at the castle. Fay told me my mother had been a scullery maid. She'd given birth to me in a small cottage inside the walls and that was where she'd died. If so, where was her grave? Not among the bleak tombstones at the edge of the castle grounds. I knew because I'd looked. Fay was not to be trusted anyway.

Perhaps I was found in a quiet village and brought to

the queen. A poor orphan to serve her and protect her. Eldred could be sending me back to my birthplace. But why? What did I have that he wanted? Or that he *had* wanted?

I covered myself with the light sheet, pondering. What would the queen say if she could see me now with silk against my skin? What would she say if she knew her knight had almost kissed me? But I realized, with surprise, that these thoughts brought me no joy, instead only hollowness.

My door creaked open. I froze. If it were the old lord, I would fight him, even if it meant the dungeon for me. But it wasn't the old lord I saw in the lantern's light.

I shut my eyes. I felt him looking at me, studying me, trying to decipher me. A strong rush of feeling poured from him, suspicion still, but something else, too, that I couldn't figure out. My own feelings toward him were just as mixed.

How did I *know* this?

Sir Kenway continued to stand over me. I could hear him breathing. Did he think he could know my mind by watching me sleep?

He crept back out and closed the door.

Chapter Fourteen

Light taps on my door pulled me from sleep. The moon was still up.

It was Sir Kenway. I felt my cheeks warm as I remembered last night.

He lifted his chin. "It's time." His eyes were red, his face drawn. I doubted he'd slept at all. I smiled and stretched, feeling refreshed. Ah, no wonder the queen didn't wish to rise in the morning — her bed was too soft.

I dressed in clothes that had been left for me. Another linen shift. A light blue dress, fashioned of silk. A wool cloak, soft and thick. Slippers for shoes. Fine leather gloves. Clothes not practical for traveling.

I smoothed down the sheets before I left.

A yawning stable boy was waiting for us, holding the reins of two black horses. Strands of blond hair hung over his pinched and tired face. He hustled away as soon as we were up in the saddles. As we clip-clopped our way through the narrow streets, I thought of Kenway's slumbering sisters in their beds. Innocents. To what world would they wake?

We rode in the cold dark, not saying a word. But the sun soon rose, softening the sky with pale pinks. *This is the color of a mother's love for a child*, I thought.

The land was rolling into low hills, with the mountains of the north in the distance. We took little-trod paths, staying off the main roads, riding at a brisk pace. We traveled mostly through forest, but occasionally rode long stretches through clearings. Sir Kenway was the most anxious during these times, watching all around us, listening.

It was difficult to look at him and not think of last night, how we'd almost kissed. He'd felt the same desire I did, I had seen it in his eyes. But this morning, he was short-tempered and distant. His coldness from the day before had returned.

I remembered how he'd ordered me about when his father interrupted us. He may have almost kissed me, but he still thought of me as lowly Shadow. That realization rankled.

But I would not let him affect my delight over this bright day. Deor might be in decline, but its forests and hills were beautiful. I'd felt no connection to this country, for it had treated me very poorly, but I was finding I appreciated its loveliness.

I lingered to look at a fox peering at me from the brush. I'd never seen a fox. What a rich red coat he wore! He scurried off when Sir Kenway yelled, "You're lagging behind!"

He couldn't have been more than thirty feet away.

"Perhaps if you told me where we were going, I would feel more inclined to do as you say."

He came toward me quickly. His face was dark, reminding me of his father's. "I will tell you nothing, and you'll still do as I say."

I looked to the heavens.

Grabbing my reins, he yanked me closer. I felt my horse resist the pull. His front hooves flew in the air. I clutched at the saddle, the animal's black mane, anything, to keep from falling. Down the horse came, neighing loudly, and I lurched forward. Then again he reared, and I slid back and back.

"Oof!" Pain shot through my backside when I hit the ground.

Sir Kenway was off his horse, trying to calm mine down. "Get up," he ordered.

I shot him an angry glance and stood up slowly, wincing. Such throbbing pain. Fury poured through me. I'd been a fool to let him close to me. "Do *not* take your father's wrath out on me."

He reddened. I knew my barb had bit deep. "Which you discovered while spying on me, as you did when I was with the queen."

"I have no interest in what you do," I said.

Grabbing my arm tightly, he gave me a long look. "We both know that's a lie. Get on your horse."

I yanked away and, quite slowly, did as he said.

The silence was cold between us. Sir Kenway had indeed ruined the lovely day.

◦◦◦

When the sun was overhead, we stopped by a clear lake. The horses took long drinks, sending ducks quacking to another part of the water.

I retreated to rest under a nearby elm. Sir Kenway came over to me. He laid his new sword down beside him as if he thought he might need it at any moment. I took the dried figs and bread he offered.

He was alert, looking toward the woods and out across the lake. His vigilance amused me. If Fyren wanted us captured, we'd already be in his hands.

Sir Kenway leaned against the tree, his feet out in front of him. He hadn't said a word to me since I'd fallen off the horse. I saw no reason to speak to him. His mood was withdrawn and dark.

"The horses need the rest," he said, "but we should not stay long."

I bit off a piece of bread and kept silent.

"I didn't mean for you to fall," he continued.

I narrowed my eyes, suspicious.

"You were clumsy," he said.

"How you charm me," I said.

He looked discomfited. A knight, even an arrogant one, did not like to be thought uncourtly. *Or at least not this one*, I thought. "Your looks have improved," he said as if this would please me.

A sweet feeling tingled in my stomach. But his compliment was not for me; rather, it was for my fine dress. The rich are always fascinated by rich things. I was no different from the poorly clothed girl of the day before. I sat cross-legged underneath my silk skirts, leaning over my food. I must admit, though, I liked the feel of the silk.

"Your father's wife is not your mother?" I asked, trying to provoke him. I stuck a fig in my mouth. It was so sweet.

His eyes flashed. "My mother died when I was five."

We had something in common, at least. "You do not like your father's wife?"

"She's common, not worthy to be the wife of a lord," he said.

"Then your sisters are common, too?"

His face twitched. So he did love his sisters. I thought better of him for loving someone other than the queen.

"I don't understand," I said, looking at him directly. "Why didn't you stay with your father? Eldred is dead, and so are his schemes. You and I don't have to follow his wishes anymore."

He snorted. "That is exactly how I would expect you to see it."

"Yes, that's how I see it. But I asked why *you* do not."

"Where is your sense of duty? Deor is your country, too."

I gave a quick nod. "Kind of you to acknowledge it." I was a little surprised he thought the kingdom belonged to all countrymen, not only the nobility.

"You don't deserve it."

"Perhaps it hasn't been as good to me."

He watched me closely. I was accustomed to the look. It was distrust. "You are friends with the regent," he said.

I gave out an unladylike snort. "We are not friends. He is the regent, and I am lowly born, as you said."

"Why did he visit you in the dungeon?"

I looked up into his narrowed eyes.

"He freed me," I said carefully. "Eldred and Piers were with him."

"Not that visit. The one before that."

I could only stare at him. How had he known? The only secrets in that castle were the ones kept from me.

"What bargain did you make with him, Shadow?"

"We made no bargain."

"Why did he visit you then?" he asked coldly. I could sense something in him, like jealousy. But it could not be that.

I thought about my answer. If I kept the truth from

him, he would suspect me of worse. Still, I was reluctant to give him any information. He didn't have a right to it. "He wanted me to do something for him, it is true, but I refused."

"What did he want?"

I shrugged. "He didn't tell me."

"And you didn't *ask*," he said.

"I did, but I was afraid to know."

His mouth was set in a grim line. "You could have saved her."

"Saved her? The queen?"

"Just days before her murder, he asks you for a favor. You! What favor could you give him that didn't involve the queen?"

Must he always accuse me? "I concede, Sir Kenway, I might have found out something useful. But I thought it best not to be entangled in any of Fyren's schemes. What could I have done? I am not one of you."

"You might have pretended to go along so you could discover what he wanted. But instead you did nothing." He stared at me. "You killed her anyway."

I shook my head. "No." But I again remembered her that last night, when I ignored her cries. Had she been dying? "No," I whispered. But his words settled into me. I could not shake them out.

"How am I to believe anything you say?" he asked.

"I have told you only the truth," I said, my thoughts still on his accusation about the queen.

"You may deny it, but your friendship with the regent was known by everyone. You flaunted it, especially in front of Queen Audrey. You only spoke to *him*. Does that not look suspicious?"

I looked up, irritated. "He was the only one who spoke to me." I didn't mention I also talked with Piers. I knew Sir Kenway didn't consider him to have any worth. "If I was kind to him, it was because he was kind to me."

Kenway studied me. "You show little warmth toward others, Shadow. People don't befriend you because you are too cold, too severe in your manner."

This riled me. "It is because I am common and of no consequence to you nor to the queen nor to anyone. Just as your *stepmother* is of no consequence to you."

I could tell he hated me in that moment, but I had lost my patience with him. Must I listen to these accusations, one after the other? He would find fault with me no matter what I did.

"Where are we going?" I called after him as he strode to his horse. He wouldn't answer me. And I was left to wonder again about our destination. But I could not think of where it would be.

We talked no more. He was still very anxious, and he pressed us hard, afraid of ghosts on our heels. What could we have that Fyren would want? Did Kenway carry some valuable object in his saddlebag?

I cursed silently. I didn't know why we were being chased. I didn't know where we were going. I didn't know why Kenway had taken me with him. Here I was, trapped again, just as I had been in the castle. He almost kissed me last night, and today he accused me. It was clear what he thought of me. I was not to be trusted, but would be used, one way or the other.

I studied his proud, straight back, knowing I should try and escape. But where would I go? Were there villages close by? I could not survive in the woods on my own.

Now was not the time. I would know it when it presented itself.

We rode until almost nightfall and settled down into our thick wool blankets on a bed of brown needles in the forest. I lay on my back, feeling my body sink into the shape of the Earth. Tall thin pines swayed in the wind, lulling me as if I were a babe in a cradle. Back and forth, they rocked and creaked. Their sharp scent floated down to me.

Hot tears stung my cold cheeks. Why was I crying? They were not tears for the queen. I did not believe it. It was not my fault she had died. Nothing could have cured her of the poison.

I did not rejoice over her death, but I *was* glad to be away from her. It was not evil of me to think so, after what she'd done to me, was it? I just wanted peace. Could I not have that? Just a quiet place of my own, where I was not subject to the will or suspicion of others. Was that too much?

"Shadow." It was Sir Kenway's voice, although softer.

I swiped at my cheek, saying nothing.

"Are you all right?" he asked.

"Yes," I said.

"Are you afraid?"

I wanted to laugh at his terrible guess. "Are you?"

Even with the light of the full moon, I couldn't read his face. I imagined his look of irritation: his lips twisting as if he tasted something sour.

"You're not easy to like, Shadow. You seem to enjoy insulting me."

I felt a pang of discomfort at that. "Why should I be kind to you? You, who detest common people so much, even your own sisters."

"I love my sisters," he said in a low, angry voice.

"How can you love them when they are common like me?"

"They have noble blood running through their veins."

"Not tainted, then?" I asked.

He sat up. "You deliberately try to provoke me."

The pine needles danced above us. "I liked you better when you were wild and young," I told him.

He was still. "You remember me then?"

"Yes," I confessed. "You had a fire in you."

"It was my father's shame that sent me there. To the castle," he said. "I know what they whispered behind my back."

I was silent, wanting him to speak again. The moon was a round open eye, watching us.

"My father was King Alfrid's protector," he said at last, in a hollow voice. "His most loyal knight. And friend. He failed him."

The king had been murdered just three months after his wedding day. Stabbed through the heart. The murderer was never found. The queen's ladies liked to gossip about that day. Ingrid claimed it was then the kingdom began to die, but Hilda said otherwise.

"It was so long ago, Sir Kenway. Who remembers that part of it?" But I knew they did remember it.

"Some even say it was my father who killed the king."

"There was no proof of that."

"Of course not. My father was loyal to the crown. But he did fail his king, his country, his family! It was his fault the king died. His fault Queen Anne grew so weak from grief she died in childbirth. His fault the country died with her."

His voice ached with sadness. I felt as if it were my own sadness, as if the wind were blowing it from his soul to mine. I tried to push it away.

I wanted to reach out to him and touch his hand.

But I did not.

"We need to sleep, Shadow." He turned his back to me. I was thankful for the silence and closed my eyes.

Chapter Fifteen

Hot breath in my ear, a hand over my mouth. I was ready to bite fingers when I realized it was Sir Kenway. "Fyren's spies," he whispered. "Lie still." The moonlight caught the glint of a knife in his hand.

And with that he was gone, slipping into the darkness of the pines.

I waited, my heart beating wildly. The night was still. Who were these men? Kenway had said spies, which made no sense. Why would we be *spied* upon and not just taken?

I did not move. I thought he meant me to be the prey. The longer I waited, the more agitated I became. How long did he expect me to lie here and do nothing? Where was he?

I heard the snap of a twig and shot up. All I could see was darkness. I listened hard, but it was eerily quiet.

If I was being watched, then let them come for me. I would not feign sleep any longer.

When I stood, one of the horses let out a breathy snort. I went to the trees to which they were tied, feeling safer at the edge of the clearing. I looked through Sir Kenway's saddlebags. There were no weapons there.

He had taken his father's jeweled sword with him.

I stayed by the horses, anxious. I couldn't wander off on my own. Even if I took my horse and left, where would I go? I didn't know these woods. I swore. No weapons, no sense of where I was — my vulnerability was alarming.

The horse shifted beside me. I put my hand on his nose and whispered softly in his ear, trying to calm him. The warmth of him soothed me as well.

What if Sir Kenway was killed? A pang of worry shot through me. I knew it *did* matter to me what happened to him, greatly.

It was as if he were seeping into me, getting too close. I shivered.

I must look after myself. My friend Piers had known that.

But that wasn't true, and I knew it, no matter how many times I told myself otherwise. I saw his little face in my mind's eye, heard his voice in my head: *We must look after each other, Shadow.* Of course he had not understood. He had not. And I had left him.

I closed my eyes, trying to still these thoughts. Guilt over Piers, even the queen, and now I was to worry about Kenway as well? What was this new doubt plaguing me? I had always been able to set myself apart from what others thought of me or did to me or did to one another.

I must put my mind to only what was before me. I needed to look after myself. It was the one thing I did well.

Noise erupted behind me, in the direction Sir Kenway had gone. I moved behind the tree, and the horse stepped toward me, wanting my hand upon his nose once more. Cowardly thing. But wasn't my own heart pounding?

The rustling of branches was distinct and loud.

Kenway emerged from the forest. I let out a sigh.

"Are you hiding?" he asked. "Because I can see you."

Sweat poured off his face, despite the cool of the night. He was flushed.

"Did you find them?" I asked, looking at his sword and knife. No blood that I could see.

"No."

"You let them get away?"

He shot me a look, but said nothing. I wondered if he had indeed imagined it. I hoped he wasn't that skittish.

"How did you know we were being watched?" I asked.

"I woke to a stirring in the woods and thought I saw a figure there," he said, pointing to the south edge of the clearing.

"You thought?"

"There *was* someone there."

I watched him take a drink from his flask. "When you woke me, you said spies."

"What?" He wiped his face with a cloth from his bag.

"You said that Fyren's spies were here. Why did you say spies and not his soldiers or his men?"

Something came into his eyes, briefly. I knew he was keeping something from me.

I studied him for a moment. He didn't look away. Instead, he searched my eyes as I searched his, both of us seeking answers. And then it seemed as if he had decided something.

"Eldred told me . . . ," he began, then looked as if he might not speak after all. I kept all expectation from my face and waited.

Finally, he spoke. "There is someone else we must find, who will come with us."

"Someone else? Pray, who?"

He said nothing.

"Where is he?" I asked.

He turned from me.

I stilled my lips. I knew Kenway wouldn't tell me much. He was still trying to sort me out. But that he revealed what he did meant he trusted me a little.

But I had to ask one more thing. "After we find him, where will we go?"

He sat down and leaned against a tree. "Go to sleep, Shadow."

I stared at him for a moment, then gave up and lay back down. So we were only being followed because we were leading Fyren to someone he wanted?

Interesting, but at least it didn't concern me.

Chapter Sixteen

I shifted uncomfortably in the saddle. I was not accustomed to such long rides, and my backside was still bruised from my fall. It was early afternoon. We were both tired from the sleepless night before.

We rode in a wide valley. It might have been beautiful once. I saw patches of wildflowers sprinkled along the graceful curves of the land. But the beauty was infrequent. Our horses trampled through brittle grass and dried-up streams, and our path led upward into dark, ominous hills. The mountains loomed over us.

I could not help but watch him. His strong hands upon the reins, eyes forward, alert, scanning the path before us. And yet, despite his vigilance, he rode with an easy grace and calm, as if he was ready to meet any challenge. I saw it in the set of his shoulders —

"Shadow," he said, his eyes suddenly on mine. Startled, I looked away, cursing under my breath. My feelings always so plain, right there for him to see.

He paused, then smiled a little.

"What?" I asked, my cheeks hot.

He shook his head, looking pleased at my discomfort.

"Are we still followed by your spies, do you think?" I asked.

"Yes."

"Yes?" I asked.

"We are being followed," he said quietly, "whether you believe it or not."

"Perhaps they're only," I said, dropping my voice, "spirits."

He gave me a quick look. "You may mock me, but I am right."

I grew serious. "Then shouldn't you confront them?"

He said nothing, just continued to lead us toward the northern mountains of Deor, which stretched from coast to coast. I was curious about this part of the kingdom. The nobility cared little for the people who dwelled in the mountains. They were rumored to be wild and not easily ruled. *Good for them*, I thought.

But subtle hints from the tutor, and even from Eldred, had suggested that *all* Deorians were descendants of the mountain people. The nobility were ashamed of the Northerners, considering them to be rough and not enlightened. They were the past; the south, Deor's future.

We took a narrow path with sheer rock walls that were high and close. This cut twisted and turned so I could not see what lay in front of us. I glanced back at Kenway. "Those men will trap us here."

"So you finally believe we are being followed?" he asked, giving me a steady look.

I pulled on the reins and turned to him. "They can more easily kill us here."

"If they wanted to do that, they would have done it already."

"They need us to lead them to this person they want?"

"I didn't lie to you. They will not harm us, yet."

I paused.

"There is no time, Shadow." He nodded, saying, "Go."

I prodded my horse, conceding Kenway was right.

After a while, he spoke again. "Just up ahead, to your left, there will be an entrance to a cave. It will be dark, too dark to see. Lead your horse into it."

"Too dark to see?" I asked over my shoulder. "How will we not get lost?"

"I know these caves. We will not get lost." He paused. "But they will."

I was intrigued. "How will we find our way beneath the Earth without light?"

"The caves are not beneath the Earth."

I flicked the reins, still not convinced.

The next entrance was more tall than wide. Beyond the jagged opening was nothing but blackness. I looked back at Sir Kenway.

"It's the one," he said, nodding.

I grinned, feeling a little thrill. Perhaps I should have been frightened, but I only felt excitement at what we might discover.

He smiled, shaking his head. "I am glad you are pleased. Shall we go on?"

I urged my horse forward.

We were plunged into darkness. I could not see, but I could tell we weren't going down into the Earth. The ground was level.

It was eerie riding without seeing. My horse was calm, for which I was glad. I could hear Kenway behind me, and that was all. The cave was dark and quiet, but in an inviting way. I was not afraid.

The corridor was narrow. I could reach out and touch the sandy walls. We moved slowly. After we turned a few more corners, light flooded in from above, giving the caves a reverent beauty. I looked up and there was the sky, visible through large holes in the roof.

"These walls are limestone," said Sir Kenway. "The caves are aboveground with passages weaving through them. Go to your right."

The entrances of three caverns were easily seen in the light from above. The right one was more narrow than the other two, and the darkest.

I did as Kenway bade me.

Again, we were plunged into blackness.

That was the way it went. Sometimes we walked short distances in the dark, sometimes we moved through lit, open chambers. The numerous paths split off in many directions. At each fork, Kenway would tell me which way to go.

And finally, the path ended.

I slid off my horse. We were in an open area enclosed by large, rounded rocks. A dark blue sky was above, and a deep pool before us. My horse ambled over and began drinking. I took a few handfuls of the water myself. It was cold and delicious.

This place was still and serene. I breathed in the natural peace, feeling it soothe my tense thoughts. I glanced back at Sir Kenway and could not help but smile.

He was off his horse, leading her around the water. I grabbed the reins of mine and followed him.

We came to an area of smooth rock, set off a little from the pond. Kenway began pulling blankets and supplies off the horses. I joined him. Silently, we fed the animals and brushed them down. I spread out our blankets on a flat area of the white-gray rock.

"No fire again tonight," said Kenway.

I nodded. Surely we didn't need it in this magical place. I half-expected a smokeless fire to appear before us.

I continued to look around, letting the loveliness sink in. "I do believe you were right, Sir Kenway," I said. "No one can find us here."

"Luck is with them if they do."

He handed me some food, and we settled on the rocks. I envied him his freer clothes as I smoothed my skirts down to put my bread and hard cheese in my lap.

"I did not kill her, Sir Kenway," I said. "The queen. I did not kill her."

His head came up. "So you said."

"You don't believe me?" I asked.

"I'm surprised you want me to," he said.

"I don't." The cheese was crumbly and mild. "But I didn't."

"It is true Eldred trusted you."

He had such faith in the old man. Why did he revere him so? "And if Eldred trusted me, then you'd follow his lead?" I asked. "I don't understand why you used him as a guide."

"Why did you dislike him?"

"Why did you trust him?"

"I'm not sure I do in every matter," he said, staring at me. But I caught a smile and realized with a sweet pang he was teasing me.

"Perhaps that's wise."

"You didn't answer me," he said, serious again.

I paused. "He was always watching me, telling me to do this or that, to protect the queen, to be with her always. Protect the queen. Protect her from death, from harm."

"You were jealous of her."

"She was jealous of me!"

"Yes," he said, "she was."

I looked at his sober face, surprised. Did I not truly believe it? Even when I had said it myself? "But I had nothing. She had everything. How could someone who has everything be jealous?"

"People always want more."

"Yes," I agreed, watching him. "What do you want, then?"

"I want what's best for my country, my family. I want to honor both."

"Deor, Deor, Deor," I said.

"Yes," he said. "Deor."

"Why is this place so important?" But as the question left my lips, I was aware again of the beauty around me.

"If you do not understand why, if you do not already feel it, I cannot make you understand."

"Now you sound like Eldred, even Fyren."

Kenway was silent for a moment. "It was Eldred who had you released from prison, you know."

"Eldred? That couldn't be."

He nodded. "It was."

I would not feel gratitude to Eldred for that. He wouldn't have released me because of any care for me.

I watched Sir Kenway cut a piece off an apple with his knife. He stuck it in his mouth and I again thought of our almost kiss. He looked at me, our eyes meeting. Flustered, I looked down.

He was still. I didn't want to look up at him. I didn't like these feelings.

I was aware of our isolation from the world in this quiet place. No father to interrupt us. No queen between us.

I felt him looking at me. I forced myself to look up and meet his eyes. He sat with his legs drawn up, his arms on his knees. His hands weren't moving now, the knife, the half-eaten apple in his relaxed hands.

He put the apple down, the knife down beside it. I thought he might come to me, but he didn't. He kept watching me, and I, him.

Finally, he stood. Without a word, he walked off from me, going down to the pond. He cupped his hands and splashed some water on his face. He stayed there, looking out at the water.

Chapter Seventeen

It was barely light when we saddled the horses. Sir Kenway led this time, taking us through the dark caves. We left by a different opening than we'd entered.

"Do you think we've lost Fyren's men?" I asked.

He nodded. "Let us hope."

We went south out of the mountains and into the rocky hills. We were no longer on a path and rode side by side. The wind was calm, and our pace slow.

It was a long day.

"We're almost to the village," he said.

"Village?" I asked, glad for the news. I was ready to be out of the saddle.

"I have not visited in a year or more," he said, his voice tired. "It rests beside a river, which used to be wide and deep. But I hear it's much different now. We'll stay there the night and start again early in the morning."

"Do you know someone there?" The person he needed to find couldn't be in this village. I'd assumed Eldred had sent Kenway for someone of wealth or standing. Perhaps a powerful lord with an army at the ready? But how could I not have heard of such a man?

Kenway paused. "I do know someone there. Malcolm worked for my father for many years. He taught me to use a sword when I was eight. He's a skilled fighter."

"Your friend, then?" I asked.

He shrugged a shoulder. "We're not of the same rank, but I like him well enough."

"So we are to visit him?" I asked.

But Kenway would say no more.

The hills grew less riddled with rocks and had little vegetation. We wound through them and headed toward a particularly large one. I could see it flattened out, with white boulders atop it. I wondered if we were close to the village because Sir Kenway seemed more alert.

Soon, we were on the hill, pushing our weary horses up.

"Erce is on the other side," Sir Kenway said.

"Erce?" I asked. "That is our destination?"

"You know it?" he asked, his eyes suddenly on me.

"Only recently," I said, watching him back. "Fyren mentioned it to Eldred."

He was startled. "What did he say about it?"

I prodded my horse, trying to think. But exhaustion pulled at me. I wanted to be at the top of the hill. It was not a steep incline, but this day's journey seemed endless. Knowing we were close to food and rest made me want it all the more. "Much has happened in the few days since then. . . . If I remember right, Fyren asked if Eldred had heard anything about Erce."

Kenway was clearly bothered by this news.

"What is it?" I asked.

He did not answer.

"Must you always keep me in the dark?" I was exasperated with not knowing.

He hesitated, looking over at me. "Erce is the ancient name of the village. It was renamed years ago — it is now called New Place. I didn't think Fyren knew that."

"Do you think his men will be there?" I asked in a rush.

He gave me a quick look. "Eldred knew this? That Fyren knew of Erce?"

"Yes."

"You are certain?" he asked.

"Certain. It was the night I was released from the dungeon."

He said nothing else, so I was quiet as well. But he was clearly more agitated.

Unease came over me as we rode on. We were almost to the top, which I was thankful for. But something felt very wrong. *Felt, felt. So frustrating!* I was turning into such a sensitive creature. I did not understand, nor want, these new feelings.

I tried to still my unease by thinking of the peaceful pond within the caves. I remembered that calm, holding it. That peace sank deep inside of me and rested.

But then — something else was there, at the edges. I tried to push it out. But it was dark, and it chewed and scratched. What was this *feeling*, so intense, so relentless and fevered? And now, it was no longer at the edges. It soared into me, dark and black, like flying ashes.

"Kenway?" I asked. "Are we still being followed?"

He looked around quickly. "Why do you ask? I see no one." His eyes combed my face. "What's wrong, Shadow?" He grabbed my reins and slowed both our horses. "You are so pale."

"Kenway."

"What is it? Are you ill?"

"The village . . . all is not well there."

"We cannot even see Erce from here. It's on the other side of the hill," he said, waving toward it.

"Do you smell smoke?" I asked.

He stared at me and something came into his eyes. He pushed my reins into my hands and rode quickly up the hill.

I was right behind him. At the peak, we looked down.

Below us was the idyllic spot where a village once rested. Erce — tucked into the bend of what used to be a wide river, now trickled down to a stream. Silver birch forests stretched out to the east and to the south, with no end in sight. The range of mountains lay to the north.

"What's happened?" Sir Kenway asked. He slapped his horse and tore down the hill into the charred remains of the town. I followed more slowly.

Black huts were in shambles on both sides of the road, their collapsed roofs still smoldering. Fragile flakes of ash blew into my face, upon my lips, as I tried to find Kenway. I arrived at the heart of the village: a simple stone meetinghouse, gray and whole.

The stench was great.

Kenway stood in the doorway, the color drained from his face. I could not see inside the dark room, but I knew those inside were dead. Still, it wasn't bodies I smelled, but something else.

"Come away from there," I said, a heavy dread upon my heart.

"I have to see if anyone still lives, Shadow." As he crossed the threshold, I dropped to the ground. Then, I followed him.

At first, all I saw was red and gray. Blood on stone and skin.

A ghastly scene.

So many. This one stabbed in the stomach. Here, a throat deeply cut. There, a slice across the chest. I covered my mouth, unable to move. Sir Kenway hurried from one to the other, touching a shoulder, moving hair off a face.

Women, too. Open eyes, glassy and blue.

No children. I sighed in relief.

Broken spears and bloodstained daggers were scattered across the room. Sad light strained in through the few windows, their glass shattered, bows and unused arrows beneath their sills. What madness happened here? A village, destroyed. I knelt down, touching the stone floor.

I felt their sharp fear before they died. Their fear for one another. The panic. *Pain in my stomach.* I fell to my knees. I could not remove my hand from the floor. It seemed frozen to the stone. I was connected to every one who lay there, dead. I felt the confusion here in the last moments of their lives, their agony as they watched one another die.

Such loss. How they *loved* one another: fathers, wives, friends, neighbors. All gone. They'd died together.

Sir Kenway was beside me. "Come. Let us leave. Not one of them still breathes."

I looked into his eyes, trying to find something to hold on to, something to keep from falling into this blackness. "They were so afraid," I whispered.

He nodded, not knowing what I felt.

While he put his ear to one more mouth in hopes of finding breath, I leaned over a woman in the corner of this tragic place. Around her neck was an iron-engraved medallion, similar to the wooden one Elene wore. I was drawn to it. Touching the metal, despite the blood upon it, I felt the fear abate and a sense of peace wash over me. I slipped it off her still neck and slid the necklace into my own pocket.

Chapter Eighteen

Sir Kenway led the horses to the slow-moving stream in the middle of the riverbed. He had not said anything about the man he'd known.

I sat on the bank, my back to the town, my hands shaking with rage. I could not see Kenway's face as he fed the horses.

Was Fyren capable of ordering this horrific act? Such a thing didn't emerge from a mere lust for power or a desire for vengeance or the need to restore the true line to the throne. All of which could be the motive, though not the excuse, for Fyren's murder of his cousin and the men around her. But the massacre in this village was nothing but evil.

We'd found a large fresh grave behind the meeting-house. The murderers, it seemed, took care of their own.

"At least the villagers killed as many of them," Sir Kenway had said, his face still pale, as we walked around the large hole.

He approached me now, leading the horses. I noticed the bloodstained weapons he'd bound and tied to his saddle.

Still trembling, I stood to take the reins. "Why would Fyren massacre a village?"

"Have you been to Erce before?" Sir Kenway asked, his eyes blazing.

"Here? I've never left the castle."

"Did you know someone here?"

"Why do you ask me?"

"Before, when we were approaching the town, you seemed to know something not before your eyes. Do you know what took place here?"

I hesitated. "No," I said, which was true. But I couldn't confide in him about this sickness that had me in its grip, this strange sensitivity now possessing me.

"You never know, do you? All these things, your secret rendezvous with Fyren, your sleeping as the queen was murdered, your panic as we approached Erce . . . and you claim you don't know *anything*?"

I stared at him in disbelief. This was too much. "What do you accuse me of? Attacking the village? While I was running from the castle with you?"

"You admitted you were friends with Fyren, the man who ordered *this*," he said with a vicious voice, waving his arm toward the ruins of the town.

I felt the heat in my cheeks. "I am sorry about your father's man — Malcolm, was it? Although I cannot believe that *you* would feel pain over the death of a mere villager."

He flew up into his saddle. "I think we've said enough here. Get on your horse."

"We cannot leave them like this!" I yelled as he rode away. The thought of them lying dead, not tended to, dug deep into me. They needed a proper burial, to be laid to rest.

He turned in his saddle. "Come on!"

I followed him, across the stream and into the hills above it. Did he really think I was involved in such wickedness? His constant suspicion tore at me.

I brooded as we rode through a forest filled with silver trees. These birches hovered over us, flourishing on this side of the old river as well. Light filtered down through their soft green foliage. This was a beautiful, but sad and haunting place.

I didn't look at Kenway. He said nothing to me.

The images of the dead kept returning. I no longer felt their fear, but I remembered feeling it. I knew those people's minds, or at least their feelings, in their last moments. I panicked a little to think of it now.

I tried to sort it all out. I knew so very little. The queen was dead. Eldred was dead. We had come to Erce, a town Eldred and Fyren had just discussed. It had to have some importance. But what?

Maybe it wasn't the town, it was the person. Was it this Malcolm? I did not think he was among the dead. Surely I would have noticed if Kenway had seen his body.

Was it he whom Eldred had sent us after?

Sir Kenway and I were on this mad journey because of the adviser, who was living beyond his grave through us. Kenway carried this knightly oath of duty too far, I thought. Why did we trust the old man so?

I could not remember a time when Eldred was *not* there, at the side of the queen, and so beside me, too. How I'd hated those watchful eyes of his, following me everywhere. The queen's ladies could be right in their laughing guesses:

Maybe he was my father. Absurd, I knew, but it would explain his hovering.

I did not like the way he'd treated me, but then I saw Lord Leofwine's treatment of his son. Perhaps that's what fathers did to their children.

I admired the wise counsel Sir Kenway had given his father despite the abuse the old lord had heaped on him. But I didn't understand his concern about his father's past. Why did he worry so about a man who was so cruel to him? I would not.

We were moving quickly now. My pride kept me from asking Kenway any questions. I was concerned we'd be ambushed by those who'd attacked the town. Were they the same men who had been following us? What I didn't understand was why we were headed south, back toward the castle.

At an overgrown area, Kenway dismounted and dropped to the ground, with his fingers to the earth, pressing a hoof-print. Then I knew.

"You cannot, Sir Kenway. You cannot mean to do it."

He ignored me and got back on his horse. We pushed on through the woodland.

"An army of men must have attacked them, to have killed so many."

He stopped then and pulled my horse short. "I must do this."

"I understand your desire for vengeance," I said. "I feel the same. But this is a poor decision. You are just one knight."

"Can you ever just agree?" he snapped. "I will hear no more about it."

We continued to ride until the horses were exhausted. I wondered if it was Lord Leofwine's cruel accusation of cowardice that pushed Sir Kenway on so relentlessly. This was madness. We would both be killed. Or captured and returned to the castle.

But I could not leave him. I feared it was Kenway who would be hurt. And I knew he was right in his desire to punish those who had committed such evil.

It was not until the sun was low that we found them.

The smell of cooking drifted to us. Loud male laughter and the whinnies of horses could be heard. We exchanged a quick glance and slid off our horses, leading them quietly back down the path. Tying them up a good distance away,

Sir Kenway told me to stay where I was. He would be back.

I sighed. "I'll come with you," I said, stunned at my own words. I felt as if I'd been in Erce when it was attacked, not just *with* the villagers as they died, but one of them. It was as if I were a part of them, or they were a part of me. I wanted their murderers punished, even if it meant my own death. "I can help you, Kenway."

He untied the bundle of weapons from his saddle and lowered them to the ground. "How will you do that?"

"Give me a dagger."

"Have you ever used a dagger?"

I had not. I picked up one with an unbent blade and a black handle. I wiped it against the bark of a tree, to chip off the dried blood. It stubbornly remained. "This one is good."

He rummaged through the pile, taking three more daggers.

I put my hand on his arm. "Have you taken a man's life before?"

He gave me a long look, which revealed he was not new to killing. "Are you certain you can do this, Shadow?"

"I'm ready."

I followed him through the trees. The underbrush was thick only in one spot around the perimeter of the men's camp. It was there we huddled together, listening and peering in at them.

These warriors wore the royal colors of red and black, blood still on their tunics. Six of them sat on logs around the large fire, taking deep drinks of what was obviously spirits. Twenty horses or more were tied to trees beside the camp.

A lone soldier stood watch over the prisoners. My heart dropped when I saw there were only two men, a girl, and two women. This was all who survived the attack? Where were the rest of the children?

The villagers had their hands tied behind their backs. They sat on the forest floor, their worried faces glowing in the firelight. One of the men spoke quietly to the others. He had thick black hair and a commanding presence I could detect even from a distance. A large woman with a weathered face stayed close to him and to the flaxen-haired girl next to her.

The other man was injured, blood across his belly. He rested against a rock, breathing deeply, but watchful.

Another woman, young, slender, with high cheekbones and a lost look, sat between the men.

"Bring me some supper," said their guard to his comrades. He looked longingly at the roasted rabbit, licking his lips. "And some wine."

"There'll be no wine for you on your watch," said one man, more clear-eyed than the others. He removed his chain mail, the only one to wear it. His rich and fine clothes suggested he was the leader.

"I don't know why I had to take the night watch, my lord. I killed more of them than anyone. Why, it was me that captured this one whole." He gestured a dirty thumb toward the black-haired man.

A soldier with a broad, flat face snorted. "You just grabbed his daughter and threatened to cut her throat! Some bravery that was!"

One of the other men laughed so hard, he fell off his stump. How could they jest after what they'd done?

The woman's face lit up a fiery red, and she whispered to her daughter. The girl, maybe twelve or thirteen years, pulled back from her mother a little and scowled at the soldier. She was long and lean, with an angelic face, but dark eyes. Her father put his head against hers, as if to calm her.

These must be Fyren's men. I thought of Sir Kenway's earlier words, accusing me of allegiance with the regent. I didn't believe Kenway meant them, but I felt slightly sick anyway. I *had* been too kind toward Fyren, in light of what I knew now. But he and I were not the same. I was not of his ilk. I was not.

My initial indifference to his murder of the queen nagged at me. Was I as hard-hearted as Leofwine had accused me of being? Shame came over me, briefly.

I pushed the shame away, impatient with myself. This brooding would change nothing.

"All of you have had enough to drink," said the leader. "We ride before the sun comes up tomorrow."

"I don't think they'll want to see us, my lord," said the guard, darkly. "With more than half our men gone. And only two men as prisoners. And one of them might not make it back alive the way he's bleeding."

"Have you finished?" asked the young nobleman.

The guard spat and said no more.

We crouched there, quietly watching them. They

continued to drink despite their leader's orders. He didn't seem to have their respect. Perhaps the heavy price the soldiers had paid for victory ate away at their willingness to follow him.

I noticed Sir Kenway studying the lord closely. I watched him, too. Although young, he was not as foolish as the others.

Soon it was dark, except for the light of the moon. Many of the soldiers had fallen asleep where they drank, snoring, with their mouths open. The lord was in his blankets, a few feet away from the fire and the men. He kept his shiny, silver-sheathed sword close.

The guard was also watching his leader. Earlier, he'd been given bread and some of the leftover rabbit, but only water to drink. The prisoners were given no food.

Sir Kenway pulled me back into the woods. "See the guard eyeing the wine? He's tempted. In a moment, he'll retrieve it. When he does, you must cut the twine of the villagers. Release Malcolm first. He's the black-haired man." He gave me the knives. "Give these to Malcolm and his wife, Ete. They'll know what to do."

"Ete is the older of the two women?"

"Yes."

My heart raced. "You'll kill the young lord."

"That is my hope," he said. "Maneuver yourself around to the large oak right behind the villagers. When the guard gets up, you must move quickly."

"Yes."

"One of the men is injured. You and the other woman need to help him to the horses."

"All right."

He paused. "Eldred would be angry if he knew I was endangering you. But I can see no other way."

"Eldred's dead, Kenway."

"You must move quickly to the horses."

"I know my part."

"It'll happen fast," he said. "If all goes right."

"And even if all goes wrong," I said, smiling a little but feeling pressure in my chest.

He pulled a dagger out of his belt. "Come."

I moved quietly through the trees toward the sprawling oak, keeping low to the ground. It was dark in the shadows and difficult to see. I tripped over a large root, but recovered my footing before I tumbled to the ground. I saw Malcolm's head jerk up. I hoped the guard hadn't heard me as well.

But he was only interested in the wine. He stood and

ventured toward the circle of sleeping men. I crept closer to the villagers, my heart pounding. Malcolm whispered something in his wife's ear, and one by one, they told each other.

The guard looked back, but I was hidden by the rock the injured man leaned against. The darkness helped conceal me as well. I waited until he turned his attention back to finding a flask not empty.

When I touched Malcolm's shoulder, he didn't flinch. No one said a word.

The blade was sharp, and the twine fell away.

"Wait for Kenway," I whispered in Malcolm's ear. They took the daggers from me, hiding them behind their backs. Even the girl was given one.

I crouched behind the rock. The guard returned.

I heard the nobleman cry out. Malcolm stood, and in one swift violent movement, slit the throat of the unsuspecting guard, who slumped to the ground. I jumped up. I could see Sir Kenway struggling with the leader.

"The prisoners!" yelled a soldier. The horses began to stir.

Malcolm gave out a guttural sound, filled with rage and pain. He flew toward the warriors, his dagger raised.

The younger woman sat frozen to the ground. I shook her shoulder and bade her to help me. We put our arms around the wounded man. He leaned into me. Ete had grabbed a spear and was fighting alongside her husband, as was the girl. I couldn't see Sir Kenway in the flying arms and weapons.

We stumbled to the horses.

"Here, Ard, get up," the woman said. She put his foot in the stirrup and pushed him into the saddle.

"I thank you, Lulle," he mumbled. She swung into place behind him, her skirt bunched up around her.

I untied my horse and resecured the bundle of weapons, but not before Lulle grabbed a dagger of her own. Her eyes, so vacant just moments ago, were now filled with rage. I thought she might leap down and join the melee.

I got on my horse. We waited.

Chapter Nineteen

Sir Kenway came out of the trees into the moonlit clearing on a dark horse. I gave a start when I saw the blood across his tunic, but he didn't appear to be hurt. He wore a serious but satisfied look.

Malcolm and Ete rode close together, the grime of battle smeared on their faces. Their daughter trailed behind. There was no rejoicing over victory. All were somber. I didn't doubt they had killed them all.

Ard fell forward against his horse, letting out a sigh. Lulle put her hand briefly on his head. She and I exchanged quick nods.

We left that place.

Not more than an hour later, we stopped by a green pond tucked into some trees. Lulle tended to Ard's wound as best she could. She had a gentle way about her, and Ard seemed to breathe easier under her care.

Sir Kenway and the others washed the bright blood from their hands and faces. All but the girl did. She lay down on wet leaves and stared at the stars until her mother stood over her. "Ingen, clean their red muck off of you! I'll not carry any part of those animals back home with us."

Ingen knelt at the water's edge. Cupping her young hands, she dipped them into the pond and poured water over her pale face. When she did so, one long thin braid fell forward. I had seen such a braid before. Ingen scooped up the hem of her light cloak to dry with and then laughed at her mother.

"Ah, Ingen," said Ete with a sad smile. "It's time to sleep."

They bunched up brown leaves, making a soft place to lie. We shared our blankets with them.

Sir Kenway sat under a tree and put on a fresh tunic.

"I'm glad to see you again, sir," said Malcolm, with his hand resting on Ingen's shoulder. "I thank you especially for saving my daughter."

Sir Kenway gave a brief nod, looking exhausted and pleased.

They all fell asleep quickly.

I listened to the sounds of the forest. The silver birches were like candles, shining brightly under the cold moon. Ladies of the wood, protecting us. I looked upon the sleeping faces of Malcolm and his family as they huddled together and felt a pang of jealousy. But it was tempered by a sense of contentment.

I saw Sir Kenway watching me.

"You can sleep, Shadow. They are all dead."

I nodded and did just that.

"We didn't have much warning," said Malcolm, his face haggard. "They attacked at dawn."

He and Kenway led us on wide paths through these peaceful woods. Birds chirped and flew overhead. I felt as if they followed us. They nested in the silver trees, which were spaced far apart with little underbrush between. It made for easy, pleasant riding.

Sir Kenway's exhaustion showed on his face. Despite our leisurely pace, he was still vigilant. But hadn't he killed all those Fyren had sent?

Lulle and Ard still shared a single horse. Neither said a

word. Their faces were twisted in a silent grief, it was plain to see. I pushed away my own memory of that tragic scene in the village. These people had been there, lived through the horror of it. Would they ever be able to forget?

Ingen rode close beside her father. I wondered about her simple braid, similar to the one of the dead woman in the dungeon: narrow, longer than the rest of her hair. Perhaps that woman Maren had been from this part of Deor and these women wore their hair that way. It *was* curious.

Suddenly, Ingen spurred her white horse on, riding this way and that through the tall, elegant trees, her worn cloak whipping around her.

"Ingen!" Malcolm bellowed.

But she either did not hear or pretended not to. Her long blond hair flew behind her. She was a blur of white and yellow.

Her father twisted in his saddle. "Do you not see, Ete?" He waved a large hand at the girl. "Can you not keep her still?"

Ete clucked her tongue at him. "If you weren't so easy on her, she'd do what you asked." Ingen made another circle around us, a grin broad upon her face. I wondered at the joy she felt, coming so soon after such loss.

"Ingen!" Ete called out.

The girl's head whipped up. Smoothly, she brought her horse back in line with ours and wiggled between her mother and me.

She stared at me outright, those dark eyes flashing, so odd in a face so pale. I did not like her staring. It reminded me of my closed-in life in the castle with cold eyes on me all the time. I was *free* of that now. I would be left alone.

"You must've known they were coming," said Sir Kenway. "The children escaped?"

"Yes, by heaven's mercy. We'd heard rumors about kidnappings in other towns, so we set up a watch on the hill."

"Kidnappings?"

"Someone's taking the men from the towns," Malcolm said, looking grim. "You've not heard?"

Sir Kenway was deep in thought. "Shadow, did Eldred and Fyren discuss this?"

"They said nothing of kidnappings," I replied. "I have never heard anyone mention it."

Malcolm snorted a laugh. "And who of the nobility would care about Northerners?" Then he glanced at Kenway as if he shouldn't have spoken.

"You're not Northerners," said Sir Kenway.

Malcolm opened his mouth as if he might reply, then shut it.

I noticed Ingen, riding alongside us. Her eyes danced with amusement. "We're all Northerners, Sir Kenway."

Sir Kenway bristled at that.

"Go away, child," said Malcolm.

She did as he said, but wore a small smile as she dropped back. Malcolm mumbled an apology for her rudeness. I thought the girl was very irritating, but her words were not alarming. What if she was right? It didn't matter one way or the other.

"With the river dried up," Malcolm continued, "we knew we were in danger of an attack from the south. When the alarm was sounded, we sent the children and their mothers and the elderly into the mountains."

"The rest of you remained to fight?" Sir Kenway asked.

"Yes. But it didn't end well, sir."

They fell into a thick silence.

Ingen was back beside me, too close.

I whipped around. I couldn't bear this girl's scrutiny any longer. "What do you find so intriguing about my face?" I asked.

The men looked back at us. The girl shrugged, tucking her hair behind her ears with long fingers. Kenway's eyebrows shot up, but I knew he would like this close attention no better than I. Then I remembered what he'd said to me, about me watching him and the queen. My face still warmed at the memory.

Ingen whispered something to her mother, who shot me a quick glance. "No, girl. Don't be silly." But she rode up to her husband and leaned her mouth to his ear.

His face grew red with anger. "You're foolish to follow a faith that has deserted us, Ete."

"It's not a foolish faith!"

"Stop filling our daughter's head with it. She's already puffed up enough as it is."

Ingen continued to stare at me and was not deterred by the hard looks I gave her.

The closer we drew to the village, the quieter our small group of riders became. Such misery on my companions' faces. We arrived at the top of the hills overlooking the town. Lulle jumped down. Lifting her skirts, she ran across the stream to the only building not a pile of ashes.

"Her husband's there," said Malcolm. "They were wed last summer."

As we rode across the dried-up river, her wails pierced the air. Ard put the back of his hand to his mouth. Ete wiped silent tears from her rough cheeks.

My own eyes stung. I fought the sadness.

"All will be well," said Ingen, looking only at me.

We all gathered in the graveyard, except for Ard, who rested under a shade tree by the riverbank. He stared hard at the hills, as if there were answers there. Lulle's husband's body had been wrapped in her cloak and placed at the bottom of the first grave to be dug that day.

Ingen sat in the freshly turned-up dirt and sang in a clear, high voice, but in a language I didn't recognize. I thought it might be a song of grieving, that she was mourning for her village, because I heard her sing, "Erce, Erce, Erce."

Malcolm said a few words in memory of the dead man. Lulle knelt down and threw a handful of dry dirt atop the body. She did not yet want the grave to be filled, so we moved off a distance and gave her some peace with her husband.

"Sir Kenway, I know you've not heard of the kidnappings," said Malcolm, leaning on his shovel in his dirty, bloodstained clothes. "But can you think of a reason the queen's army would be taking the people?"

"It's not the queen," said Kenway, his look somber. "We'll fight against this army when the time is right, Malcolm. We need men like you to help us."

"Not me, sir. I think your land doesn't want us here. We'll be returning to the mountains. No use trying to grow things out of a ground no longer giving."

"The mountains?" asked Kenway, surprise in his voice. "That was a hard life, you told me once."

"And this one's harder," he said.

"May I have a private word with you, Malcolm?"

He nodded.

They spoke by the bank of the river. A little distance from them, I washed my hands and face in the brown shallow water.

Sir Kenway had one hand on Malcolm's shoulder and was gesticulating with the other. He spoke with great animation. The older man shook his head vehemently. He seemed about to erupt in emotion, and I wondered if

Kenway were not a knight if Malcolm would have already done so.

Ete emerged from the meetinghouse. I couldn't see her face, but I felt her sorrow. She wore it like a cloak wrapped around her.

I hadn't gone back to that sad place myself. I could not.

"Wife!" Malcolm called out, waving at Ete to join them.

She approached slowly. This made Malcolm impatient. He kept gesturing to her. "Come, come."

When she reached them, she put her hands on her hips. As Sir Kenway talked, she dropped her arms and her shoulders drooped. She looked up at Malcolm.

"Foolishness!" he yelled. He glanced at Sir Kenway, then away. Sir Kenway, who was taller than Malcolm, put a hand on the older man's shoulder. He bent his head and talked to him most urgently.

At one point, the three of them all looked up together. I followed their gaze to Ingen. What was this about?

Soon after, we said our good-byes to Malcolm and the others. As we left, I glanced back at Lulle, sitting still beside her husband's grave. A sharp pang went through me, and I almost gasped in pain. With a force of will, I pushed the

feeling away and turned to look at the forest we were riding toward.

"Where are we going?" I asked Kenway. He looked
deep in thought, so perhaps he hadn't heard me. I had many
questions for him. I would wait.

Ingen followed as we rode east from the village, into a
second forest filled with birches. At first, I thought she
would turn back, but she did not.

"Why is she following us?" I asked Kenway after a
while. "Don't you see her there?" Her pale face and clothes
and white horse hid her in the silver trees.

"Why does she bother you so?" Kenway asked.

"Your mother wants you, Ingen!" I called out, wanting
her to go back to Erce.

She came up beside me swiftly. Startled, I drew back,
unable to get away from those dark eyes. So black and
deep, like the night sky, whose mysteries no human
understands.

"You need to go to Erce," she said. "Don't fight us."

"Erce? We just left there. Leave me be, you
strange girl."

She leaned in, our horses almost touching. "I can help
you," she whispered. "I know what you feel."

Shivers ran up and down my arms and neck as if a cold wind penetrated my cloak. "I feel nothing," I told her. I didn't need anyone's help.

"Ah," she said, falling back, hiding from us again.

"She's mad, I think," I said to Kenway's questioning eyes. I wasn't sure if he'd heard her words.

"You should be flattered by her attention," he said. "She's a priestess, of some old religion from the mountains." But I could tell he was skeptical.

"Ha! After seeing her fight those soldiers, I think she is a warrior, or a leader of warriors. What gentle qualities does she have that would make her a priestess?"

"Some people live in a spiritual place beyond our earthly understanding."

A spiritual place? That sounded like death to me. I was just discovering the depth of beauty of this Earth. I wanted to live *in* it, not beyond it.

"Ete saw that early in her daughter," said Kenway, shrugging, "although Malcolm doubts. He's less of a Northerner than he'd like to admit."

Ingen was so quiet I forgot she was there for a time. But when I noticed her again, I turned to Sir Kenway, amazed he had let her come this far. "She must go back."

"She can't, Shadow," he said. "She's coming with us."

I was speechless.

He laughed. "Nothing to say?"

"But —"

"She comes with us." He rode off in front of me, leaving me to stare after him. *Ingen* was the person Eldred sent us for? This young thing?

I watched her riding through the trees. How could she be so carefree in the midst of all this death?

A chill went through me. There was something in all of this, something dark and personal, something beyond my understanding. It unnerved me. What was all this about? And why was I here? It could only involve sacrifice, for no one valued me but me.

My eyes drifted to Kenway.

Eventually, the line of birch trees stopped at a wide marsh. It was like a great mud sea. A thick oak forest lay on the other side. To get there from where we were would be a trial.

I said farewell to the silver trees, the ladies of the wood.

I will leave my memories of Erce and those troubles here with you, I thought. I wondered if that was possible since we had one of her people still with us.

The marsh was not easy riding, and the horses didn't like it. Kenway said that a foot of shallow water had once stood in this muddy field. It had since dried up. Frogs and toads hopped all around us, and black snakes slithered along the ground, frightening my horse. Not a tree nor a bush, just mud and more mud. We finally made it out, much dirtier and wearier than when we'd started.

This forest was darker, with thick underbrush and a narrow path. Soon the path disappeared.

"I have lost the path, Ingen," said Sir Kenway. "Which way?"

She shrugged.

"You don't know?" he asked, an edge to his voice.

"You've lost the path," she said.

He opened his mouth to reply, then snapped it shut.

"I can see why you said she lives in a spiritual realm," I said.

He ignored me.

Using a knife, he hacked away at some overgrown areas. We ducked under twisting vines. We got off our horses to lead them over long-fallen trees.

By nightfall, we still had not found the path. The night was cold and getting colder. I huddled, chilled, under my wool blanket, as close to the fire as possible. Sir Kenway handed me a cup of hot wine. It scalded my lips, wonderfully sweet. He'd stolen it from the soldiers, I knew. Ingen took another cup from him and sat quietly, sipping.

Kenway gave me a distracted smile. I peered at him over the rim of the cup. "You're not worried about the smoke being seen?" I asked.

He shook his head. "We've lost them or killed them, and we need the fire."

"Were those soldiers you killed also the ones following us, then?"

He poked a long stick in the fire and played with the burning embers. "I don't think so."

"You're not sure?"

He looked up at me. "I'm not. Eldred warned me we might be followed because Fyren wanted Ingen. But her father said the soldiers weren't after her. They did not treat her differently."

I looked at Ingen, still trying to accept she was this valuable. She stared back, saying nothing.

"So the men following us —" I began.

"They are no longer tracking us," said Kenway, "not since the caves."

"But it makes no sense," I said, closing my eyes. I was so tired. "If . . . Fyren already knew of the town, why send spies after us?"

"I can't figure it out, either," he said.

We both looked at Ingen. "Fyren didn't know where I was," she said.

"He did know," I said, but halfheartedly. I did not want to talk anymore. I wanted to sleep.

"He did not," she said calmly.

"But he asked Eldred, the queen's adviser at the castle —"

"I know who Eldred is," she said.

Kenway looked as baffled as I. "Ingen," he said, "*why* does Fyren want you? Eldred did not tell me. There was little time."

She leaned closer to the fire, her young face glowing. "I'm the connection to Erce." A chill ran down my spine. She'd said it with such fervor.

"Erce," Kenway repeated, not hiding his skepticism. "Your small village?"

"You have a narrow view of things," she said. "I've no patience for your stubbornness."

This amused me. If I were not so weary, I would have laughed.

"What?" Kenway asked me.

I shook my head, wanting to fall into the quiet of the forest. The flames were enticing, especially after such a long night and day. I watched the flickering as I thought about what Ingen said. I should feel relief. The more I learned, the more Eldred's plans seemed to have little to do with me.

The medallion I'd taken felt heavy in my skirt. I would have taken it out, but I didn't want Sir Kenway to know I had stolen it. Fumbling for it in my pocket, I tried to trace its ridges, but my fingers brushed against a roughness on the metal. Dried blood, I knew.

A pain suddenly pierced my heart, as if I were a mother whose baby had been ripped from her breast. I released the medallion. Holding my stomach, I stood up, stumbling away from the fire.

"What ails you?" asked Kenway.

Ingen stood.

"Nothing, I . . . just want a handkerchief." I went over to the saddlebags, thrown against a tree.

"You'll freeze," Kenway said in a weary voice. "Come back to the fire."

With the white cloth in my hand, I scooped the medallion out of my pocket, not wanting to touch it again. I breathed easier when it was in my saddlebag, where it would remain. I should have left it in the village.

"I cannot protect you from harm if I cannot see you. And I cannot take you to Kendra if you are dead. Come, Shadow. I fear these woods aren't safe."

"Kendra?" I asked, coming back to him. Ingen watched me openly. "Who is Kendra?"

"A woman who lives in the mountains."

My pulse raced. "But who is she?"

He shrugged. Ingen smiled at me.

"What does she want with me?" I asked.

"I don't know." He smiled.

"That is all you will tell me?"

"That's all I know."

"You enjoy teasing me," I said.

"I do," he said with a gentle smile. "But truly, I do not know."

Kendra.

I lay down and listened to the fire.

If we had not been so tired, we might have heard them coming.

Chapter Twenty

Sir Kenway was shouting. His sword was out. He stood in front of me and Ingen, as if to protect us. I jumped up, my blankets falling to the ground. It was barely dawn.

Two men faced us. One had a sword. The other, an axe.

They were dressed in the skins of wild animals. Heavy beards hid their features. All I saw was wild hair and shiny blades. These were not Fyren's men.

The man with the sword was a giant. I had never seen such a man. He looked ready to attack, but he was focused on Ingen, not Kenway. The other man swung the axe up over his head.

I had no weapon. I looked behind me for a stone, a stick, anything. There was nothing close at hand.

The stocky man ran toward us, axe up high. Sir Kenway was at him in a flash. He brought his sword up to meet the axe, but he moved at the last second, and the axe came down hard, digging into the Earth. The man tumbled.

Sir Kenway jabbed his sword at him, but the giant stepped forward and blocked his move. The blades sang in the air as they fought.

The stocky man had pulled his weapon out of the ground. He grabbed Ingen around her wrist. She reared back and hit him in the jaw with her fist. He did not seem angered by this, just more determined. He went toward her again. I grabbed his arm, but he threw me to the ground easily.

Sir Kenway's sword flew out of his hands and into the air. The giant lunged at him, slicing his upper left arm.

"No!" I screamed. I pounced on the giant's back, biting him in the neck, tasting sweat and grime. He brushed me off as if I were an insect and backhanded me across my face, whipping my head back. Pain shot through my jaw.

Arrows began flying through the air. They seemed to be coming from every tree, every bush. One hit the stocky man in the shoulder. He leaped onto my horse and rode off.

The giant grabbed Sir Kenway's sword and disappeared into the woods.

Ingen looked like she might follow them.

"No!" I yelled at her, my jaw throbbing. "Kenway is hurt."

I ran to him. He was leaning against a tree, his horse standing beside him. "Let me see your arm," I said, reaching for him.

"No," he said. "Come here." He turned my face. "Are you hurt?" His eyes were wild. "Is Ingen?"

"We are unharmed." I brushed him off. "You're the one who's injured."

He touched my cheek lightly with the back of his hand. "You mustn't be hurt." I wondered if he worried only out of duty, but his touch was gentle, and so were his eyes.

He rested his head against the tree. He was pale, breathing quickly.

"Let me tend to you," I said. His sleeve was ripped and bloody.

"It's not deep, Shadow," he said.

Out of the forest came a man and two boys, all holding longbows.

"Sir, are you all right?" asked the man, running up to us. He winced when he saw my face. "And you, my lady?" He glanced at Ingen, still breathing hard from the fight.

I looked at the small boys. I had thought them an army.

Sir Kenway nodded weakly at the man. "You saved our lives."

"But not your horse, sir," said the man. He had an open face — a gentle mouth, warm eyes. I trusted him immediately. A strange new feeling for me.

His long tunic was patched and worn and fell to his knees. The boys' tights were ripped, almost in rags. They were both redheaded and had freckles sprinkled across their flushed cheeks. Twins. Their bows were almost as big as they.

"Or my sword," said Sir Kenway, shaking his head.

But I'd seen the way that giant had looked at Ingen. And the other man had grabbed her. The attackers had been after her, not the horses nor the sword.

"Sir, you must come with us. Goodham, my village, is but an hour away. My boys and I were out hunting when we heard the attack."

"No, no," said Sir Kenway, waving his hand.

"This forest's not safe, sir. You shouldn't be traveling in it. Filled with thieves. Especially these last few years."

"We must go," said Sir Kenway, trying to stand. He fell back against the tree.

"We'll go to your village," I told the man. "Can you see to the wound first? We must stop the bleeding."

It was a struggle to get Sir Kenway to agree, but finally our rescuer, Stillman, was able to rip off his sleeve. Although the cut was not deep, it bled too much. The boys ripped up a tunic they found in Sir Kenway's bag. Stillman bound the wound.

"Tayte, my wife, she's a good healer. She'll tend to him."

"Help me get him on his horse," I said. Sir Kenway didn't protest. Once in the saddle, he fell forward. We draped his cloak around him.

I whispered to him, "Are you all right?"

"I'll rest a moment." He closed his eyes.

I worried he'd fall, but he clutched the saddle with both hands. I led the horse through the woods, following Stillman and his boys. I kept a hand on his leg. He'd respond briefly when I questioned him. Ingen was last, talking softly to her pale horse.

Shortly, we were on a wide path, the one we couldn't find last afternoon. Stillman plucked several leaves off a tall bush and put them in his pocket.

"Tayte can use them," he said. "She'll make an ointment for the young knight." He held out one of the leaves to me. "Here. Take a sniff."

I put the sweet-smelling plant to my nose as we walked. It was wonderfully fragrant. I felt its scent in my nose, down my throat, filling my lungs. I pulled it back and looked. It was just a bit of greenery.

Ingen reached over and grabbed the plant from me.

"Those men were after you," I said to her. "Weren't they?"

She sniffed the herb and continued to hold it to her nose. Then she caught my eye and nodded.

"Why?" I asked her.

She leaned over and whispered in my ear, "Because *they* believe."

I turned away from her. She seemed as fanatic about faith as Kenway was about Deor.

She laughed at me, then grinned playfully at the boys. Their names were Rowe and Roe, and they couldn't keep their eyes off of Ingen.

It took me a while to understand that there was a difference in their names, since they were pronounced the same way. The boys chattered at me about the names, pressing me to acknowledge the difference.

I knew the importance of a name.

We had walked about a mile when Sir Kenway called for me. He felt feverish to the touch.

"Lie still, Sir Kenway. We're almost there."

He raised himself up and grabbed my hand. "We need to find Kendra." With that, he fell forward again.

I was worried. "How much farther is it, Stillman? He's very hot."

Stillman didn't answer. I looked up and saw the three of them staring at me.

"What is it?" I asked.

Rowe spoke. "Kendra? You're going to see the witch?"

Ingen smiled and nodded.

Chapter Twenty-One

Goodham was situated in a valley no longer green.
But beauty could be found in the snowcapped mountains,
which soared above the small cluster of buildings. The pass
to the north out of the village was wide enough for horses,
Stillman told me, and was often used by travelers to the
mountains.

His cottage was long, with a hard-packed dirt floor and
a fire pit in the middle. Smoke drifted up, past dead animals
hung from a peaked ceiling and through a hole in the roof.

The single room was about eighty feet long. Large straw
pallets were at one end, stuffed in the corners. A cow lived
at the other end.

The smells were strong — simmering rabbit over the
fire, cow manure, sweet herbs hanging by the door. Sir
Kenway coughed and gagged. Ingen and I helped him to

one of the beds of straw, away from most of the odor. Stillman told me he would care for our horses, and then he took the boys and left us with his wife.

Tayte bustled from one end of the cottage to another. She glanced at Sir Kenway's arm, then ran back to the fire. She barely acknowledged us before she started work. She took Stillman's leaves and threw them into a stone pot. With a stick, she removed a hot rag from a pot of boiling water and skittered back to Sir Kenway.

I helped her take off Sir Kenway's tunic. Ingen knelt down beside the pallet and watched us. Tayte removed his bandage, which was wet with blood. Pressing the now-warm rag into my hand, she said, "Clean the wound *gently*." As if I would do it otherwise.

She hurried back to finish making the ointment.

Sir Kenway moaned while we worked. Tayte said the loss of blood had weakened him. The wound mustn't get infected.

It was odd to see Sir Kenway so vulnerable. Lying on a straw pallet with his shirt off, in a peasant's cottage, he did not look himself.

I could not stop staring at him, for he was lovely. If there were such creatures, weren't the rest of us — who were not so fortunate — supposed to look at them? Still, I was very glad Sir Kenway was unaware of my gaze. But when I looked up, Ingen's eyes were on me. I felt my cheeks grow hot. Could the girl not leave me be?

Tayte applied the ointment and bound the wound, and covered Sir Kenway in blankets warmed by the fire. Then she hustled us away from him. Her eyes darted as quickly as her hands. She had a kind manner, but was twitchy and easily agitated. Her hair was flaming red.

Ingen and I went outside to eat the hard black bread Tayte had given us. She might be a good healer, but alas, she was not a good cook. It was still early. The chilly open air was welcome after the shut-in smells of the hut.

I sat on a stump outside the cottage. Ingen plopped down in the dirt, still strangely quiet. Villagers watched us warily from their windows or the small plots of land they tended, but didn't approach us. Stillman returned and nodded at us as he went back into the hut.

A brown dog sniffed my feet. I ran my hand over his cold wet fur. He smelled as if he had been swimming in a river. I threw a stick and, with his tail wagging, he flew after it. I envied his freedom.

But if that was so, why was I still here? What lofty thoughts I'd had in the castle, telling myself nothing would keep me from escape. But here I was, free to leave *again*, and yet I stayed. Surely I wasn't shallow enough to stay because of an attraction I didn't understand. But I knew it was much more than that now. I felt uneasy and didn't want to look too deeply at my feelings.

The twins came running from around the corner of the cottage. Seeing us, they skidded to a stop, their eyes mostly on Ingen. Their cheeks were flushed, and they must've been cold without warm cloaks. But they didn't seem to mind the chill.

They looked very much alike, but I found I could easily tell one from the other. Rowe had longer hair than his brother, and he could not be still. He rocked on his feet, found a pointy stick on the ground, squashed a bug with his heel, jabbed his brother, and spoke continuously all the while. He peppered me with questions — not waiting for an answer before he asked another.

He wanted to know about Kendra, the witch. He looked at Ingen when he asked, but she only smiled.

"I know nothing of her," I said to him. "Have you seen her?"

"No, but she used to be one of us," he said, grinning. Mischief twinkled in his eyes. "The villagers threw her out when she was thirteen." He pointed. "Sent her to live up there."

I gazed at the mountains, feeling a pull toward them. "How did they know she was a witch?"

Roe spoke this time. "She could see things before they happened." Next to his restless brother, he seemed so still, except for one hand playing with something in his pocket.

"Is that all then?"

The boys looked at me askance.

"She seems a harmless witch to me," I said, biting hard into the bread, tugging a piece loose. "Not a very powerful one."

"Ha!" yelled out Ingen, startling the three of us. Then she looked off as if she'd said nothing.

"You shouldn't say things about Kendra," said Roe to me. "She can hear from miles and miles away."

"I should like to meet her, I think."

His mouth dropped open. "Is that where the knight's taking you? To meet the witch?"

"Yes," I said, glancing at Ingen.

"You're not afraid?" he asked, taking something out of his pocket and squeezing it in his hand.

I shook my head.

Rowe spat on the ground. "She took that orphan boy Piers."

"You know she didn't," said Roe. "The tall man in the gray cape took him."

Rowe grinned. "It could have been him."

I grabbed his arm. "What man?"

"How would I know his name?" he said, twisting out of my grip. "He was old, and from the castle."

"Eldred?" I asked. "Was his name Eldred?"

"I think that was it," said Roe, squinting at me.

Could Eldred have visited this small village? If it led to the pass into the mountains, to the witch Kendra, he could have been here. But this Piers, it must be another boy. Not my Piers. It was a common enough name.

The door shut behind me. Stillman stood there, with purpose in his eyes. "What stories are you boys telling now?"

I glanced at the open window. Had he and Tayte been listening? Maybe everyone in the village had. An uneasy quiet was in the air.

"About Piers," said Rowe, looking up at his father. "How he was stolen."

Stillman squatted down in front of his son. "You know he wasn't stolen, Rowe. The queen's adviser took him to give him a home." He said it as if it was of no importance, but wouldn't look me in the eye. "You know Eldred?" he asked.

He had heard.

"I know him," I replied, looking at Ingen. She said nothing.

Stillman tousled Roe's hair with a shaking hand. He was hesitant. I waited.

"You're from . . . the queen's castle?" he asked, his once open face now closed up tight.

I nodded, watching him, sensing his fear. News of the queen's death had not yet reached this small village. Would it matter to them that she was dead?

I wondered if Stillman was afraid of the army. Malcolm and the others knew about the kidnappings; I guessed Stillman did as well. Perhaps he also thought the queen was behind the attacks. As if she could have devised such plans.

"Do you know Piers?" asked Roe, so serious.

"I knew a Piers, but he couldn't be the same one." I felt sure of this. Piers was no great friend to Eldred.

"Piers was conniving and quick," said Stillman, sitting down in the dirt. Roe sat beside him and laid his head on his father's knee. "But he had a hard life. Sad."

I didn't want to hear about this Piers's sad life.

"I remember his mama calling him, Father," said Roe. "And wherever he was, he would run to her. Isn't that right?"

"She called when she was hungry," said Rowe, digging at the hard earth with his toe.

"Rowe," said Stillman, "you didn't know her when she was young. Blythe was a sweet girl. She had pink chubby cheeks." He reached down and pinched Roe's face. Roe pushed his father's hand away, smiling. "But she changed."

Rowe tugged his father's sleeve. "After Piers's father was taken? Isn't that right?"

Stillman glanced at the door. Rowe followed his eyes and nodded. Some unspoken thing had passed between them.

Another villager taken? I wondered when this man had gone missing. We had lived in selfish ignorance in the queen's castle on the hill.

Again, I looked at Ingen. Sadness drifted across her eyes, but then it cleared. "All will be well," she whispered to me.

"Blythe did change," said Stillman. "As if her soul left her body early. Piers took care of her. He fed them, by stealing. He slipped inside people's cottages and took bread, eggs, clothes for his mother.

"The village was larger then, more of a town, but small enough we knew who it was. Most turned a blind eye, but others were . . . not so kind."

"They beat him," said Rowe, eyes flashing.

"With sticks." Roe bit his lip.

I winced, almost feeling the blows on my own back. Not my little Piers.

"When Blythe died —" began Stillman.

"She got sick," Rowe said. His brother's eyes were large in his small freckled face.

"— Piers fled to the forest. Tayte tried to get him to live with us, but he wouldn't. He came back from time to time."

"Came back to steal," said Rowe.

"He was so brave," Roe said. "He wasn't scared of anybody."

"It couldn't be the same boy," I said, shaking my head. "The Piers I know is easily frightened. Small with gray eyes."

"Our Piers had gray eyes," said Rowe. "Just like his mother."

"When was the last time you saw him?" I asked.

"He left with Eldred two summers ago," said Stillman. That was when Piers arrived at the castle.

"He said he was going to kill the regent," Rowe said.

"Shh," said Stillman, looking around. "Don't say such things, Rowe."

"He said it. He hated the regent."

I felt an ache inside of me and folded my arms across my stomach.

Piers.

Chapter Twenty-Two

I sat up, confused. Where was I?

Straw poked my bare legs and through my shift, making me think I was on my pallet in the castle, sleeping by the queen's bed. But the earthy scent of animals and wild grass clung to the ice-cold wind blowing through the window — smells I was not accustomed to. I pulled my blanket up around me.

Ingen was beside me on the mat we shared. The twins and Sir Kenway slept on another mat on one side of us, and Tayte and Stillman slept on the other side.

Rowe turned over, his red hair bright in the moonlight. One closed hand rested by his mouth. So sweet he looked. I lightly touched his cheek, but then drew back, remembering another boy. I felt Piers strong in my heart.

"Audrey!" Sir Kenway cried out. "No!"

I could see him in the moonlight, closest to the wall. He tossed his head back and forth, moaning. I rolled the twins gently to the edge of their mat. Sir Kenway was hot to the touch. I glanced at Tayte, snoring on the other pallet, her hand flung across her husband's stomach. She looked so peaceful after her long day's work. I didn't want to wake her.

Shivering, I immersed a rag in a bucket of cold water and dabbed Sir Kenway's forehead. "Shhh. It is all right."

He stilled my hand with a grip so fierce it hurt, but looked at me with unseeing eyes. "I let her die."

He was out of his mind. "You did not."

He asked for things. *Can I have a cool drink?* I dipped water from the pail and put the cup to his lips. He pushed it away, splashing it on himself, gasping at the water's coldness. *Can I have a roll, warm and fresh?* I gave him all I had, stale bread, but he spit it out.

He thrashed about, throwing off his blanket. I put it back, dabbed his face, and waited. When he relaxed, I closed my eyes again. Over and over, we did this. Finally, he lay still and fell into a deep sleep. Exhausted, I did the same.

But darkness haunted my dreams. I kept waking, not able to remember my nightmares, but thinking of Piers.

In the morning, Tayte tended to Sir Kenway, applying the sweet-smelling ointment, giving him fresh bandages, feeding him a yarrow broth.

I sat watching him. His mouth was relaxed. His cheeks, pink again. He seemed past his pain. He wouldn't be pleased to know he had slept on a straw pallet, nursed by a peasant woman. I wondered what he would say when he discovered it.

When Tayte's back was turned, I pushed his hair off his forehead and ran my fingers lightly along his face. I traced his lips and then my own and shivered as if we'd kissed. *Longing* swept through me. I wanted him to wake and touch me as gently as I touched him. That desire was so sharp, and so unrequited, hot tears popped into my eyes. I wiped them away, feeling foolish at my emotion.

His eyes fluttered open. I blushed deeply, worried he'd sensed my feelings. He looked at me for a long moment and closed his eyes again. He was so dazed I doubted he was much aware of what was going on around him.

Stillman and the twins were out in the field with the other villagers, plowing. Getting ready for the winter harvest. Ingen had gone with them.

"The only thing the fields give us anymore is rye," said Tayte. "And that was a poor crop this year."

She was cautious with me. Last night, after our meal of rabbit stew, Stillman whispered to her as she washed the bowls in a large barrel. I saw him mouth the word *castle*. It frightened her, I could tell. He held her hands, trying to calm her.

Did they think we meant them harm?

Stillman seemed to trust Eldred, though. He hadn't been concerned about Eldred taking Piers.

Piers had never mentioned it was Eldred who'd brought him to the castle. The first time I'd noticed him was when he was a kitchen boy. Not long after, he became Fyren's personal servant.

He had played me for a fool. Had *he* befriended me and not the other way around? Had he been watching me, just like Eldred? The thought made my stomach turn.

But I was the one, not Piers, who'd escaped. I had left him there. If Piers was in with Eldred, then he might be dead. My eyes burned. I shook my head, frustrated by these emotions making me so vulnerable I was beginning not to recognize myself.

Tayte grabbed an old bucket hanging on a nail by the door. "I'll be back. I need water."

I reached for it. "I'll go." I wanted to be outside.

She hesitated, glancing at my silk dress.

"Where is the well?" I asked her.

She pointed with her head. "Down the road." She grabbed a small pouch of dried herbs from a table by the door. "Here."

The herbs smelled sweet.

"Give that to Erce. There's a shaft by the well."

"Erce?" I asked, suddenly alert. "Like the village?"

"That was the village's old name, yes. It was named after her by those who are from the north. The mountain people place a strong hope in Erce."

"Erce . . . is a woman?" I asked.

"No, my lady." Tayte pushed her bushy red hair out of her eyes. "Why, she's the mother of the Earth."

"The mother of the Earth," I repeated. It is what Elene had said.

"We give Erce gifts, so that she'll give back to us," she explained, looking at me as if she expected some acknowledgment.

I nodded. *So, this must be the old religion.* And with a shock, I realized this was who Ingen referred to. I thought back on what she said, but I could not remember what she had rambled on about. I had been so tired that night.

I doubted this Erce existed. If she did, why was the land no longer fertile? Had Eldred sent us on a fool's errand?

I looked at the herbs. "What shaft?" I would do as Tayte asked of me.

"By the well, my lady. As I said."

I felt her eyes on me as I left.

I raised my skirt out of the muck in the path, amused by the muddied silk. What would Lord Leofwine think of me dirtying up his gift of a dress?

I passed thatched-roof cottages and muddy pigpens. Most of the villagers would not look me in the eye. They were working — sweeping dirt floors, hacking at the soil in their gardens, grinding grain in wooden bowls. All women and children.

The well was in an open square, surrounded by a small tavern and a few huts. Some of the buildings lay in ruin. Perhaps they were once shops and this plaza had bustled with people clinking coins in their hands. The only movement now was the flapping of a wooden door in the wind.

The shaft by the well was circular and about six feet deep. Peering in, I could see rocks, a comb, red and blue bird feathers, spoons, animal bones, and one shoe on the bottom. I threw in the herbs. No rumble from the Earth. No lightning in the sky. I sat on a bench. The mountains rose behind me. Before me stretched the valley, resting under a deep blue sky, unbroken by clouds. The air felt crisp and cool.

I counted about twenty men and boys in the crop fields or herding the sheep. Not many, compared to the number of women and cottages. I could easily pick out the twins. Their red hair stood out. As did Ingen's long blond hair. The three of them ran around Stillman as he and another man pulled at the oxen in front of the plow. I wondered if the boys were any help to their father at all.

He needed their help. The army had been here, too.

I pushed those thoughts away.

A sweet boy helped me carry the heavy bucket of water back to Tayte. A simple kindness, but one I was not used to.

As the day passed, Sir Kenway improved. He began to sit up, then to move around the cottage, finally settling on my stump outside for most of the afternoon, in deep thought. I sat in the dirt and chewed a piece of straw, feeling like a villager.

"Last night," he asked, "you nursed me?"

"Yes."

"And this morning, too?"

"I . . . yes." My cheeks grew hot when I remembered my thoughts about him, my fingers caressing his face. I should not have been so intimate with him. Did he know?

He looked at me closely. "Are you well?"

"Yes." I nodded. "Yes."

His brow furrowed as if he was trying to find a memory. "Did you —?"

"What?" I asked quickly.

He smiled a little. "Nothing."

I turned my head and put my eyes to the heavens. Why was I so awkward with him?

"I remember talking," he said, finally, "but not what I said. Last night."

"You — you called out for Queen Audrey."

At her name, his face fell. "Yes."

I looked at the ground. Again, I felt a tightness in my own chest at his pain. "I know how you loved her," I mumbled. I felt sad and lost and didn't know if it was because I worried over him or rather that I mourned her myself.

"I didn't protect her," he said. He was so pale. Not better after all.

"All of us could say the same," I said, wanting to put my hand upon his arm. "I slept beside her."

He gave me a look that silenced me. He thought me glad of her death. But I didn't like to think I wanted my freedom so much that I'd wish her dead. But hadn't I? I remembered my joy at our escape from the castle. Would I give my freedom back for her life? I pressed my lips together to keep them from trembling. I thought I would not make that trade and that filled me with sadness.

"You were not told to protect her, Shadow."

"What?" I didn't say that Eldred had told me to do just that. "Why must we dwell on this?"

"I didn't love her as you think I did," he said suddenly.

Our eyes caught. "Yes . . . you did."

"Not the way you imagined," he said, his eyes not leaving mine.

A hope stirred in me. "No?"

He said nothing, but shook his head a little. I wondered

if it could be true. The way he looked at me now, with such gentleness, I thought perhaps it might be. There seemed to be something in his look, more than just the desire I saw that night in his father's castle. I smiled at him, and he returned it and did not look away.

But then, as fate would have it, Ingen came out and sat between us. "We have much to do," she said.

A look of irritation crossed Kenway's face. Then to my surprise, he laughed. I caught his eye and laughed with him.

At supper, he didn't complain about the smells in the cottage. He didn't turn up his nose at the black bread and thin stew. Instead, he thanked Tayte and Stillman for helping us. When I raised my eyebrows in surprise, he noticed, but didn't say anything to me.

In one way, he was the same.

"Shadow," he said later, as we sat on the stump looking at the stars. "We leave on the morrow." Always duty first.

We were to meet the witch.

Chapter Twenty-Three

Tayte thrust her finger in his face. "You're not well enough, Sir Kenway." He was under her care, she told him. He'd not spoil her good work by collapsing in his saddle on the difficult trek into the mountains. "You can't go yet, sir. Not yet!"

One look at her red, puffed-out face made Sir Kenway back down. We would stay another day.

The boys each took me by a hand and led me to the river. It was wide and low, filled with cold water from underground springs. Ingen had followed us in her quiet, bemused way. She was there, watching, but detached. I wondered at her thoughts. Sometimes an eerie feeling came over me when she looked at me. It was as if she knew my mind.

She was mostly by my side.

The four of us picked flowers growing on the bank. Made stick houses. Played war games, hiding behind trees and throwing stones at one another. I did not like that game, but Ingen and the boys did.

I slid off my silk hose and put my dusty feet into the green water. "Ahh," I said, laughing. "It is cold." I left them there, letting them turn numb.

"It'll freeze your feet off," Roe said, sitting beside me. "You'll be walking on stumps."

I smiled at him. "Will you help me hobble around on my ankles?"

He nodded shyly, his hand back in his pocket.

"What do you have there?" I asked.

Without hesitation, he pulled out the contents and showed me. Four rocks, of different colors, shapes, sizes. "I picked out one for each of my family." He put his small finger on a dark gray rock with sharp edges. "This is Rowe's."

"Yes," I said, "I can see that would be his. Which one is yours?"

"Not one for me. But for my mother and father. And my grandmother, who died," he said, pointing out a smooth pink one. Ingen reached down for it, but he drew back, not letting her take it.

A family of stones, kept together by this small boy. Who would I carry in my pocket? Piers? Could I claim that right now?

"They are lovely rocks," I said. "A treasure, for certain."

"A treasure," repeated Ingen.

Roe ran off to chase a croaking frog on the bank. His twin joined in and dove for it, but the frog made a slippery escape from Rowe's hand.

These redheaded brothers looked nothing like my pale, gray-eyed friend, my little ghost. But they were boys, and so reminded me of him.

Ingen laughed at them, while running her fingers down her long braid.

"Why do you not cut that piece of your hair?" I asked her. "Is it the way of the women of the mountains?"

She looked at me. "Of some."

"I've seen another wear her hair that way."

"Maren."

The shock took my words.

"A gentle woman," Ingen said.

"I'm sorry . . . Ingen, but I must tell you that —"

"I know she is dead."

How could she? I studied her, trying to figure her out. "How did you know Maren?"

She leaned in to me. "Only priestesses wear their hair this way."

"And . . . what do priestesses do?"

"I will tell you when you believe," she said.

"Convince me."

"I see the look in your eyes." She smiled. "You are like Sir Kenway. Neither of you has faith yet." Her face was radiant. "But you will, Shadow."

Discomfort squelched my curiosity.

She leaped up and ran after the boys: one moment a thoughtful girl, the next a playful child. I envied her, and the twins. I had not been a child in a long time, since the day I was locked in the queen's trunk.

But as I watched them, my heart lifted, suddenly light and unburdened, as if all my cares were dropping away.

I sat on damp needles under an old cypress tree. Thick gnarled roots crawled along the dirt. I lay in between two huge ones, propping up my arms. The Earth held me in its palm, the roots like fingers wrapping around me. I closed my eyes and listened to the *plunk, plunk* of the boys' stones hitting the water. Something tight inside me was releasing.

A light sweet tickle brushed my nose and cheek. A leaf? A blade of grass? I laughed and pushed the hand away. My eyes flew open. It was not mischievous Rowe, but Sir Kenway who dangled a yellow wildflower over my face. I smiled but felt shy as he lay down beside me amongst the roots.

"You like it here," he said, telling, not asking me. "In the village."

Roe had slipped off his shoes and stuck his feet in the water, getting his hose wet. He looked back at me with bright eyes. His brother tried to push him in, but Roe fought back. He was stronger than he looked. A laughing Ingen grabbed Rowe's shirt, trying to pull him off his brother. Rowe jerked away from her and went after his twin again.

"Yes," I said, watching the boys tussle in the dirt, but much more aware of Sir Kenway's presence. He held his left arm stiffly to his side. Tayte had ripped his sleeve to accommodate the bandage. "You're different here, too."

"How so?" he asked.

"Less distant." I looked away. "To those you don't consider your equals. Like Stillman and his family. You're not so . . . severe." I smiled.

He shrugged. "They're good to us. Perhaps it's because of our rank . . . I mean, my rank, and the duty they feel they owe me."

I sat up, exasperated. "Perhaps they are just kind people."

"Perhaps," he agreed.

He pulled a metal flask from his boot and took a long drink. He offered it to me. I sipped the cold water.

I did not love her as you think I did. That is what he had said. Had I misread his feelings all along? Had he only been protecting her for his father's sake?

Ingen gave out a shout and I watched her run with the boys. "I wanted to talk to you about Ingen," I said.

"She is a mystery."

"She said she was some sort of connection to Erce. Do you remember?"

"I remember," he said. "The village has no strategic importance. No riches are there." He shook his head. "I wish there'd been more time for Eldred and I to talk."

"What if Erce isn't a village?"

He hesitated, watching me. "What is it then?"

I shrugged. "Tayte said that Erce is the mother of us all."

"What?"

"The villagers believe she is a goddess, I think."

He laughed. "You don't believe in that Northern religion? I know you, Shadow. You don't believe in what you cannot see."

I shrugged again.

He chuckled a little more.

"Enough of your mocking, sir," I said, giving him a small smile.

He studied me for a moment. "Does that hurt?" He reached over to me and placed his fingers on the tender spot on my cheek. "That giant gave you quite the blow."

I tried to speak, but at his touch could only stare.

He froze, his eyes on mine. We were both quiet. His hand lingered, then moved slowly across my cheek. Such a touch, such a gentle touch. I was afraid to drop my eyes, or speak, or do anything. I couldn't bear it if he took his hand away.

How could this light caress be so deeply felt?

I was aware of a hushed silence. The twins and Ingen stood in a row, staring at us.

Kenway looked their way and then back at me. His eyes smiled briefly before we broke apart. He stood, and I took the hand he offered me. When I was on my feet, I felt his fingers caress my palm as his hand slowly left mine. A tingle of pleasure rippled through me. I could not help but smile.

Rowe was at Kenway's side, jumping from foot to foot. "Are you really a knight?"

"Father wouldn't like you to ask that," Roe said. "Isn't that right, my lady?"

I realized he was waiting for me to answer. "What? I don't know."

"Why are you looking at Sir Kenway like that?" Roe asked me.

Kenway glanced quickly my way. He looked pleased; his smile tentative and sweet.

"Well, Father's not here," said Rowe with a scowl for his brother. Red splotches appeared on his face. I noticed the shy look he gave Ingen.

"If you *are* a knight," he asked Kenway quickly, "why don't you have a sword?"

"It is curious," I said.

Kenway looked at me askance, but I saw his lips flirt into a smile. "I have a dagger," he said, pulling one out of his belt.

Rowe stepped forward. "I saw that." He trailed Kenway out from under the long branches of the cypress. I thrust my bare feet into my shoes and stuffed my wet hose into my dress pocket. Roe, Ingen, and I followed.

Sir Kenway held out the steel blade.

Rowe ran a careful finger along its length. "Ah, sir. The blacksmith did fine work." Ingen reached over and touched it as well. Roe hung back.

"You know something about blacksmithing?" Kenway asked the boy.

"Yes, sir. Well, no. Our smith, Godwine, is gone." Rowe glanced at me. "Piers's father. But I like fire. And I like weapons. I'd be a knight, but I'm not allowed because I'm just a peasant."

"That is the way of things," said Kenway.

"It's a stupid way!"

Roe shook his head. "You can't say that. He's a knight."

"I can say it," Rowe said, glancing at Ingen again. "I just did say it."

"No —"

"Boys, would you like to hold the dagger?"

They stopped arguing. "I would, Sir Kenway," said Rowe, a new respect in his voice.

Sir Kenway presented him the dagger as if it were a great treasure. If that was all a knight had left, then I suppose it was a treasure.

With both hands, Rowe oh-so-carefully took the weapon. He gripped the jeweled handle and gave a short jab into the air. He looked back at Kenway, who nodded at him. That was all Rowe needed. He began to thrust the weapon up and down, left and right, turning and twisting as if he were fighting a real opponent. Ingen smiled at him, which made him puff up with pride.

He jumped up on a thick root, balancing, then pushed the dagger forward. But he lost his footing and stumbled forward and the blade spilled out of his hand.

Roe laughed, pointing at his brother in the dirt. I smiled at the shy boy, glad to see his seriousness gone for the moment.

Rowe turned a violent red. He came at his brother, smacking him hard on the arm.

"Ow!" yelled out Roe. But he looked at me with twinkling eyes.

Rowe picked up the dagger, brushing the dirt off. "I'm sorry about your knife, sir."

Sir Kenway took it from him. "No harm."

"Perhaps I'll be a knight someday, sir," said Rowe with a child's hope in his voice.

Sir Kenway hesitated.

And I worried what he would say.

"You certainly have the spirit of a knight," he said finally. "If the day comes, it would be an honor to be at your side during battle."

Rowe beamed.

The boys ran down to the water, pushing and shoving one another. Soon Rowe fell in, making a show of it, with flailing arms and legs. Ingen clapped her hands. She grabbed Roe's arm and began to pull him toward the river. Laughing, he twisted from her grip. But Rowe climbed up the bank and dragged his younger twin in.

Kenway returned his dagger to its sheath. "You are smiling at me."

"I'm not."

"Do you think I cannot be kind to peasants?"

"It is a surprise when you are."

He laughed a little. "You judge me too harshly."

"On the contrary, my thoughts are kind toward you. At the moment."

"Your mood could change?"

"Not my mood," I said. "Your attitude."

"Do you not know how to do anything but argue?"

"I'm giving you a compliment!"

He laughed again. "Ah, this is the way you compliment."

Rowe and Roe came up beside us, soaked from head to toe, shivering. They pushed into me, twirling me around, getting me wet, too. Sir Kenway and Ingen stood off to the side, watching.

Rowe jerked my sleeve. "Come with me. I'll show you something."

I had little choice as he yanked me along. Once on the outskirts of the village, we didn't take the main road, but walked around the perimeter. We cut down a narrow, overgrown path. The deserted huts were like tombstones in a little-visited graveyard, sad reminders of what once was a living, thriving town.

"No, Rowe," said his brother, stopping on the path. "Don't you take her there! I don't want to go."

"Go back home then!"

"She's still in there," whispered Roe, his eyes wide.

"Are you always afraid?" asked Rowe.

Roe didn't answer. Ingen shook her head.

"Get out of here, then!" yelled Rowe.

Roe ran back toward home, his little heels kicking up dust.

"Come back!" I shouted, but he didn't stop. I whirled around. "You shouldn't taunt your brother."

Rowe's eyes glinted under his wet hair hanging down. My lips twitched into a smile.

We arrived at a small hut, with a low thatched roof that buzzed with wasps. A worn stone seat rested on one side of the door, piled-up firewood on the other. Cobwebs covered the wood. Sadness seeped out of the dark gray walls. I fell back a step. Ingen touched the door, looking back at me.

"You asked about him," said Rowe. "You want to see his house, don't you?"

Piers's home.

I pushed hard against the door and the sorrow. The cottage was dark, and smelled of rotting straw. Its two square windows were covered. A trestle table stood in the center of the room, broken plates upon it and a chest beside it for a sitting bench.

Rowe hovered outside the door.

"Has no one been here?" I asked.

"Not since his mother." He edged closer to the threshold, but didn't cross it.

Sir Kenway pulled back the skins, letting in more light, revealing not much else. A lone candlestick on the hard-packed earth floor. Pallets and blankets tossed in the corner. A weaving loom, still filled with yarn. Ingen ran her fingers along the wool.

"The villagers won't use any of her things. Some say she was a witch like Kendra, that she should've been thrown out of the village like Kendra was. She could tell your future just by looking at you. Well, at least, sometimes, she could. Once Piers's father was taken, she started talking to ghosts, right here in this cottage."

"Ghosts," said Kenway.

I knelt down over the pallet where they slept.

"She did," Rowe insisted. "I myself heard her talk to Piers's father all the time. I stood by that window there" — he jerked his head — "and it was Godwine this and Godwine that. Piers came at me then, throwing stones at me." He scowled. "He was always angry."

No, no, not the Piers I knew.

I picked up the blanket. A pain shot through my hand

and traveled to my heart. My eyes welled over with the hot tears of a child. He was so lonely. But there was something more I could not bear: These feelings were inside of me, like an ache in my own heart, as if they were *my* feelings. But I felt as fragile as a child. I dropped the blanket as if it had burned me.

Kenway was at my side. "Are you crying, Shadow? What's wrong?"

"Piers," I whispered. My mouth felt dry, as if I had not drunk for days, and my body began to tremble.

Ingen picked up Piers's blanket and put it to her cheek.

Kenway took me by the elbow and pulled me away. The farther we moved away from Piers's hut, the easier I breathed, but I could not stop shivering. We returned to the river.

"Are you ill?" he asked, placing his palm upon my face. "You are not feverish."

"I cannot tell you," I whispered. It was like someone else had moved inside my soul, living with me now, causing me to doubt myself in ways I never knew before.

"You keep something from me," he said, rubbing his hands up and down my arms. "Let me help you."

I couldn't tell him this. It was all too strange. Was I going mad? I'd had little sympathy for the queen's dark visions. Was this what she had felt? Was I being punished for my hard heart?

And so I didn't answer, and he stopped questioning me. The trembling finally ceased and we walked back to the hut in silence.

That evening, we joined the villagers out in the open square. Out came a toothless man with a fiddle and a boy with a flute. They stood on the crumbling steps of the tavern and played while old women and young boys danced in the dust.

It was last summer that the old mayor had died and was buried in the cemetery. And though he had been beloved, he had not allowed music and dancing. The old villagers were now teaching their young the songs their bodies and voices remembered.

There was one dance that I'd never seen, not once in the queen's court. The couples formed a circle, the women with ribbons of scarlet and green streaming from their hands and hair. Into the middle they moved as one, skipping in and out again, in time with the lively music. In the center, each woman twirled, so beautifully, the streamers over her head, wrapping around her body.

Rowe danced with his mother, swinging her in circles and sending her wild hair flying. Stillman clapped his hands, while Roe waited for his turn with his mother. Ingen danced alone, apart from the crowd, turning in circles.

Sir Kenway bowed before me. "Will you dance?"

I looked at him in surprise. He would dance with me?

"But you're hurt," I said.

He held out his hand. "Then we'll move slower than the others."

"I don't know how." I'd watched him and the queen many times, but I had never done it myself.

"This one is new to me, too, but we'll learn it together," he said, pulling me off the stump. A girl in a tattered skirt shyly handed me a ribbon.

Sir Kenway's hand clasped mine, only releasing it when I twirled alone. I looked up, growing dizzy with spinning and watching the ribbons flying.

This was joy, laughter bubbling up from the heart, like a spring flowing out of the earth. I felt it each time Kenway brought me close, our eyes locking and our bodies together for just a *moment*, before he pushed me out again. Even when I'd spin alone, I would catch his look, again and again, his eyes following me. I saw a hunger there, a need. I knew it because I felt it when I looked at him.

Was this what it meant to love another?

As the sun sank, we danced by the light of the torches and the moon. The notes of the music drifted up, up into the sky, turning into bright stars. I soared up, too, no longer Shadow, no longer in my own body, but dancing among the new constellations we created that night.

On the way back to the cottage, I tossed my ribbon to Erce.

✤

I lay on the bed of straw, listening. A cricket sang the fiddle's tune in my ear, Stillman's cow lowed in rhythm, and an owl hooted from a nearby tree. I could hear Kenway in his silence and knew that he and I were the only ones awake.

I sensed him there listening to me listening to him.

Something had changed between us.

Chapter Twenty-Four

As the sun rose over the trees, we said our farewells. The boys wrapped their arms around my waist and squeezed. Their affection made me blush, but I didn't push them away. I felt a small ache in my heart. I didn't like that part of saying good-bye.

Ingen was on her horse, prancing back and forth, impatient. Roe gave her a shy wave. Rowe raised his palm, then dropped it quickly. He looked sad to see her leave.

Kenway and I rode the other horse, me in the back, my cloak and dress bunched up around me, hiked up, revealing my calves. I cared little about that, although Tayte cast a reproving look my way.

I had suggested to Kenway that I ride in front, because he was still recovering. He grimaced, shaking his head. "I am well enough." His eyes flashed. "We danced last night, didn't we?"

He did seem better, with more color in his cheeks. But his eyes were red and tired. The world he knew was no more.

All was quiet as we left. Looking back at Stillman and Tayte in front of their hut, I saw a neighbor with them, pointing toward us, or perhaps in the direction we were headed. Something was wrong.

A crowd of villagers huddled around the shaft by the well, talking loudly and gesturing with wild arms. We jumped off the horse. They backed away as we approached, as if they were afraid. Hadn't we all danced together in fellowship just last night?

"What's wrong?" Kenway asked.

The people moved aside to show us.

Ingen let out a gasp and jumped off her horse.

A wild bush of blackberries spilled forth from the hole in the ground. The leaves were dark green and plentiful. The berries looked large and luscious. I dropped down to get a closer look, breathing in a fresh sweetness. The roots of the plant ran along the black soil of the shaft. Thick roots that looked as old as the trees by the river.

"This bush wasn't here yesterday," said Kenway. He plucked a large blackberry, squishing it in his fingers. My favorite fruit.

"It is wonderful," I said, reaching for one, full of wonder.

Ingen wore a radiant smile. "All will be well," she said, looking at me.

Then I noticed. They all stared at me. The old man who'd played the fiddle. The boy who carried my pail of water from the well. The girl who gave me the bright green ribbon.

"I saw you," she said, stepping toward me, her shyness gone. "You gave your ribbon to Erce. You tossed it in the hole last night."

"I saw her, too," said a mother with a babe tugging at her skirts. The other villagers nodded.

"All of you gave things to Erce," I said, rising.

I stepped back from their eager faces. What did they want from me? Erce had given them a blackberry bush. Or maybe it was the witch who had done this thing. Not me.

No one spoke. I glanced at Kenway. He was looking at me in the same way they all looked at me. As if they expected something.

I backed up, trying not to stumble over my feet. They

circled me as I got on the horse. Why weren't Kenway and Ingen coming?

"I pray you, stay," pleaded the old fiddler, pulling the reins from me. "You're in Erce's favor. We need you."

I jerked the reins back, but he grabbed my hand.

His fingers bore into me as if they were roots, crawling under my skin, winding their way into my veins, twisting around my lungs. Desperate faces all around me, pushing me toward feelings I didn't understand. I was a child at the foot of a father's grave, a wife mourning a husband taken away. I felt panic. They were reaching for my soul.

I tugged at the front of my dress. I couldn't breathe.

"Let's go, Kenway," I pleaded.

He did as I bade him. Ingen swung up on her horse, a wide smile on her face. We left a silent square, so different from the one filled with music and laughter the night before.

I tried to shrug off the unsettling feelings. I found I was clinging to Kenway, my arms wrapped around his waist. Embarrassed by my need, I released him.

"Are you all right?" he asked.

"Yes," I said, breathing a little easier.

Quickly, we left the village behind and took the pass up into the mountains. It was a good trail, although rocky and steep in places. Ingen was in the lead. I wondered if she knew the way. Then I remembered her people were from the mountains. Did she know this witch Kendra after all? Perhaps she was our guide.

Kenway fell back against me as our horse moved up the path. He smelled of soap and sweet herbs. I felt a little dizzy and put my forehead on his back.

"I don't understand," he said. "How did that bush grow overnight?"

I kept my head against him. "I don't know," I whispered, not wanting to talk. I didn't understand, either, but the bush wasn't what troubled me.

It was those feelings, digging into me, like I was the soil that would feed them. Only a witch could make me suffer so. What did this Kendra want from me? This newfound interest in my person amazed me. I had always been nothing to those around me.

Eldred had a hand in this. The past would not stay behind me, no matter how far I traveled.

It was almost midday when we stopped by a bubbling stream of clear water. It was so quiet. No birds that I could see. No deer. No rabbits. Only red ants crawling on rocks.

The sun was out, but it was getting colder. I pulled my cloak around me.

Kenway and I sat on a gray boulder beside a scrawny bush, the horses not far from us. Ingen squatted down and peered into the water. Kenway handed me some of the remaining figs in his bag. I took them, squishy as they were, but lay back without eating them. A breeze whispered to me, blowing strands of hair across my face. I fancied I heard the soothing sounds a mother makes to her child.

"That blackberry bush," Kenway said. "I have never seen anything like it before."

"A witch's trick," I said, trying to listen to the breeze. "Eldred's sorceress."

Ingen took some figs and ate them as she walked on rocks in the stream. When she playfully jumped from one slippery rock to another, I bit back chiding words. I was not her mother. If she fell in, it would be her own doing.

"So you believe this Kendra we seek is a witch?" Kenway asked.

"Whatever she may be, she's allied with Eldred."

"What could she want of you?"

"I don't know," I said, not wanting to think about it.

Perhaps she wanted Ingen, not me? Then why was I here, too?

"You were so afraid this morning, in the square. The bush, the words of the townspeople . . . it was disturbing. Is that what frightened you? Or was it something else? Was it . . . this Kendra? Do you think she's responsible for the blackberries?"

I turned on my side toward him, propping my face upon my hand. "I was *not* afraid, just confused." I handed the uneaten figs back to him. I wasn't hungry.

"You do have a strong heart, which I've always admired," he said. "I confess I don't understand it, though. You come from nothing."

I clucked my tongue. "You still only see rank, even after staying with Tayte and Stillman?"

"It's what I've been taught, I guess. We're each born to our station."

"Rowe's a brave boy. He comes from nothing."

"Yes, but *he* is loved and wanted. You were neither." He flushed. "I'm sorry —"

"It is all right, Kenway. Don't bother with it." I lay back down and took in a breath of blue sky. This was my tonic: the boulder I lay upon, the air around me, the sun in my face. "I don't know how to explain it to you. It . . . seems odd, I know, but I think I am being watched over." There, I had said it. The silly thought I had refused to voice, to even think on.

"You mean, as if your mother were still here?"

I looked over at him, curious. "No, she is gone, and I never knew her anyway." I wondered if he thought of his own mother. His face was soft as if his mind was lost in a child's memory.

When I caught his eye, he smiled, somewhat sadly, it seemed to me. "If not your mother, then your father?" he asked.

"I don't think I had one of those," I said, laughing.

"That could be fortunate," he said. "So *who* is watching over you?"

I shrugged. "At times it feels as if it is the Earth itself."

His lips quivered into a smile. "Do you mean Erce?"

"Perhaps the villagers are right, and she's real." I was starting to believe it. It could be Erce taking care of me. Maybe she had sent me the blackberries. I hoped it was her, not Kendra. Eldred's witch wanted something, or Eldred would not have sent me to her.

"I find it difficult to believe Erce exists," said Kenway.

"And yet you believe in ghosts and witches."

"A ghost has visited me, Shadow."

I nodded, wondering if he would tell me more. I thought back to the night his father struck him and called him a coward for being afraid of ghosts.

"It was my mother," he said, not looking at me. "Right after she died."

I wanted to ask him, but he was very guarded. My curiosity felt wrong, like I was intruding on something private. "Perhaps you'll tell me about her one day," I said.

"Perhaps." He smiled at me, twisting the gold ring on his finger.

"Your father is wrong, Kenway. You are very brave."

"I think *you* fear nothing. Not Erce, Kendra, Fyren."

"Only living a life not my own."

There was a pause. "I can see how your life must've been at the castle."

"Can you?"

He lay beside me, his sleeve against mine. His skin, so far from my skin. "I have a confession."

"What?"

"Remember when I accused you of . . . watching me when I was with the queen?"

I blushed, flustered again. "You are quite sure of your-self, Kenway."

"I'm not fin —"

"You must think all the ladies are in love with you."

I'd embarrassed him. "You don't know me as well as you think you do. You think me arrogant —"

"Indeed you are arrogant."

"Not any more than you."

I sat up. "Me?"

He gave me a crooked smile.

"How can I be arrogant? You yourself have let me know many times how lowly I am."

"Well, I'm sorry for it."

I narrowed my eyes, suspicious.

"I am, Shadow," he said, sitting up. "But despite my feelings about it, you never felt that way. I saw your eyes when you were yelled at or slapped. There was defiance there and a steady will. You've never believed you are less than anyone else."

I thought of his father hitting him and his defiance. I remembered how he had stood up to those in the castle who beat him and called him a traitor. "We are not so different, I think."

He reached for a strand of my hair, twirling it in his fingers. I thought of the queen and how he did this to her and pulled back from him. I lay down on the rock.

"I didn't finish my confession, Shadow," he said softly.

"Confess, then. I will give you absolution."

"You weren't the only one spying. I used to watch you when you'd lie just like this."

My heart skipped. I felt his eyes on me, but I couldn't look his way.

"You were not like the queen or her ladies, who were always so proper."

"So I wasn't proper?" I asked.

"No," he said.

I laughed and stole a glance at him.

"You were brazen," he said with a smile, "lying on the ground, with dirt smudging your skirts and leaves in your hair."

He reached toward me, and my heart sped. He smoothed back some loose strands of my hair, his touch tender. He wouldn't meet my eyes. I was glad for it because he would've seen the depth of emotion there.

But I couldn't stop looking at his face, the beauty there, the kindness.

He lingered for a second before dropping his hand. "You seemed so far away." Then he looked right at me, and my feelings were there for him to see. "You were there, but never really there," he said softly. "What were you thinking of so intently?"

"Escape," I whispered. I had thought myself so watchful, so clever. I had not been. I had misread Piers, Fyren, Eldred. And Kenway, too. My mind had been too cluttered with dreams of escape.

"It was on our picnics," he said. "Do you remember?"

"Those were the queen's picnics." I had been wrong about much, but I knew one thing. "You did love her," I said, sitting up. "I saw the way you looked at her."

"I was desperate to protect her because she was my queen and . . . and to please my father."

It was more than that, I thought.

"She was beautiful," he admitted.

"Was she?" I picked up a rock and studied it.

He gave me a look I couldn't read, but I might have said that it was *knowing*. I lifted my chin. Did he think me jealous of his feelings for her? I felt my stomach twist when he didn't drop his gaze.

"She was cruel to you, and you didn't deserve that."

He looked away. "But she was more than what she showed you."

I remembered when she and I were children, when she cared nothing about our ranks of queen and shadow. At night, she'd lean over the side of her high bed, her blond hair flowing down like bright gold water, and whisper to me so Ingrid wouldn't hear. I felt a pang at the memory. I missed the child that she was.

But she grew up. I threw the stone hard and fast at nothing. It hit the rocky ground and bounced along. It was my own fault for trusting her.

"I was committed to her," he said, watching me closely. "But not in the way she imagined, that I think you imagined. It didn't matter anyway. She was destined for a prince."

We were silent. I felt his eyes on me, looking at me in a different way.

"What?" I asked, blushing.

"You confuse me. I wish you were . . ."

"Yes?"

"I'm a knight. I have a duty to my family."

"Now you confuse me, Kenway."

"I have no choice in whom . . ."

"In whom . . . ?" I asked.

Standing, he held out his hand. "We must go. We need to reach Kendra's by nightfall." He called to Ingen, who had ventured far up the stream. We took the horses to her.

We moved higher up into the mountains. An icy wind blew against my cheeks and ruffled my fur-lined cloak, but I welcomed the chill. Unexplainable warmth filled my chest, like my heart was on fire.

How had I lived for fifteen years and not seen such beauty? The heavy stone blocks of the castle had not hidden us from harm, but only from wide rivers, sweet blackberries, and yellow wildflowers.

Toward late afternoon, we'd almost reached the top of a peak. The horses struggled so much that we got off and led them up. A smell I did not know was thick in the air. I felt a rumble in my chest. Piles of snow lay on the ground.

We were at the top. The wind whipped around us. We were flying in the deepening blue sky, touching wispy clouds. Craggy hills and more mountains stretched out on all sides. Straight before us was something I had only heard about, but had never seen.

Water going on and on until it fell off the Earth. I ran, hearing Kenway calling me to stop. At the edge of the cliff,

I looked out on the deep blue ocean with its white-capped waves. Elegant birds swooped down and back up again. The salty smell, so rich and full of life.

Kenway joined me at the high cliff. I looked back to see Ingen holding the reins of the horses, her long hair flying in the mountain wind.

"Have you never seen the ocean?" Kenway asked, putting his hand on my shoulder. That simple touch sent a thrill through me. I felt a fight within me — a longing to reach for him and a strong resistance to that yearning.

"I've never seen anything," I said, trying to keep my unruly hair from blowing in his face or mine. The wind gusted cold and strong.

And then he wrapped his arms around me and pulled me to him, enveloping me into himself. I'd never been held like this before. Not by anyone that I could remember. It felt strange, disorienting. I gave in. I leaned into him, no longer caring if he knew of my feelings. He tightened his hold on me and nuzzled his scratchy face into my cheek. "Shadow," he said.

I could feel his heart beating. I could feel my heart beating.

I turned my face to look at him. He looked back.

"Shadow," he said again, as if it were the only word he knew.

He leaned down to me. His lips gently touched mine. Sweetly, and I wanted more.

Out of the corner of my eye, I saw her. "Ingen is watching," I said.

"I don't care," he said, not taking his eyes off of me. He put his hands in my hair and pulled me in, the next kiss less gentle, but still so sweet.

Finally, he spoke.

"I have to do it," he said, his words warm and thick in my ear. I cared little what he said, just wanted him to keep speaking. "It's my duty. I've failed at so much. I have to do this last thing for Eldred. For the queen."

I didn't understand it, so I said nothing.

"I will protect you," he said, with emotion. "I promise you."

"I'm not afraid, Kenway."

"I know that." He turned me around, but kept me close with one arm draped around me, and pointed to a cottage perched on a lower hill, precariously close to a cliff overlooking the sea. "That's our destination."

Chapter Twenty-Five

The cottage was made of gray weathered wood and had a thatched roof. It was sealed none too well. Through the cracks, I glimpsed something moving inside. The witch.

Kenway gripped my arm as if to hold me in place. The door opened.

She was tall. White hair flowed down her back, almost to the ground. Her eyes were a calm green, like a resting pond, and wide set over a perfect nose. Her skin was lined, but soft and white.

She put her fingers to her forehead, letting them linger there for a moment before pulling back her hair. The gesture reminded me of someone.

Kenway saw it, too. He bowed. "You are so like the queen. Who are you, my lady?"

"I am not royal," she said in a low voice. "Do not bow to me."

Her cottage was smaller than Stillman's. A square shape, with a fire in the middle. Smoke drifted up.

A single cot was shoved against the far wall. A gray table with two benches on our right. A long window on the left faced the ocean, but the shutters were closed. Food had been set out for us.

She had known we were coming.

Ingen wandered in, moving about the hut. Kenway and I sat beside each other on one bench. He ate the dark grainy bread and sipped the fish soup and drank the ale. Wind whistled through the cracks in the walls. Kendra sat across from us. We watched one another.

"You are like your mother," she said to me. "I'm surprised no one saw it." Out came a weary laugh. "People see what they want." She looked at Kenway. "Noblemen only see things by . . . rank. Is that right?"

Kenway studied her warily, no longer deferential.

But I was drawn in. "You knew my mother?"

"I knew her." Her eyes were no longer green, but now a jarring blue. "Anne."

My heart thumped fast. "Anne?"

Kenway leaned impatiently over his mug of ale. "Who are you? Are you related to the queen?"

She stared at me, not him. "I am the mother of the girl who was poisoned."

"Queen Audrey's mother?" he asked. "That's not possible."

"No, not Audrey's mother." With that, she left. Through the open doorway, I could see her staring at the sea. Her robes snapped violently in the high wind.

I saw the truth, but didn't want to see it. It could not be so. I closed my eyes, trying to piece it all together, while my heart pounded in my ears. I felt as if I moved through mud and could not think.

"Kendra looks like the queen," said Kenway. "But she's not Audrey's mother. Queen Anne was her mother." He was suddenly quiet.

I thought back on all my years, and the clues I had missed. The sameness of our pasts. Both mother and father dead. Or so I had thought. Her mother was here. Mine was truly dead.

The old men including me in all her lessons, pushing me to understand what she could not. The leaders of other countries. The number of their ships. The size of their armies. All while the queen looked out her window at Sir Kenway riding his steed in the lists.

Eldred, always watching. He'd been protecting me, not her. Not protecting me from jabs, slaps, pokes, and loneliness. Only from death. I was to live. And I had lived, while she died. She was sacrificed for me. My eyes stung. My cheeks hurt. They had all been sacrificed.

All that I knew was false.

I'd only had my imagination to create a mother. In my mind, she was a simple woman, of lowly station, who loved the baby she had to leave. But now I knew my mother wasn't a scullery maid buried in an unmarked grave. She'd been a queen.

I felt at once hot and cold, panic rising. I'd always kept myself apart from others, for others only caused me pain. But how could I do that now? The world was reaching in, grasping for me, just as those townspeople had done. *A queen? A queen? It could not be.*

Kenway took my hand. "Your mother was Anne? Who was she?"

I pulled away, not wanting to be touched.

Ingen was then beside me, standing close, but not touching me.

Kendra came back into the cottage and sat across from us again. Her face was bruised and puffy, like a plum. She saw that I knew.

"You are clever," she said. "Eldred said that it was so."

"What was your daughter's name?" I asked her. I had to know her real name.

"Devona," she said.

"Protector," I whispered. I thought of her perfect face. "Did she know?"

"No." Kendra's eyes were cold.

"And so, my name is . . . ?" I could not say it.

"Audrey." She said it with a dead voice.

Audrey. Not Shadow.

Kenway stood up, knocking over his ale. The amber drink flowed across the table. He stared at me. "She's the queen?"

"She is our queen, your queen," said Kendra. "But she's more than that."

Chapter Twenty-Six

"Your mother's spirit left her body before you were switched with my Devona."

"Who switched her? Eldred?" Kenway asked. He was back beside me on the bench, stunned. He stared at me as if he didn't know me. Ingen was on my other side, looking at me as if she'd known these secrets all along.

Kendra went to the window and opened the shutters. The cold wind whooshed in, sending her hair flying. The ocean opened up before us. "It was Larcwide."

"Larcwide?" Kenway asked. Then he nodded. "Yes, I can see him doing such a thing."

I could believe it, too. Larcwide was the most scheming of all the advisers. Silken words slid out of his mouth into Eldred's ear.

"He was my husband," Kendra said.

Larcwide was Audrey's father? Devona. Devona's father. I didn't doubt he'd want his own daughter as queen. It must have given him such pleasure to watch her order us all about.

"I was the one who suffered. Not only did I have my daughter taken from me, I was the reason for it."

I felt her grief in the wind, flying through the air, pounding at us. The dishes flew off the table, crashing against the wall. I gripped my fingers around the bench, waiting. The wind subsided.

"I told Larcwide I had foreseen your death. It would happen before your sixteenth birthday. He wanted to know how it would happen, who would do it. I tried, but I couldn't see it. He and Eldred had a plan."

"You're a witch?" Kenway asked. He watched her closely.

"A prophetess. I see and hear things. Know things."

"But you make the wind move," I said, trying to slow down her story. I did not want to hear it.

"Nature — the waves, the wind, the clouds — senses my feelings and reacts. I cannot control it. I cannot control anything."

It grew dark in the cottage. I could hear the sea slapping the cliffs. The fire glowed low.

"Larcwide brought me back to this cottage where I'd grown up. He told me if I returned to take Devona, they would kill me and she would be motherless. But, if I waited, when the danger had passed, they would bring her to me."

Grabbing candles, she lit them in the fire and placed them on the table. "They promised to keep her safe." She sat down and leaned toward the light. Her eyes were growing black, from corner to corner.

"I'm sorry," I said, feeling the words like cold stones in my mouth. She was accusing me, I knew. I lived while her daughter had died.

She put her hands to her face. "I saw her death." The words seemed to weep as she spoke. "I saw her lying still. I saw you touch her."

The wind was dead now. The flames of the candles did not flicker. I felt Devona's coldness on my fingers.

"Larcwide gave up his daughter for his kingdom. But I betrayed her by letting him use me." Her eyes grew even blacker.

"What's wrong with your eyes?" I asked her.

"It's your own feelings you see there, not mine."

"It was not my doing, Kendra."

"You are alive and she is dead. Now you must do what you were meant to do."

Whatever she thought I must do was not my desire, I knew that much.

"You cannot escape it," she said.

She was wrong. I was free of duty. I had left that at the castle.

"It's my choice what I do," I told her.

"You sound like your mother." She spat the words. "So selfish."

I stared at her with hard eyes. "You may call me selfish, but I don't think my mother deserves that."

"She is more selfish than you."

Is? I dragged my fingers across the grooves on the table. A splinter pricked me.

"Queen Anne is dead," said Kenway, almost laughing.

"In a sense," Kendra said.

"What . . . do you mean?" I asked slowly.

"Your mother was not that human form. That died, but her spirit still lives."

I stood up, suddenly trembling.

Kendra came at me, poking my chest with her long nail. "You feel her."

Kenway rose, grabbing her hand and thrusting it back at her, but she kept her eyes on me.

"She comes to you. She's in the trees, the rivers, the wind."

I stepped away from her, back and back until I bumped against the wall. I wanted her to stop saying these things. An hour ago, I was a queen's shadow with no mother or father. Now I was to believe this? I shook my head at her. She was a liar. I wanted to believe she was a liar.

"Listen to me, Audrey."

I flinched at the use of the name. I'd yearned for a real name, given to me by a loving mother and father. But I didn't want this one.

"You feel her, Audrey," she said.

I sucked in a painful breath, knowing the truth of it. I did feel her. I'd always felt her.

"You're mad!" Kenway yelled. "That's why Larcwide left you here."

"Then why did Eldred send you to me, boy?"

"Queen Anne lived!" he said. "She married. She birthed a child. She died."

"Audrey's mother took a human form to marry the king. That was her first selfish act. When she did so, our kingdom began to die."

"What was she then, if not human?" I asked, finding my voice.

"You don't believe her!" Kenway said.

"You know already, Shadow," said Ingen. "She is earth and sky. She is the air we breathe and the water we drink. She nourished us and fed us."

"Then she saw your father and loved him more," said Kendra. "But her king died." She gave Kenway a wicked smile. "Murdered by Fyren when your father turned his back."

Kenway's hand went to his belt as if there were a sword still there.

"Oh, I know he didn't mean to. None of us meant to be in this place. There's guilt enough for all of us."

I collapsed on the bench. "Erce," I said. She'd been coming to me. Even when I was in the castle, I had sensed her there. I looked at Ingen, into her dark eyes, and knew she was indeed here because of Erce.

"She grew weak when your father died," said Kendra.

"Her human form wasn't strong enough to survive your birth. So her spirit went back where it belonged."

"Then why is the country still dying?" Kenway asked, not giving in, not believing.

"She hides away, not giving us what we need. Except she left us one who can make it right."

I turned to Ingen. "You're her priestess."

She smiled. "It's not me Kendra's talking about."

Kendra reached down and grabbed my hands, but I jerked away. "Think of who you are, Audrey. The union of nature and man. You're our connection to the Earth and to one another."

"No," I whispered, feeling the fear of the villagers inside me again.

"Only you can unite us. Only you can bring your mother back to us. When you do that, we'll be able to defeat Fyren."

Her words squeezed my lungs. I sucked in air.

"Fyren raises an army as we speak!" yelled Kendra. "You *know* he's the one who kidnaps the villagers, whose soldiers slaughtered those in Erce. If anyone refuses to go with Fyren's soldiers, he is killed. Fyren doesn't care for Deor's people, Audrey. He only wants more power."

"It is not my concern," I said in a voice that felt no part of me.

She grabbed my shoulders, shaking me. "He will send Deorian troops in ships to attack our friends to the south, to try to take their lands. His evil will bleed out beyond Deor."

I yanked away from her. "I don't want to hear any more."

"Fyren believes in Erce, just as his mother did," Kendra continued. "He is seeking priestesses to reach her. He attempts to gain more control through Deor's goddess."

I looked at Ingen and back to Kendra.

"Yes," said Kendra. "Ingen is the last priestess. There was another, but she died in the queen's castle not many days ago."

"Maren," I said.

"I felt her spirit leave her body," said Ingen. "You did, too, didn't you, Audrey?"

I trembled, remembering.

"He seeks to reach Erce, by any means," said Kendra. "He wants Ingen. Thankfully, he does not know about you." But her voice was filled with despair, not relief. "Eldred and Larcwide succeeded there."

"I am . . . sorry for it," I said, trying to just breathe. "But I . . . cannot help you, Kendra."

"Fyren killed your father!" She came to me, trying to stroke my hair; her fingernails were like claws on my scalp. "You and Erce will defeat him, Audrey."

"Not I," I said.

"You have no choice."

Chapter Twenty-Seven

I left the cottage, desperate to be out of that closed-in space. Too many thoughts swirled in my head, making it pound and ache.

I was the daughter of King Alfrid and Queen Anne. Had the king known his beloved Queen Anne was a goddess? Had he loved her still?

What had he been like, my father, murdered before I was born? Eldred had assumed the murderer was Fyren, but had no proof. Fyren had been powerful even then, with many lords loyal to him. He was also the cousin of the king — the only son of King Alfrid's dead aunt, who'd died not long after being denied the throne by her father.

Fyren was to be crowned king, but history turned as it is wont to do: My mother discovered she was with child. I could imagine the ire Fyren must have felt at that bit

Just as Erce had left me behind. Was I so like her?

Piers had saved me, really. He had kept my heart from withering, and I repaid him with disloyalty, adding to his mother's and father's abandonment.

The sand was fine, so white. I knelt down and ran my fingers through its cold softness. The salty spray of the waves settled on my lips. Sea birds with large cupped beaks flew overhead in communion. I envied their peace so much it hurt my heart. I could stay here, live here. Push all the madness away.

I climbed onto a black rock jutting out into the sea. Yanking out the medallion, I hurled it out into the blue water. Once back on the sand, I closed my eyes, trying to push it all away.

"Do you think you can rid yourself of her so easily?"

I whipped around. It was Kendra, yelling above the sound of the waves crashing on the shore.

"She disposed of me that easily."

She came close to me, looked at me with those bewitching eyes. "You know nothing of a mother's pain."

"I don't believe motherhood was in her schemes," I said. "She wanted a king, not a daughter."

"You didn't know her."

"Then tell me: What was she like? Like nothing I have imagined, I am sure."

"You imagined a frail human mother whose body couldn't survive your birth? That was an easier mother to love."

Tears pricked my eyes. "An easier one to understand, at least."

"You look so like her. Your eyes, your hair, the way you move. Even your voices are the same."

"And were any of those things a part of Erce?" I looked toward the waves. "Did she create a body out of the sea? What does it matter if I look like that body she made?"

"It is true your humanness is similar to a body not truly hers. But that resemblance is uncanny. It is as if I stand before her again, sixteen years ago."

I eyed her then. "You were friends?"

She laughed. "No. We weren't friends, Audrey. I'm a peasant — it was a scandal that Larcwide had married me at all — and she was the queen and more like my Devona in her manner. Proud. And, yes, selfish.

"You're the exact image of her, but your strong spirit matches your father's. A perfect blend of nature and man.

You were meant to be queen, no doubt. Destined for this moment."

"No. I'm plagued with weakness."

She studied me. "You are confused, not weak."

But she didn't know the cause of my agony. It wasn't only *my* feelings that haunted me like ghosts. Everyone's feelings emptied into me as if I were a vessel made just to contain misery. But I was a weak vessel, cracking, drowning.

"I am weak, Kendra. All the vulnerability I saw in others has now laid claim to me. So, you see, this blend you speak of is a flawed one. I was not meant to rule a *country*. The only way I can live in peace is to embrace a solitary life."

"I cannot see you at a nunnery."

"You may laugh at me, but I know the truth of what I say."

"I think there are other plans for you," she said, nodding at the sandy ground.

I felt it knocking against my soaked shoes even before I looked down. With shaking hands, I picked up the wet medallion, no longer stained with blood.

Kendra left me on the beach. I sat on the rock staring

out into the sea, searching for her. Why wouldn't she come to me?

Kenway was at my side. He wordlessly took my arm and led me back up to the cottage. Once there, I put the medallion away.

Kenway was restless. He tossed on his pallet, but didn't cry out as he had in the village. His anger and guilt raged inside *me*, making it difficult to think. He carried the blame for Devona's death deep in his heart as if it were his doing, the feeling so intense it was almost as if he'd poured the poison down her throat. His pain felt like a piercing high note of a song that would not stop. I hadn't known his feeling of shame was this sharp and lonely.

Kendra's despair crept toward me from her cot. It was bleak and bitter. I could taste it in my mouth.

Fear rose into the air, from far away. I smelled death and ashes and terror. A fire, once blazing, now gone out. The odor became stronger and stronger.

And from Ingen, poured out need. It was strong and vivid and tugged at me. I didn't understand it, but its power was frightening.

Chapter Twenty-Eight

"You must bring back Erce," Kendra said.

"Bring back Erce," I repeated, not understanding.

The four of us sat at the table. A fire blazed under a pot of fish soup, its warmth easing the cold of the morning air. The cottage stank of fish.

"What do you mean, bring her back?" asked Kenway from his place beside me. He hadn't looked at me in the same way since we'd learned who I really was. "You said she's been watching out for Shad — the queen."

"Erce is a wounded spirit," whispered Ingen, putting her hand over her heart.

"She must be providing for Deor," said Kenway. "Or else there would be no rain. Nothing would be growing at all."

"She's dying," said Kendra.

"How can she be dying?" I asked, not wanting to accept it. "She's a goddess."

"She *can* cease to exist," Kendra replied. "At present, she's very weak. Some of the mountain people say she's too human and that drains her of life."

Ingen shook her head. "That's the part of her I like best: the nurturer, the giver . . . human qualities. Not like the other gods."

Nurturer, I thought. *I see little of that.*

"What other gods?" asked Kenway, a scoff twisting his lips.

"An unbeliever, I see," said Kendra. "That's why Eldred didn't reveal much to you."

"He told me enough," said Kenway, suddenly defensive.

"And what did he say?" Kendra asked, rising from her seat.

"He entrusted me with Shadow, telling me to get her out of the castle, to protect her," he replied. "He told me to bring Ingen to you, that she would know where to find you."

"Ah," said Kendra, ladling soup into a bowl. "But he didn't trust you with what's most important: that Audrey is the true queen and the child of Erce." She tried to give the bowl to me, but I turned up my nose.

"Too early for fish."

Ingen took the soup and spooned it to her mouth with loud slurps.

"No, but he chose me —" Kenway began.

"And he didn't tell you about Ingen."

"He knew I knew Ingen. She came to my father's castle when she was five or so."

"But he didn't trust you completely, Kenway. He didn't tell you everything." Kendra handed the next bowl to Kenway, who did not refuse it. She took her own and settled back down with us.

"He told me we might be followed," he said quietly, looking down at the bowl while he slowly stirred his soup.

I didn't want to get drawn into their exchange, but my curiosity was too great. "How did Fyren know about Ingen?" I asked reluctantly.

"He first discovered Eldred was meeting with Callus," said Kendra.

I remembered Fyren's accusation. "So Callus was helping Eldred?"

"Callus has become too careless in his old age," Kendra said. "His ability to guard secrets is less than it once was. The regent has spies everywhere. *Many* have betrayed the realm. Although some are just misguided, wanting to restore Fyren's mother's line to the throne."

"That is not without merit," I said. "She was the true heir, not my . . . father."

The prophetess gave me a long stare. I glanced at Kenway and Ingen, their faces a mixture of disbelief and sadness.

"Do you think, Shadow," Kenway began, "that Fyren is what's best for Deor?"

"I didn't say that. But he is the *true* king."

His eyes filled with disappointment as he looked at me. "He has lost that right," he said simply.

I didn't want to talk about it. "Those spies," I asked Kendra, "what did they tell Fyren?"

"That Erce is dying, and that Ingen is the key."

Ingen gazed at us with innocent eyes. I knew better than to believe the innocence. This girl was a warrior.

"Why is she so valuable?" I asked.

"She can talk to Erce," said Kendra, offering me some dark bread.

Kenway and I exchanged a look.

"Skeptics," said Kendra. She pushed the bread into my

hand. "Eat." My stomach didn't want even this, but I knew I should eat something, so I nibbled at it.

"Why shouldn't we be suspicious?" Kenway asked. "All we have as proof of Erce's existence is one blackberry bush. You could have done that."

"Is it easier for you to believe in a witch than a goddess?"

"It is. A witch is human, just born with gifts others do not possess. But a *goddess* of the Earth?" Kenway scoffed. "This old religion is not for the educated."

A smile played at Kendra's lips.

Ingen's eyes caught mine. "Audrey knows the truth."

She was right. I felt it. I grasped the medallion around my neck and felt a surge of something deep and strong ripple through me. I did not like the feeling.

"Show him," said Kendra.

I narrowed my eyes at her, but pulled out the necklace for Kenway to see.

He took it in his hand, looking from me to it and back again. "It is you." I felt him pull away from me.

I slid the medallion back under the front of my dress. "It is Erce — her human form."

"What human form?" he asked.

I looked at Kendra. "How did she —"

"She's a goddess," said Kendra, waving her hand. "I don't know all her ways."

I could see it in her eyes. She knew more than she was saying. But I was Erce's daughter. It was my right to know everything.

"You must seek her, Audrey," said Kendra.

"Seek her?" I asked with a bite to my words. "I thought she was all around us."

She ignored me, looked at Kenway. "You will take Ingen and the queen to High Pointe. There, you will find Erce."

The queen.

"High Pointe?" I asked.

"The highest point of Deor," Ingen said. "Erce's spirit is strongest there. It is like . . ." She looked away. "Like her heart. Her energy pours out from there."

"Where is this place?" asked Kenway.

"Not far. A full day up the mountain," said Kendra. "But you must be careful. Others also seek Ingen."

"Who does?" he asked.

"The mountain people," said Ingen, "like the ones who took your horse and sword, Kenway. They think I'm a charm, that I'll bring good fortune to their people." She got up for more soup. She filled the bowl to the brim and then carried it to the table with both hands cupped around it. "They believe I belong to them."

"Obviously they thought the same of my horse and sword," Kenway said soberly.

I gave him a small smile, but his eyes were serious and he did not return it.

"You once did belong to them, Ingen," said Kendra. "Before your father took you from your mountain home."

"He has little faith." She blew on her soup. "But I do remember Maren. My father says I couldn't because I was young when I left her temple. But I remember her voice, her hands," she said, looking at her own, "the things she taught me about Erce. I was with her until my father brought us to Kenway's castle."

"Ingen is a special priestess," said Kendra. "Maren was angry at Malcolm for taking her from the mountains."

Ingen nodded, taking a big spoonful of soup. "Mmm." She took another. "Maren told my mother I had the strongest connection to Erce she'd ever seen."

"So you have spoken to Erce?" I asked, ignoring Kenway's look.

Ingen nodded. "But not since I was a child."

"You're a child still," said Kenway.

Ingen's forehead furrowed, but then she went back to her soup. "The fish is sweet and tender." She looked at Kenway. "I haven't spoken to Erce since I was five. But I remember it."

"What did she say?" I asked.

"She was very sad," said Ingen.

Kenway sighed. "This is . . . ," he said, gesturing with his hands out, then clenching them into fists and dropping them to the table.

"You haven't talked with her since then?" I asked.

"I've tried. My mother and I have taken trips to the temple. We would meet Maren, sometimes Kendra, too, at High Pointe. But Erce was silent."

"But you think I can talk to her?" I asked Kendra.

"If her daughter cannot, who can?"

"And what shall I tell her?" I asked.

"To return to her people. The land needs her. She must put away her grief."

"And after we . . . *talk* to her?" Kenway asked. "What next?"

"Erce can defeat Fyren. We can put Audrey on the throne where she belongs."

"And how will Erce do that?" I asked. "How will she defeat him?"

"Nature is powerful."

"And if we aren't successful?" asked Kenway. "Do you have another plan?" He obviously did not have much faith in this one.

"It will be up to Audrey then," said Kendra.

They all looked at me.

I could not return to the castle. But I could not confide in them about why. They would think I was going mad if I told them I was haunted — and not by ghosts, but by the feelings of others.

Perhaps I'd discovered the true nature of ghosts.

Chapter Twenty-Nine

Kendra told me to use her gray horse, Mirth, for the ride to High Pointe. She gave us thick wool blankets, feed for the horses, and a cloth pouch overflowing with salted fish.

When Kenway mounted his horse, his hand went to his wound. But he didn't complain. He never complained. Kendra had given him fresh ointment and clean bandages the night before.

We said little to one another as we rode.

I was lost in my own thoughts. For the first time, I felt uncertain about who I was. Part of me accepted Kendra's claims. Her truth did explain some of the mysteries of my life. But I also resisted. *A queen? The daughter of a goddess? How could that person be me?* It fit, and yet it didn't. It explained things, but it was a wild truth and not what I wanted, not who I'd been for the last sixteen years.

So why was I going with them? I was a queen. No one could make me do anything anymore. I could truly choose my own path.

I glanced over at Kenway, who was deep in thought himself. Sweet warmth rippled through me, just watching him. In the beginning, I came with him because I wanted to be with him. I also wanted my freedom, but perhaps I thought I could have both. I had a great faith in my ability to survive and, in some respect, to ultimately get what I wanted.

But I could *not* have both. The thought jarred me, as if a cold hand had grabbed my heart. Kenway would never leave duty behind. Deor, not me, was first to him. But wasn't I the same? I was choosing freedom over him. But I had to. I would be of no use to anyone if I was not true to myself. A ruler must want to rule. I had no desire for that.

And even if I wanted to, I could not in my present state.

So now I stayed for Erce. I did want to know her. I had always thought of my mother. I had never imagined this, but this is what I had, what was before me. If I had the chance to speak with her, I would take it.

After High Pointe, I would leave.

I looked again at Kenway, and he looked back at me, finally. But his face was a mask of knightly distance and obedience. It wounded me, this change in manner toward me. I knew he must be scheming, trying to think of ways to convince me to do what he felt I must do for Deor.

If only he would leave with me! We could be together. Perhaps Piers would come live with us in Goodham, in a cottage by the river. And Tayte and Stillman and their boys would visit us. And we would farm. And catch fish. And hunt for our supper. I would like that life.

But Kenway would never do that.

Ingen was leading us. The path forked and twisted, but she continued to take us higher into the mountains. Midday, we got off the horses and let them drink from a cold stream. We fed them, and ate fish in quiet.

On this journey to Erce's temple, I found I was trying to let go of the mother I'd created. It wasn't at all who she really was. I had imagined her vulnerable and frail. But also loving, and not choosing to leave me. But she *had* chosen.

So I now mourned a mother who never really existed. It

was a humbling and unsettling feeling for someone who put much faith in her own judgment.

I tried to replace her with the queen-goddess Anne-Erce. This creature wasn't strong, either — she was as weak as I had imagined a human mother to be. Weak, not loving, but capable of great power.

Ingen's face was scrunched in concentration on a piece of fish. She picked something off it and flicked it away. She saw me looking, smiled, and said, "A gnat."

I wondered how this enigmatic girl could connect with a goddess.

We were back on the horses.

The path continued to be well-worn. Many had traveled this way, on horseback and on foot.

We came to yet another fork: One path went up, one down. I thought Ingen would continue to follow the most-traveled path. Instead, she took the lower one. We descended a little, then traveled around the perimeter of a rock that jutted out.

The view opened up when we turned a corner. We were on a ledge overlooking a vast valley. The trail wound around the side of a mountain. On the other side of the valley was another mountain. Connecting the two was a narrow bridge of rock. The trail ended at that bridge and continued on the other side. We were meant to cross it.

Kenway's horse was skittish on the ledge. The other two horses were more sure-footed.

"Is she all right?" I asked him, concerned for his safety.

He nodded his assent.

The ledge was not as narrow as I first thought. Two riders could easily ride side by side. Still, we rode one behind the other, Ingen in the lead, Kenway behind me. I was glad there was only a slight breeze — it was cold enough without a gusty wind freezing our faces.

As we rode, I'd glance back at Kenway. His horse stopped frequently and he had to urge her on. He touched his shoulder once, and I wondered if his injury still caused him pain.

The height and beauty of this place was magnificent. A narrow strip of water flowed at the bottom of the gulch below. The sky was a beautiful blue with not a cloud to mar it. It felt as if we were indeed riding to the home of the gods. Kendra's horse was calm and not hesitant. She had been this way before.

Crossing the rock bridge was a challenge for Kenway's horse. She didn't want to make the trip, even after the other two horses had easily crossed. I watched her every step. Kenway's face was one of intense concentration. He handled his horse well. I let out a breath of relief when he finally joined us.

We rounded the next mountain on an identical trail. This one went slowly up and up and then turned away from the edge.

Scrub bushes got larger and larger and soon we were riding through trees. The trees became a dark forest, and it was colder here away from the sun. Patches of snow hid in the shade.

The sun kept sinking. Clouds had now rolled in, disturbing the pure look of the sky.

We finally made it to more level ground, at the top of the mountain, still surrounded by forest.

"We're on foot from here," Ingen said, gesturing to the path. It was no longer wide enough. We tied the horses' reins to thin trees.

We walked through trees and bushes and around rocks. The wind had picked up and blew ice-cold against my face. One part of the path was very narrow, pressed against a rock wall. We went one by one, and watched our feet carefully, for it was a long way down.

I looked up as we rounded the corner, and I saw it.

Erce's temple.

It was circular, with large gray rocks set one to the other to make the perimeter. There was no roof. I approached it slowly, feeling a tug in my chest.

Inexplicably, wildflowers covered the ground around the temple. One unruly bush with purple blossoms spilled over the side of the stone.

Ingen touched the flowers. "Erce loves these, so the mountain people named them after her."

"She loves purple flowers," I said, "but not her own people."

Ingen looked at me curiously. "You care about the people, Audrey?" She plucked a flower and brushed it against my nose.

"Don't," I said, pushing it away.

Kenway's eyes were on me, too.

"The people of Deor," I said, "are in Erce's care . . . not mine." But I looked away so they wouldn't see the doubt in my eyes.

"Ah," Ingen replied. She tucked the flower into my hair. I pulled it out and tossed it on the ground.

The sky was now gray, with clouds thick around us. We couldn't see below or above, just the close area around the gray rocks. I felt hemmed in, trapped like I was still in the castle.

"Why is there no snow," asked Kenway, "anywhere around here?"

"Erce doesn't like snow," said Ingen, slipping through an opening in the rocks.

Kenway slid a disbelieving look my way before we followed her.

In the center was a circular hole, about three feet deep, its diameter the length of two men. Purple flowers sprang up everywhere, despite the cold. The temple was beautiful in its simplicity, but it didn't reflect Erce's spirit. She was not simple.

"So where is she?" I asked, holding my arms out. I felt that same strange pull inside of me. It was not pleasant. It made me want to stay and to run, both desires strong and rooted deep, entangled together, and pulling me apart. I sat on the ground.

Kenway was beside me, looking at me carefully.

Ingen stepped down into the circle. "It's late."

I laughed. "So she only appears during the day? What kind of goddess is she?"

"You are tired. You must rest."

"Me?" I asked.

Ingen sat in the center, cross-legged.

So this was the place of Erce's power. And all I had to connect me to her was a rush of confusing feelings. I had expected clear answers, not more uncertainty.

"We can't sleep out here," said Kenway. "We'll freeze."

Indeed, Ingen's teeth were chattering. But she had her eyes closed and was ignoring us.

"Ingen," I said, not letting my feet even dangle over the edge. I didn't want to go in. "Ingen!"

Her eyes popped open.

"We need shelter," Kenway said. "Come on, Ingen. Get out of there. You're turning blue."

Ingen smiled as if we were children, but she stood slowly. The girl rarely moved very quickly.

We made our way to the horses. I didn't look back.

We then went in the opposite direction, but kept to the top of the mountain. The trail was wider here, but we walked the horses. We came to a small hut, accessible by stone steps up to its door. It was perched on a jut of rock, with little level land surrounding it before it dropped off to cliffs on three sides.

"Protected," said Ingen. "They can only approach us from the front."

"Our only escape as well," said Kenway, opening the door.

We put the horses in a lean-to not far from the hut, situated by a small spring. Kenway tended to them while Ingen and I went to get us settled for the night.

It was not much warmer in the tiny hut. A small table stood in the corner with bowls, plates, spoons, and candles stacked upon it. There was a rim of stone in the middle of the room for a fire. Wood was stacked by the door.

"The mountain people provide for me," said Ingen. "They visit the temple frequently."

"How frequently?" I asked.

"They'll leave me alone here."

I nodded, not sure if I believed it.

Soon a fire blazed, and despite the hole in the roof, the room became smoky and close. Kenway came in, saying little. After spreading out all but one of my blankets on the earthen floor, I went out into the cold night air with the last one pulled about me. My hands were warm in the leather gloves given to me at Kenway's castle.

The clouds were gone.

I sat on the top step, looking out into the dark and seeing nothing but the stars and the bit of moon above and the dark figures of the trees below us.

Kenway joined me. He gave me a bowl of slightly warmed fish, while commenting on our oversupply from Kendra. "She means for us to eat it morning, noon, and night," he said in a distant tone. He stood off from me a little, which was not easy to do in this narrow place.

I took the food, not happy with this gesture of his. It seemed out of duty, not out of kindness. Something a knight would do for a queen, not . . . whatever it was we had been to each other before. Sadness tugged at me.

"Have you seen any signs of these mountain people," I asked, "or anyone else following us?"

Kenway shook his head.

We were quiet while we ate our supper.

When I finished, he reached out his hand for my bowl.

"You don't have to wait on me," I said.

He paused, a look of uncertainty crossing his face. Then,

he sat beside me on the step. I was glad for it, but kept my distance.

"You're worried about Erce," he said.

A tentative feeling of relief came over me. This was more like the Kenway I'd grown to . . . know this past week. "Why would I worry?"

"Shadow," he said, taking my bowl anyway and setting both of them down.

"You mean Audrey," I asked, "Queen Audrey, don't you?"

He said nothing.

"Your Highness, Your Majesty . . . any of these will do."

"I'm sorry," he said.

"Don't apologize!" I said. "Stop treating me differently. I am no different."

"Everything is different."

"No, it's not. I won't let it be."

"And how are you going to do that?" he asked.

I looked away, not wanting him to see my eyes.

"You are the queen," he said. "You can't change that." He touched my arm. "Shadow?"

"I'm not crowned queen. I don't have to accept that . . . burden."

"What do you mean not accept?" he asked. "You would refuse?"

I looked at him with purpose in my eyes.

"You cannot! You have an obligation to Deor."

"An obligation? What has Deor done for me?"

"I don't believe you would shirk your duty," he said.

"You confuse my values with yours."

"And what will Deor do without you? Let Fyren rule?"

"Depose him. Give someone else the throne."

"Who?" he asked. "The royal line dies with you."

"I don't know," I said. "What about your father? Don't you have any royal blood?"

He shot me an angry look.

"There are many lords willing," I said.

"Not just one would want to take it. Several would. You would throw us into civil war."

"I don't believe it," I said, shaking my head.

"You mean you won't concern yourself with it," he said. "Why are you here then?"

"What do you mean?"

"If you don't care about our country's fate, why come here with us?" He stared back at me, his eyes looking into mine, as if he were trying to read my thoughts. Did he think I would say I followed him here?

But that wasn't the reason anymore. I cared for him. I did not deny it. And the thought of being without him clawed at my heart, scratching off bits of it. But I had to survive. If I went back, my soul would shrivel up, so tiny nothing would be left of me. I could not be queen, or I would be a queen without a soul.

"You're not going to answer me." He looked away. "You have always kept your own counsel."

How I wished for his understanding.

The night was quiet and cold. I pulled the blanket tighter around me. Kenway reached over to help, his gloved hand grazing my chin. I reached, taking his hand between the two of mine. I looked at him, silently willing him to look at me as he did before.

We stared at each other. I was conscious only of his eyes and my own breathing. I leaned forward, touching my lips to his. Very gently we kissed, the warmth of it a pleasant shock against the cold. I felt a surge of need to have him close, as close as I could get him. My arms went around his neck, my blanket dropped. He drew me to him, his arms keeping me tight against his chest. One kiss followed another.

Then suddenly he pulled away. "No, Shadow."

But I couldn't. I kept reaching for him. I had never felt this before, never known what it was like to be so physically close with another.

"Shadow!" He put me at arm's length. Hurt washed over me, but I buried it in anger. I tried to get to my feet, but he pulled me down. "Shadow. Listen to me."

"What? What is it?" I asked. "What you wanted just yesterday you no longer desire?"

He shook his head. "Things are different now. I have much to sort out."

"When you thought *she* was queen, it made no difference."

"Yes, and look what happened."

"You think that's your fault? You make too much of yourself."

I went inside, pulling the door shut behind me. Ingen sat cross-legged on her blankets, poking at the fire. She did not look at me.

I buried myself in my covers and turned my face to the wall. I felt the exhaustion in my bones and sighed deeply. I was already half asleep when Kenway came back in.

Chapter Thirty

We woke with first light.

Kenway hovered close, but I would not look at him. I wanted to be ready for this day, not distracted and confused. The three of us sat outside the hut and ate more fish. The sun came up, coloring the cold sky.

After caring for the horses, we hiked to the temple. With the gray clouds now gone, a stunning view of the mountains and the ocean had opened up around us. A wind blew in from the sea and was gentle.

Ingen jumped into the circle and went right to its center. "You must join me, Shadow."

I eyed her warily, but climbed down.

"No, Kenway," said Ingen, her palm out. I looked back to see him at the circle's edge.

I took her outstretched hand. We stood side by side. I felt that same strange pull, as if something were trying to yank me into the Earth, into an early grave perhaps. I hid my panic.

"Sit there," Ingen said to Kenway, pointing to a rock. "You shouldn't stand so close."

He did as she bade him, folding his arms over his chest. His mouth was tight with concern. He gave me a look that I could easily read.

"It's all right," I said, trying to reassure him. "You don't believe in all this anyway."

He looked unconvinced.

Ingen's face was so open, as if she was ready to give anything asked of her. "Close your eyes, Audrey," she said, shutting her own. She suddenly looked more vulnerable, and I realized her dark eyes gave her face its depth and strength.

All was quiet except for the *whish-whish* of the wildflowers dancing in the soft breeze.

"Close your eyes," Ingen said again, her own still shut.

As soon as I did, my fingers began to tingle. It was Erce, that quick, coming to me through Ingen. The girl squeezed my hand tighter as Erce flooded my heart, my mind, my eyes. She found empty spaces inside of me and poured into those. She was very real, very human, really.

I knew her, for I'd felt her all my life. She was the silver birches, red fruit dangling on a branch, black ash, bubbling springs, white boulders, a wooden medallion, a woman carved from stone. The sweetness and splendor of the Earth was her. To my surprise, she breathed power. But of course she did. She was a goddess, and her spirit had to be great for it filled a kingdom.

But alongside that power was the feeling of humanity. I sensed her vulnerability, choices, regrets — oh, her regrets.

The last feeling, very weak, was of a mother, just a taste of what it'd be like to have one. A tender brush of a hand upon my cheek. Oh, is this sweet feeling what it is to be a child loved by her mother?

I heard Ingen's voice inside my head as if she were in my thoughts. She spoke to Erce, calling her, worshipping her, thanking her for the beauty of Deor.

Erce grew stronger as Ingen praised her.

And then Ingen's hand was gone, no longer holding mine. But I could still feel Erce's spirit within me.

I didn't need Ingen at all. I was Erce's daughter. I was hers, a part of her spirit. But our bond was weak, broken by years apart, and something else. What was it? What was keeping me from her?

It was just below the surface, rising. I couldn't stop it.

Hadn't she deserted me? Hadn't she let her grief consume her so much she left her only child to the wiles of three old men? And to the abuse of Devona? Memories from those lonely years slammed into me. Devona had betrayed me, too, but she had been only a child herself and as manipulated as I was.

Erce . . . Erce was a mother. Didn't a daughter deserve a mother's love?

Anger bubbled inside of me.

And now Erce wanted me when I no longer needed her? *Leave me be, Erce. Out of my heart. Get out of my heart.* I felt her power ebb, her hold on me loosen.

And then she was gone.

I expected to feel satisfaction, but in her place was just emptiness.

I opened my eyes. Kenway hovered over me. I was lying on the ground, in the middle of the circle. "What did you do?" he yelled at Ingen.

I could hear her soft voice in reply, but couldn't understand the words.

Kenway put his arms behind my shoulders. I struggled to stand, but my legs felt weak.

He tried to pick me up, but I pushed against him. "No." I would not be carried.

"Shadow," he said.

I grabbed his arm and pulled myself up. He helped me walk to the circle's edge. My knees buckled; Kenway kept me from falling. He picked me up despite my protests and laid me down on the ground at the perimeter. I was dizzy still.

"What happened, Audrey?" Ingen asked.

"Don't you know?" Kenway asked her.

"I let go," she said.

"I saw," he said. "Why? That's what you were there for!"

"She didn't need me. She had to connect with her mother and know that she could do it."

"But it didn't work," he said.

I knew what had happened.

Ingen's dark eyes were on me. I didn't like looking into those eyes. There was no light there, no peace or calm . . . none of those things that were a part of her, too. Instead, I saw a need. I felt her need.

"What?" I asked her.

"You pushed her away, didn't you?"

I tried to pull myself up. Kenway reached for me, but I slapped his hands. "No."

"You can't do it alone," he said.

"I can." I sat up and held my head. It spun and spun. I swung my feet over so they were dangling into the circle.

Ingen put her hand on my shoulder. "We need her."

I shook her hand off. I knew who she meant. Again, I felt that need in Ingen. She needed Erce to come back. It was a hunger inside of her. She was driven to do it, perhaps because of who she was.

"You failed," I said to her.

"You must try again."

I shook my head.

"She won't," Kenway said, brushing dirt from my shoulders. I shrugged him off. He didn't have a say in this.

"You're a priestess, Ingen," I told her. "You can do this alone. You're the one who brought her to me."

"No. It was you, Audrey." She pulled herself up to sit beside me. "Maren and I tried together. We reached out to Erce over and over, but we failed. Our goddess only came to me now because of you." Her eyes lit up. "It was wonderful to feel her presence again."

Indeed, Ingen's face was bright with joy. She reached behind her and plucked some flowers off the vine.

"You have tried here at the temple?" I asked. "This is where Maren brought you?"

She nodded.

I grabbed her arm. "Does Fyren know about this place, Ingen? Would Maren have told him?"

"No, no," she said, tying the stems of two flowers together. "Never."

"And you are the . . . only priestess left," I said, feeling suddenly ill.

Kenway reached for me. "Are you all right?"

I nodded, but I felt dizzy. He put his arm on my elbow, steadying me.

"Why did Fyren kill Maren?" I asked. "He needed her. He needs Erce to rule."

"Fyren pushed Maren too hard," said Ingen, her eyes watering, "wanting to break her spirit. When you came to the dungeon, Audrey, she let go."

I shivered.

Ingen plucked more flowers and linked them to the others. "She knew who you were."

"You knew Maren's thoughts?" asked Kenway.

"We were bonded as priestesses," said Ingen. "The last ones. And now there is only me."

We were all silent for a moment. I could think only of Maren's face as they carried her out of the dungeon.

"What will happen to Deor," Kenway asked, "if Erce continues to weaken?"

"There may be another way to save us," said Ingen, putting her necklace of purple flowers around my neck, "that Fyren doesn't know about."

We both looked at her, waiting.

"Maren thought I could join with Erce, let my spirit pour out of my body," Ingen said, "and go to Erce and strengthen her."

"What?" I asked. "Ingen, no."

"How could it be done?" asked Kenway. "How can a human spirit leave its body?"

"Erce had to use the body of a woman," explained Ingen, "to become Queen Anne. There was no other way. That woman was from the mountains and had no special gifts. But Erce liked the look of her."

"What madness is this?" I put my hand over my queasy stomach.

Ingen looked at me steadily. "Erce had no choice but to

let the woman's spirit flow into the trees and rivers of Deor. The woman's mind wouldn't have survived living inside a body she could no longer control."

"Erce did have a choice!" I said. "You cannot defend her, Ingen." This is what Kendra had hidden from me about my mother.

But no outrage showed on Ingen's face. She worshipped Erce. She would not deny her anything. The priestesses followed a goddess who was not a very loving mother of her people.

"And what happened to this woman?" I asked.

"Her human spirit was too weak to survive the experience."

"She died," I said. "So my mother killed her."

"It wasn't her intention."

"Oh, I forgive her now," I said, removing the necklace. This creature, this selfish being, was a part of me. But I didn't want her in me. "She took a life so she could be with my father."

"Erce could not save the woman."

"Could not?" I repeated. "She *would* not."

"After the king died, Erce had no desire to stay human. She was ready to take up her duties again as the goddess of

Deor. She saw how this land was dying and needed her. She knew she had to return. And she wanted to give this woman back her life and relinquish her body to her."

"How kind of her," I retorted. Such selfishness was hard to imagine.

"But then Erce discovered she was with child," said Ingen, her voice becoming soft. "It is sad the woman's spirit died before your birth, Audrey. Erce was not pleased by this. She still carries great guilt. And she did return to her rightful place, grieving for you and the human life she took."

And she sacrificed all of that because she desired a king for her husband. "What was the woman's name?" I asked. In a way, this woman Erce killed was also my mother.

Ingen smiled sadly. "They called her Cara."

"But Cara died," Kenway said. "And so would you, Ingen."

"I'm a priestess," said Ingen, "with a very strong spirit. Not like that of an ordinary human."

"No," I told her. "We will have no more human sacrifice because of a weak-willed goddess."

"Audrey," she said, putting her hand on my arm. "I may be part-goddess, like you, descended from the sea god through my great-grandmother, a priestess."

"The sea god," said Kenway, throwing up his hands. "Of course."

"You're still an unbeliever?" Ingen asked. "There are many beings taking care of the Earth, and of us through that care."

"If that is your lineage, then others in your family would have special gifts. Why isn't your mother a priestess?" I asked.

"My father, you mean."

"Malcolm?" Kenway asked, with a derisive laugh. "He doesn't even believe in all this. He told me so."

"Men are not priestesses," she said.

"You would die just as Cara did," I told Ingen. "You must *never* try." I felt protective of this girl. I didn't welcome the feeling, not wanting to carry another in my soul. I already felt the weight of Piers and Kenway.

"But I will, if it comes to that," she said.

No, you will not, I thought. *I won't allow it*. But I knew she was stubborn.

"Why does Fyren think," Kenway asked, "Erce would ever help him anyway? He killed the king, her husband."

Ingen laughed. "Fyren doesn't know Queen Anne was Erce. He never suspected that."

"But he told me that he knew something of my mother. He offered his knowledge up to me as a trade." I felt Kenway's eyes on me.

"He doesn't know," Ingen said.

Fyren tried to trick me then, but that was no surprise.

"He thinks he's the only heir," continued Ingen. "Deor will fall into foreign hands or erupt into civil war without a king or queen. Erce would not want that."

"But that won't happen," said Kenway, looking relieved. "Our queen is alive."

"Audrey is unwilling," said Ingen. "If she won't take the throne, then without Fyren as a stable force, our enemies will waste no time."

That part was true enough. The Torsans had coveted the strategic position of Deor for decades. Our countries had no great love for each other.

"Ingen," I asked, "have the Torsans moved on us?"

She nodded. "Kendra said they attacked the port of Mays, a few days after Devona's murder."

Kenway swore.

Fyren is a fool, I thought. *He must have known this would happen. He plays a dangerous game with this country he supposedly loves so much.*

"Lords who once opposed Fyren," said Ingen, "now support him. They know Deor mustn't appear vulnerable."

"My father hates Fyren more than he hates the Torsans," said Kenway. "He will never support him."

I looked at him. "He would not side with our enemies? He wouldn't let them have Deor?"

He slowly shook his head. "Truly, I don't know what he would do."

"But the Torsans hate us," I said. "They would make us all slaves."

"I know, Shadow," Kenway said, looking intently in my eyes. "Do you now see?"

I looked away.

"I would have no choice but to support Fyren," Ingen said. "But if you should change your mind, Audrey . . . if Erce should come back . . ."

They both looked at me. How could I let Ingen risk her life? It was a simple thing to hold hands in a circle and talk to one's mother.

"I will try again," I said.

Chapter Thirty-One

We were back in the circle.

"You must forgive her," Ingen said, holding my hand, squeezing it hard. "I felt the anger in you, Audrey. I shouldn't have let go, but I knew you had to feel it so you would understand."

"*I* am to understand? Two days ago, I didn't know Erce existed. And now I am to forgive her murder of the innocent, her abandonment . . ."

"Yes."

"If it were that easy, Ingen, I would do it."

"If you don't, she will not heal."

She should heal herself, I thought. Wasn't she the mother and I the daughter? Wasn't she the goddess? Why must we coddle her? "I said I would try."

"If she doesn't heal, then Deor doesn't heal."

"I know what is at stake!"

I saw Kenway shake his head at Ingen, as if to shush her. He stood at the edge of the circle, closer this time.

As before, Ingen and I clasped hands. Erce's power flowed into me again. But it wasn't only through Ingen this time — it was from the Earth and from the air, pouring into me, but tentatively, testing to see if I would receive it.

I did receive it. I pushed my anger to a corner of my heart and kept it there by an act of will.

I called to Erce, and she came, sweeping around the edges of my heart.

A strange feeling came over me. I was at once aware of all that touched me. The breeze on my face carried a sweet scent that opened up my lungs. The soil under my shoes was cool; how could I feel it? It was a part of me, like my feet were rooting into the Earth. It wasn't my *body*, though: It was my spirit. It moved with Erce, my mother.

We were in the air, the lightness of it delightful, and in the mountain, too, its depth immense. We could do anything, she and I.

The vast green sea stretched to the eastern horizon. We soared like birds above high craggy tops, sheer slices of white and gray, patches of green, the temple of Erce covered with

301

purple blossoms, and my friends Ingen and Kenway, small, but vibrant and living.

In the distance was the village of Goodham. I heard laughter ring out. The twins played by the river. I rushed by Rowe and blew his hair with a big puff. He turned his head to look as I went by, but I was the wind to him. I caught the scent of his happiness, and it filled me up.

Don't you feel it, Erce? Isn't this worth saving? I told her to come back to Deor, that the people needed her.

I could feel the people's worship of her; how could she not love them in return? They needed their goddess.

But she wasn't thinking of them. Instead, she pulled at me. That sweet mother's touch became a grasping for my love.

Give to your people, I told her.

Give to me, Audrey, she answered.

What do you want? I asked.

My daughter back.

I am here, I said, *as I've always been.*

I want your forgiveness, she said.

You have it.

She did not answer. Bleakness filled me up.

Ingen and I were knocked to the ground. I sat up, trying to catch my breath. Ingen was sprawled next to me, her face flushed.

"What happened?" asked Kenway, helping us up.

"You must forgive her," Ingen said to me. "You can reach her, help her."

"I *did* forgive her."

"You do not," Ingen said. "And she knows it."

"This will not work."

"Shadow!"

"We must think of another way."

I could not sleep the second night in our hut.

I had come to High Pointe to find my mother. I did not like what I'd found.

In the morning, we left for Kendra's. It was dark when we arrived, but she had a fish stew simmering.

Chapter Thirty-Two

At dawn, Kendra opened the shutters, letting in gray light. She threw sticks of wood on the dying embers and poked until they caught fire. She saw me watching her.

"It's time for you to go. You need to confront Fyren at his coronation, in three days' time."

"Crowned?" I asked, surprised. "So soon?"

"Do you now see the danger?" she asked.

I sat up, ignoring her. I pulled up my knees and rested my chin, gazing at the flickering flames. The air felt cold and heavy. I longed to touch the ocean again.

Kenway was awake and putting on his boots. "Why at the coronation?"

"That's when I see her defeat him."

"*She* defeats Fyren?"

I shared Kenway's doubt. Kendra's sight must be failing her.

She sat at the table piled with cracked plates and mugs. Ingen was beside her, playing with the broken dishes.

"I saw him fall, with Audrey standing over him." I could feel the fury in her. She *hated* him. "He will reap the whirlwind."

"He must," said Ingen, without looking up. She laid out the broken plates and pieces, trying to match them up.

Reap the whirlwind? I didn't know what they meant, but I said nothing.

"My father will give us men," said Kenway. "My brother's a good warrior. He'll help."

I heard concern, mingled with hope, in his voice. He still thought he could redeem his honor.

I went to the window and stared out at the ocean.

"It's too late for your father," Kendra said. I looked back at Kenway, worried for him. "Most likely," Kendra told him, "Fyren has already defeated the old lord."

"So sad," said Ingen. "The regent loves this land, but has lost his heart. You can't rule without a heart."

Nor could you rule with a heart filled with the weaknesses of others.

Kenway's mouth twitched. I thought of his sister, so sweet to me. I wanted to reach out to him, to comfort him. But I did not.

"Did you see that in your visions, Kendra?" he asked.

"No," she said. "But if I'm right, you're putting it all in jeopardy. If Fyren has taken your father's castle, he has men there. You'll walk into a trap."

"I've already failed them once. I won't abandon them."

"You'll do what is needed. You'll sacrifice, as we all have." She moved past him, her long white hair glowing in the gray light. "You must bring Audrey to the castle. There is little time." She leaned over a pot on the fire. As she stirred, the room filled with the aroma of strange spices.

Kenway looked at me as if he expected me to argue his side. I dropped my eyes. He turned to Kendra. "We won't defeat Fyren without my father's men."

"I saw it, just last night, while you slept."

"How? What weapons will we have? And I am only one knight. How is Shadow to defeat him?"

"You must trust me," she said.

"This is madness!" Kenway yelled. "You'll get her killed." He took a step toward her. "Is that your true intent?"

She slid her eyes over to him. "I don't know if *you* will live or die, Kenway." He flinched. "But if you do as I say, Audrey will be queen, and the world will be right again.

"In three days, Fyren will attempt to crown himself king. The courtyard will be filled with people invited to join the festivities. His coronation will be held on the balcony of the Prince's House, in front of the crowd. Audrey must be there." She nodded at me. "Everyone must see you defeat him. Then they'll know you are the true queen."

"But you don't know how she will do it?"

"I cannot see it."

"Stupid woman!" Kenway shouted. He left the cottage, banging the thin door, sending one of its boards flying to the dirt floor. The wind blew the door against the wall. I saw Kenway pacing back and forth.

"You must leave now, Audrey. You don't have much time."

I looked back at the sea. A lone gangly bird flew just a few feet above the water. Kenway could take me to the village on his way back to the castle.

"Your life is not your own," she said. "It belongs to us."

She was using my own words, twisting them for her use.

Words I had said to Kenway. Was it just four days ago? It seemed a lifetime.

"It belonged to you," I said, still watching the bird. "It's mine now."

"Do you think you're the only one who has ever known hardship?"

"You are not," said Ingen, looking over at me.

"Your life is your own," I told Kendra. "You don't know what I feel."

"I was thrown out of my village by my own mother because I saw and heard things she could not. Larcwide married me for my sight and then took my child away. Now my child is dead. What do you know of suffering?"

"You let those things happen. No one tells me what I do. Not now."

I thought she might slap me.

"You desire all those you love . . . to die for your freedom?"

Through the open door, I watched Kenway. "I love no one." The words pulled at my heart.

She strode over to me and grasped my hands. I tried to shake her off, but she was strong.

"Look at me, Audrey," she said. "Look."

308

I jumped back. Strange colorless shapes swirled in her eyes. I couldn't free myself from her grip.

"Do you see him?"

I did see him. His little body curled up in a ball. He was in a small, stone room, with little light. I saw his face. His eyes were open, but there was little life there. His lips moved. He called for his mother.

A shadow fell over him. *Wake up,* said a voice I instantly recognized. Fyren. He kicked Piers with the silver tip of his black boot, and pain shot through me. I heard Piers groan as I doubled over. *Tell me where he is, boy.* Fyren's boot came back and back. This was Fyren's blackness turned against a child, seen with my own eyes. How could this be the same man who had smiled at me?

I flung away Kendra's hands. Her eyes were a raging red — I saw my own anger there.

"Piers will die without you," she said.

"You're trying to trick me," I said, holding my throbbing stomach.

"Fyren knew Piers was a spy and used him. Only you can save him."

"You blame me for Devona's death. You want me to die because of your hate."

"I want you to live and destroy the man who murdered my child."

I trembled in the cold air. "Where's Piers?"

She smiled. "In the dungeon of your castle."

I looked out the window. The bird was gone.

Chapter Thirty-Three

We talked as we broke fast together, making
plans. Ingen would stay with Kendra. They would visit the
temple again and try to reach Erce. Kenway and I would go
back to the castle. He'd help me get Piers.

But we could agree on little else.

"Ingen," I asked, "what will you do if you can't
reach Erce?"

"Whatever needs to be done."

I felt her conviction and grabbed her hands. "You must
not try to merge your spirit with hers. Don't let Kendra talk
you into some mad plan of hers."

Kendra looked at me meaningfully. "So Ingen is in your
care after all, my queen?"

I released Ingen's hands and looked away.

Kendra explained how the coronation would take place on the balcony of the Prince's House three mornings from now, right before noon. She insisted Kenway find a way to get me to the balcony.

"With the guards there? All by myself?"

"You'll do it," she told him.

He threw up his hands.

"There is no use in fighting over this," I said. "I will not confront Fyren. I'll get Piers, and that is all."

"You cannot be so selfish," Kenway said.

"Don't," I said, but felt the truth of his words. Such a storm raged within my soul.

"How can you be so uncaring of Deor's fate?" he said. "You are our queen."

I could not hear any more of this. I left the cottage and made my way down the rocky path to the shore. The sea was loud and persistent. It slid along the sand, edging toward my feet. Then it receded, tempting me to follow it. Again and again, it came to me and went back out. Would the waves rescue me from this sickness eating away at my spirit?

I couldn't cope with these feelings of others. They were crippling me. If I became a queen, with the cares of an entire kingdom upon me, I would surely sink into madness. What good would I be to anyone then?

I thought about Devona's suffering. She might have been spared that if she had not been thrust into the life of a queen. She would have lived. She would have known her mother. Kendra would have taught her that her visions were gifts and not demons trying to possess her.

Could *my* mother do that for me?

Hot tears of frustration pricked at my eyes. A simple life might give me refuge from this pain. Those stolen moments in Goodham had been the loveliest I had ever known. It seemed so little to ask for, especially when I didn't think my soul would survive if I were queen.

I didn't know what to do now. I'd always known what to do.

Who could I confide in? Kenway's devotion to duty was like that of a zealot, as was Ingen's faith in Erce. Erce was powerful, but deeply flawed. Her selfishness kept her from caring for her people. She had shown that again and again. And Kendra, there was *something* about her that was not right. I laughed through my tears. I did indeed feel like a queen with the weight of a kingdom upon me.

I sank to the ground and stared out at the sea. *Eldred,*

you manipulative old man: Where are you when I need you? I
angrily brushed away my tears.

I looked down at Kendra and Ingen from my seat behind
Kenway. The horse was restless, stomping her hooves against
the rocky ground. She wanted to be gone.

That was my wish as well. I would rescue Piers and find
a safe place for us.

I huddled in my cloak, chilled by the mountain air.
When we'd first escaped from the castle, I had welcomed
the cold. Something inside of me, then, glowing like a hot
coal from a new fire, had kept me warm.

That had been doused. My stomach was ice, and I was
chilled to the core.

"Your father was a man to admire," Kendra said. "So
tall, with broad shoulders and a golden red beard. He had
more energy than ten men and filled a room with his presence. Filled a country with his presence."

I wanted to hear more about my father. I hoped I might
be like him. In the strength I had always felt. It was him in
me. He didn't know to what fate he'd left his child.

Erce had known. She knew even now.

"He was trusting," said Kendra. "Once he gave his loyalty, he didn't snatch it back. Fyren was his cousin, his friend when he was young. The king thought well of him, but Fyren betrayed that trust."

She exchanged a look with Kenway. I shouldn't have left them alone this morning. They were conspiring against me.

Kenway prodded the horse, starting us on our way.

We didn't get very far. At the western edge of the hill, I caught a whiff of something burning. I knew it was from Goodham. I remembered another village, a place filled with the murdered.

"Stop," I bade Kenway. I sat still for a moment, my hands balling into fists, my heart beating wildly. I couldn't do this alone.

I looked back at Kendra, a pale figure against a gray sky. She walked toward us, her feet bare and white on the rocks. Kenway took us on the path back to her. Ingen did not move, just watched from her place by the hut.

When Kendra grabbed the reins, the horse neighed and pulled back.

I hesitated, not wanting to tell her.

"I've been experiencing things, feeling emotions." I bit my lip, not wanting to say more. Kenway moved in the saddle. I put my hands on the cantle behind me.

"What emotions?" she asked.

"Not mine. Not my feelings." I looked off. "They are from . . . someplace else."

Kenway turned his head toward me slightly. "From where? Erce?" I was glad I couldn't see his eyes.

I didn't want to tell them, especially him.

"From the villagers," I snapped. "From you, Kendra. And Kenway, too."

He twisted around, looking at me directly. I stared back.

"I don't understand it," I said. I grabbed at my hair, pushing it back and back, trying to push away the fear. "Why do I feel them?"

Kendra's eyes were the color of water, revealing nothing. "When did it begin?"

"I don't know," I said quickly, for that was only part of the truth.

I remembered feeling Kenway's anger and sadness, when he stood over me at his father's home and when we talked under the pine trees. But there had been moments before that, back in the castle, with Piers, when I felt I was glimpsing something inside of him. I had controlled it then.

I could no longer push it away, whatever *it* was. It was growing stronger. Flooding into me, sapping me of strength. The thought of going back to the castle weakened me even more.

Kendra finally spoke: "You dwell in the space between."

"Between? Between what?"

"You're the daughter of nature and man, so that's where you dwell: between nature and man. Between man and man."

I shouldn't have asked her. Her answers made no sense. "There's nothing but air between us."

"All that matters exists in the space between us. Men are not self-contained; neither are the things of nature. Our spirits pour out of us, through our skin, just as the clouds release rain." She leaned in and whispered, "You collect the rain."

I pulled back from her, not wanting to even feel her touch. "If this is so, why did it just begin?"

She looked at Kenway. "You cannot open yourself up to your own feelings and expect to stay immune to ours."

I saw her meaning. "Let's go," I said.

"We need you, Audrey." Her eyes were wild. I saw madness there.

And when she grabbed my hand, I found the source of it: Devona's death. It was pushing her to a dark place. I never knew a mother's love was like this — deep, strong, sharp. Too much feeling. How did she bear it? Was my own mother's love for me like this? I doubted it.

I wrenched my fingers from her grasp.

"You are our only connection to what has died. To Erce and to one another."

"Now, Kenway," I said, tugging at his cape. Kendra wasn't going to help me. I was a fool for telling her.

"You must not fight us. It will kill you, and us."

"Go!"

"Erce must reawaken!" shouted Kendra as we rode away.

I didn't look back this time.

The smell of smoke stayed with me. It sat on my tongue, in my nostrils, behind my eyes. I blew out and out as Kenway took us down the path, but I couldn't make it go away. It made me so dizzy I feared falling from the saddle.

It wasn't real smoke. I knew that.

"Queen Audrey," said Kenway.

"Don't." His manner was so courteous, deferential. "Don't call me that," I told him. "I am no queen." I longed for the old Kenway, desperately.

"What shall I call you then?"

"Nothing feels right," I said.

"My duty is to protect you, and your duty is to face Fyren."

I felt such sadness. Hadn't he heard what I just told Kendra? Was duty so paramount that it pushed out tenderness, or had there been none in his heart for me anyway?

Pulling on the reins, he brought us to a halt. The wind blew his hair this way and that. "Do you think the peasants will have freedom with Fyren as their ruler?"

"You are not one to talk of the freedom of peasants."

"I was wrong about that. I know that now. I know it because I look on one whom I thought was . . ." His voice trailed off.

"You can say it. You thought was nothing."

"But I was wrong. You are the queen."

"You should have valued me anyway!"

"You know that I did," he said. "And still do. Don't let your fear keep you from doing what's right."

"I don't fear death, Kenway. Go!"

"Then you are selfish. You're no better than what you accuse me of."

Selfish, like her. That was what he thought.

He started the horse back on the path. Our anger hung in the air.

The village was in trouble. I knew it. I felt as if, like Roe, I carried rocks, one for each person in Goodham. His rocks brought him comfort; mine only put a great weight upon me, crushing me.

Had the town been invaded? Fyren's soldiers again? Taking villagers or looking for us? I thought I might be sick and closed my eyes. The cold wind stung my cheeks. I wanted to huddle closer to Kenway, but didn't.

We did not find destruction. Houses were intact. Pigs grunted in their pens. A dog lying in the hard-packed dirt watched us as we made our way down the main road. But no one was out.

The village held the quiet of snatched hope.

I ran into the cottage. Tayte lay on a pallet, huddled against the wall. Her boys sat beside her, their hands on her body as it rocked to and fro and she moaned and cried.

"What is it?" I asked, panic rising in me.

Kenway was behind me. "What? What's wrong?"

Rowe ran to Kenway. "You must go find them, sir!" His freckled cheeks were wet with tears, his mouth a tight white line.

"What has happened, Rowe?" I asked.

But it was his brother who looked at us with eyes no longer sweet. "The soldiers took our father."

Tayte let out a wild wail. I dropped to my knees in the dirt and put my hand upon her shaking back. She was cold. I covered her, but she threw off the blanket.

"Fyren's men?" asked Kenway.

"We were out in the field. I heard the horses and told Father, but they were on us too quickly. Twenty soldiers. They circled us. Ian and Dagger, the older boys, wanted to fight. They tried to rush at them with spades. The captain said he'd kill everyone in the village. Father told the boys to drop the spades." Roe's chin trembled. "The captain read us a proclamation. Then the soldiers took them away. All of the men and the older boys."

Tayte continued to weep, burying her face in the pallet.

"What did the proclamation say?" I asked.

"The queen is dead. The regent will be crowned in

three days. He'll hold a festival," Roe said, spitting out the words, no longer the innocent boy I had left just days before. "He's promised jousts and jugglers, and fancy breads and sweetmeats. He'll snatch the men who show up for the food. I know it."

Kenway looked at me. It might have been my own guilt, but I felt he was accusing me.

"You must go after them!" screamed Rowe.

Kenway dropped to his knees in front of the boy, taking him by the shoulders. "I'm sorry, Rowe. I cannot."

"You are a knight! You can fight them!"

"I have another task I must do."

"You must do this. We helped you. My father saved you. My mother nursed you. You would have died."

Kenway looked at a loss for words.

Rowe pulled away from him. "You are a coward then! Why did I ever think I wanted to be a knight like you?" He tore out of the hut.

Despite all our efforts, Tayte wouldn't move from her place on the pallet. As the day ended, we settled on logs and stumps outside the hut, eating a little supper around a small fire.

Rowe returned to us, but he sat alone and shunned our small circle. Kenway kept an eye on him.

"Boys, you must listen to me," said Kenway. "You, too, Rowe. If Fyren's men come back, you must not fight them. Do you understand? As soon as I can, I will be back for you."

Rowe kicked at the dry earth, sending dust into the air. He glared at Kenway and went inside the hut, slamming the door behind him.

Roe stood before me, his face so small and hurt. "I guess we ended up like Piers, didn't we, my lady?"

"Oh, no, Roe," I said. "No."

He held up his closed hand, opening it to reveal one bluish rock. It was not smooth, not rough, not his largest one, nor his smallest. "It's the color of your eyes," he said. "I found it by the river."

I nodded, but could not speak.

He slipped it into his pocket and then left us.

Chilled, I wrapped myself tightly in a blanket. I felt alone, as if I were adrift upon a great dark sea.

"I was wrong about many things," said Kenway.

"It's not your fault Stillman was taken."

"And not my fault that I couldn't protect Devona nor my family?"

"You can't protect us all, Kenway."

"It is clear I can protect no one."

"Your family could still be safe," I said, although I didn't believe it. Who was safe in this new world?

"That is my hope."

"And mine as well."

"As I said, I was wrong about many things," he said. "One of those things was you."

Did he truly understand? I looked at him expectantly.

"I know your life in the castle was difficult," he continued. "And I did nothing to help you."

I watched him in the firelight. I had been drawn to him, from the beginning, when he came to the castle as a young boy. I remember when Sir Crag, an older knight, had rushed at him with a sword, trying to frighten him, make him back down. Kenway had stood there, feet planted, jaw set. His courage had thrilled me. I'd wanted to be there beside him.

And there was even more. He had defended me when the others were harsh and cruel. I hadn't needed him to do it. I was strong, probably stronger than he was. But when I had been the most vulnerable to the will of others, he had reached out for me, to me.

"You must put your old life behind you, Audrey," he said. "In a way, that life prepared you for this one. You will be a strong queen."

Oh, Kenway. I looked away.

"We need you."

I am alone, I thought. "Do not."

"It is your duty," he said. "You cannot escape it."

"Those are Kendra's words, not yours."

I left him and went to the village square. The blackberry bush was still there, smelling wild and new. I spread my blanket beside it.

I lay under the black sky, fighting Tayte's pain, feeling her sadness dripping on me from the stars above. I couldn't bear it. I rolled over, trying to hide my face in the dry dirt.

Audrey. It was Erce, whispering. *Breathe it in.*

Breathe it in? I didn't trust her. I could only survive if I fought the feelings of others. Or else they would destroy me.

Trust me.

A new breeze blew across my cheek, so delicately. It smelled sweet — of blackberries and sweet herbs, of wild honeysuckle and roses in the royal garden. Erce was here, giving me the quiet peace of the things of nature, as she had all my life. It was then I realized: Erce had never really left me. Her love had always been there, in the things of the Earth, reaching out to me.

And now, she wanted me to release, to let go, to stop holding on so tightly. I knew as I did, as I let my anger go, the agony of others would rush in, pour in, drown me . . . but *trust me*, she said, and I did. I felt their pain deep down, sharp, but then it was gone.

Taken by the wind.

When I awoke, I felt it'd only been a dream.

Chapter Thirty-Four

Tayte was still on her mat, staring at the ceiling. I placed Erce's medallion about her neck and kissed her forehead. We didn't wake the boys. The road was dark. No villagers pleaded with me to stay this time.

My eyes stung. I had slept only a few hours, despite my exhaustion. Erce hadn't returned since last night, but my thoughts wouldn't leave her. It was time for her to put aside her selfishness. Sixteen years was too long. We were all dying a slow death with her. I was weary from anger, but it clung to me.

I wore the tights and shirt of a peasant. The afternoon before, a thin, pale woman had traded her kidnapped son's clothes for my silk dress. As we rode, the material brushed guilt onto my skin.

Riding through the marsh was even more difficult

than before. I could barely stay on the horse as she plowed her way through the muck. More and more the feelings of others poured into me. How could I bear it? I remembered how I'd felt when we'd escaped. I had never known such joy. And now we were returning to that dreadful place, willingly.

The birches were still the same, eerily beautiful. I wondered if they possessed some healing power because I felt a numbing of the raw edges of my pain. Then came a whisper in my ear: "I have faith in you." I whipped around in the saddle, looking for Ingen, knowing it was her voice. But of course she wasn't there.

Were she and Kendra at Erce's temple? I worried for Ingen. What would she try to do if I did nothing?

The village of Erce was deserted. We rode through without a word. I didn't look back as we crossed the stream into the forest beyond.

We were taking a more dangerous way back, closer to the camps of the royal soldiers, not skirting to the west as we had done before. That path would take time we didn't have. Kenway put us on a little-traveled dirt trail, barely wide enough for the horse. Prickly branches scratched our faces as we pushed them out of the way.

We stopped at nightfall. Dusty and tired and sore, we almost fell off the horse. I leaned against a tree, grasping my knees.

"You are too pale," said Kenway. He sat beside me, touching my face. His hand felt so warm and soft on my cheek. "Audrey, are you well?"

"No, I am not well."

"You must eat something," he said, offering me black-berries.

I stared at the fruit, not moving. It had become the fruit of betrayal to me — given to me by Devona first, and then my mother. A substitute for love.

"I thought they might give you strength. That there might be . . . something in them."

I looked at him skeptically. "Something like magic?"

"It's *your* mother who isn't human," he said.

I ate one. I thought I might retch.

"We are close to your father's castle, aren't we?" I asked. "Did you tell Kendra your plans?"

I saw his face set in his stubborn way. "There's time. In the morning, we'll return to my father's. We need his help. Kendra's wrong to think otherwise."

I thought Kendra's plan was the more prudent one, but I said nothing.

We did without a fire because the smoke might be seen. I could have used the heat. The night air was very cold, and I was trembling.

We slept hidden in the quiet woods, in a grove of pines. Their sweet scent was too strong, overpowering, flying up into my nose and mouth. I threw my arm over my face.

A root poked me in the back all night. I couldn't get away from it. And I couldn't hide from Kenway's fear, either. That, and the root, and the smells in the forest, made me toss and turn.

We left before dawn.

It was not two hours later when we crept up to the town. We watched from a rim of trees outside the gates. Guards, in red and black, strode up and down the battlements. Like spiders, they crawled atop the walls.

"We're too late," Kenway whispered.

He looked over at me, as if he believed I would think of something. The wind whipped up around us, sending the branches over our heads swaying. I doubled over with pain in my stomach.

"What's wrong?"

Don't ask me, I thought.

"What, Audrey?"

I shook my head and sat down in the leaves. I just needed to rest. I put my face against the cold ground. Just rest. The pain did not abate.

"You sense them there."

I looked up at his wild eyes. "I feel their fear, Kenway, which means they are not dead."

He paled. "In the village, in Erce, you felt their fear, too."

The truth of this hit me powerfully. I groaned. My stomach was hot with an icy fire.

"Shh, Audrey. They'll hear you."

He wrapped his arm around me. At first, each step was misery. I thought I might collapse. But as he led me toward the horse, I felt some strength return.

"Here," he said, leaning me against a tree. I took in gulps of air. He pulled the flask out of his boot and bade me to drink. I put my hand on his and drank the cold water.

"I thank you."

He sat beside me, his face unreadable.

"What will you do?" I asked him.

"I cannot fight an army by myself." He gave a mirthless

laugh. "But it seems I must do it. Either here or at the queen's castle. At your castle, Audrey."

"I'm sorry about your family."

"I'm too late," he said.

"Fyren wouldn't harm them. He needs your father's support. He'll try to win his allegiance. If he can do that, other lords might follow. That will be his thinking."

"And how do you know this?"

"I know him," I said, resting my head against the tree.

"You always seemed to."

I looked up. "Do you think I want him to be victorious?"

He stared at me.

"I thought we had left our suspicions behind us, Kenway."

"Say you are right, my queen," he said. "Pray tell me what Fyren does, then, when my father rails against him and declares his unwavering loyalty to King Alfrid. How long will it take Fyren to decide the fate of my father and my sisters . . . ?" His voice trailed off.

"Don't think of it, Kenway. Don't let your mind go to it."

"My father was right. I should have stayed here instead of running off with you. What good came out of that?"

His words dug deep. If we had not left together, I wouldn't have discovered my love for him. How could he not feel the same? If he didn't, what good were my feelings?

"What?" he asked. "Why do you look at me so?"

I tried to answer, but couldn't.

"You think my father is right about me?" he accused.

My eyes stung. He was far away from me indeed if he misread me so utterly. "Your father no longer thinks clearly. Even about himself."

"I'm surprised you don't blame him. It was my family that made your life what it is. Without your father's death, you would not have lived the life you did."

"Your family puts too much guilt upon itself," I said, but he wasn't listening to me.

"If I try to save them, I might jeopardize it all. As much as I'm pulled toward them, I cannot do it. My father wouldn't want me to."

"I wouldn't worry about his wishes, Kenway. Do what you think is right."

His eyes narrowed. "You want me to try to save them? Why? So we'll miss the coronation and you'll not have to face Fyren?" He threw his hand at me. "You are selfish and manipulative, like every other monarch I have met."

How could he say such things to me? "I don't expect you to understand, Kenway, but I will do what I will do."

Strong words, but guilt nudged at me. How could I deny Kenway's words about Fyren? My thoughts returned to Kenway's sisters in the castle, to the slain in Erce, to our friends in Goodham. The regent's reach was far and deep.

"My duty is to protect the queen. And that I will do. Even at my family's expense." He went over to our horse. "It's time we left."

The ride to the castle took longer than we thought. Fyren's men crawled the woods surrounding Lord Leofwine's town.

We stopped to rest by the stream with the blackberries, but neither of us touched the fruit still growing there. The horse drank from the brook and grazed in the grass, but Kenway and I said very little to each other.

It was dark and cold when we reached our hole in the wall, our way back into the castle. It was still there, still open. No one had discovered how we'd escaped.

We settled into our camp for the night. I wrapped myself in my blankets, watching Kenway comb the horse. He was gentle with the animal, but he was short with me. So I stayed quiet. Sitting cross-legged, I wrapped as much warmth around me as I could. The ground felt so cold, like the snow I'd felt in the mountains. I tucked my face inside the blanket to hide from the sharp wind.

Kenway threw the currycomb back into the saddlebag. He sat on a stump and put his head in his hands. He didn't know his family's fate, and he was here, I knew, because he thought he could persuade me to change my mind.

He took a long drink of water from his flask, but didn't offer me any. "The coronation will be about midday tomorrow."

"Yes. I think it will be easy to get Piers."

"Easy? I have no sword. I am one against all of Fyren's men. I appreciate your confidence," he said, laughing bitterly, "but I think it will be far from easy."

"I meant because of the music, the dancing, the noise of the crowd. No one will hear us."

"Why should I save this boy? That's not what I'm here for."

His face showed his weariness. Each day he seemed to age another year. He now looked as old as his brother.

"I'll do it alone then," I said.

"I won't leave you. You know I'll not shirk my duty."

"I don't want to hear any more about duty, Kenway."

He jumped up and hurled his flask at a tree trunk, sending bark flying. "Do you know what I'm giving up for you?"

I'd never seen him so angry. He dropped back to the ground and ran his shaking hand up and down the back of his neck.

"What love you have for them," I whispered.

He looked over at me, but I didn't need to see his face to know the truth of what I said. I *felt* his love for them. It was strong and warm, but so far away I couldn't reach it from the icy place where I lived — the space between. I shivered and could not stop. Would he ever love me in this way?

"Why do you tremble so, Audrey?" he asked.

He picked up one of his own blankets, dusting off the dirt and leaves clinging to it, and draped it over my shoulders.

"Better?" he asked.

I nodded, but it wasn't true. The cold came from inside me.

He returned to his stump, so far from me. So far from where I needed him to be.

"Love causes such pain," I said, my teeth chattering. "How can it be worth it?"

"Audrey," he said, "it *is* worth it."

I crept closer, sitting on dead pine needles beside him, and laid my head against his knee.

He must have been surprised, but he said nothing. I wanted him to hold me as he did when we were on the mountain. But I couldn't ask him. And he didn't do it. But perhaps he lightly touched my hair?

We stayed like that for a few long moments, listening to the forest.

"I will not let you face him alone, then," I said finally.

"What?" he asked.

I looked up at him. "Kendra said I must be there for Fyren to be defeated. Before I leave, I will help you do that."

He dropped down beside me. "Before you *leave*?" He paused, then took my hands. "Deor needs her queen."

And I felt that need everywhere I went. It yanked and scratched at me. I would drown in that dark need if I allowed it to flood my soul. Erce had given me one night's peace from it. But she was a fickle god, mother or no. I had no doubt she would desert me on a whim, leaving me to succumb to madness. And I had seen what madness did to a queen. The memory of Devona's rages caused me to tremble even now. That could not be my fate. I must find a way to help Deor that would not mean that sacrifice.

I squeezed Kenway's hands. "Let . . . us do one thing at a time."

He paused, as if he might say more.

But I did not have the strength to argue. "We will find Piers first." His little face came to me again, and with it, a desperate loneliness. Now that I was so close to him, just outside the walls where he was held, I felt his absence keenly, and I knew he felt mine. "He is more like family to me than anyone has ever been, Kenway. I must save him."

"Don't cry," he said, wiping my cheeks.

"I have been a poor friend to Piers."

"You are returning for him. You love him."

I nodded. "Yes."

"Forgive me," he said, raising my chin to look at me. "I shouldn't have said such cruel things to you."

"No, you were right," I said firmly. "Fyren cannot rule."

Relief flooded his face. "No, he cannot."

"We will reveal who Fyren truly is," I said. "Once the people see that, Deor can recover."

His eyes held questions, but I had no more answers.

"All right, Audrey," he said, kissing me gently. "I will protect you."

"I will protect you," I said, putting my hand on his cheek.

"*You* will?" he asked.

"We'll do it together, like when we fought the mountain men."

He smiled. "And what did you do in that fight?"

"I bit the giant's neck."

He laughed a little, then gave me a long look. "You're trembling." He ran his fingers down my lips. "You are too cold."

"I cannot get warm, Kenway."

"Come to me."

I felt a sweet rush of yearning for him and let myself be wrapped up in his arms. I could not get him close enough. Did he feel this same ache inside? I wanted to have him with me always, but I feared my life would not ever be so giving.

Chapter Thirty-Five

A pine torch helped us find our way to the stone staircase. When I saw the steps, I felt an urge to run back to the safety of the woods. I had left a shadow, finally free, connected to no one. I'd had the freedom I'd yearned for all my days within my grasp.

Now I returned, not a queen in my mind, but no longer a shadow, and no longer free. I was entangled. With Kenway, Piers, Ingen, Stillman, the twins. Caring for them was weakening me. I felt their vulnerability in my legs, my eyes, my heart. I felt their *need*.

As we climbed the steps going up and up, the memory of the day of our escape loomed larger in my mind. I pressed my hand against the wet wall, feeling unsteady.

I remembered Eldred's face, and the moment of his death when his eyes found mine. I had seen fear in them, fear for me, as if he were reaching across the room, trying to push me from danger.

He had made me the queen's shadow for the sake of the kingdom. And I would be dead if he had not done it. And, now, he was dead, and I was sorry for it.

Sadness was cold, I'd discovered.

At the stone door, Kenway pulled an iron torch holder. The door opened.

We slipped in and passed through the small, cluttered room, then into Eldred's chamber. It was dark, with a shuttered window and a cold hearth. We moved through the queen's chambers, every room cold and drafty. There was no life here. Gone were the giggles, the sighs, the clanks of armor, the music of the harp.

I felt empty. *She* had been our queen. Not the true one, but real to us. And now she was dead, sacrificed for me. I had never been in this room without her. I hadn't expected to feel anything. Now grief — unexplainable, fierce grief — shot through my heart as if an icy arrow had pierced me.

Kenway said nothing, but his face was agony.

"You mourn her," I said, feeling his pain.

"I feel so distant from her, as if she never lived."

I felt the opposite. I had lost a protector, if not a sister.

We left her chambers.

This part of the castle was now deserted, haunted by ghosts leaving trails of cold memories. Kenway took us up tight, twisting stairs I had never climbed. Holding my hand, he led me down a long passageway and stopped at a bulky door. It was locked.

"There are swords, spears, and daggers in this room," Kenway said. "I hoped it wouldn't be locked. It was a fool's hope."

"Where's the key?" I asked, leaning against the wall.

"On the constable's belt," he said.

"The key is needed to steal the sword, but the sword is needed to steal the key," I said, giving him a small smile.

He did not return it. "Come."

Another deserted passageway. Kenway pulled me into a cluttered room.

"What is this place?" I asked.

It had few windows. Thick cobwebs hung in every corner. Wooden crates were stacked one on top of the other. Old iron torches and worthless plates and bowls were thrown here and there.

"A storage room," said Kenway. "Maybe there's a weapon."

He put his torch into an empty brace. He began digging through one pile, tossing aside spoons and combs and shoes as he looked. I searched in an old chest, finding doeskin slippers and silver brushes. I shut the lid and looked for a more promising heap.

Kenway found a sword. The blade was not sharp enough. The black leather on the handle was loose and hanging partially off. It would have to do.

"We must hurry," he said, positioning the sword in his hand.

He took us down another passage, moving so quickly I was disoriented. He stopped at a stone staircase that plunged downward. It was on an outside wall. Light came in through vertical slits.

"These stairs end at a guardroom for the dungeon," he whispered. "There are two ways into the room. These steps. And a door that leads back outside. Once outside, we will be on the east side of the castle, away from the coronation."

"I know, Kenway. I have been here, remember?"

He nodded. "There will be at least one guard responsible for the prisoners. Usually the dungeon isn't heavily guarded because we hold few prisoners there."

"I know."

"Yes." He took a breath.

"You cannot kill him."

"What?"

"The guard. You cannot."

"How do you expect me to rescue Piers? I have to go past the guard to get to the dungeon stairs."

"He's not one of Fyren's men. He's just a man working in the castle." I couldn't say it, but I felt protective.

"I would not have thought *you* to be so softhearted. Stay here."

"I must come with you."

"No, Audrey. I am to protect you. You need to stay here or you'll make it more difficult for me."

"All right."

"Audrey," he admonished.

"I *said* I would."

Before he left, he turned back to me.

"What?" I asked, wondering at his delay. "I promise."

He pulled me to him and kissed me. "I'll call for you." Then he gave me a look of warning. He still thought I would follow.

"Go," I said, but with a smile.

I sat on the top step and dropped my head to my knees.

It was so difficult to trust. At first, I heard nothing, then a shout and scuffling from below. *This would not do.* I found I had to break my word after all.

As quickly as I could, I made my way down the stairs. The staircase was well lit from the numerous shafts of light.

Emerging at the bottom, I came upon Kenway in a fight of fists and muscle. His rusty sword lay on the ground in the center of the stone floor.

The room was so small, the two men kept running into walls. The guard was larger, but had a great belly. Kenway was much quicker. He smashed his fist at the guard's nose. A shock of red erupted. The guard growled and threw his bulk into Kenway, who groaned when he was hit in the stomach. He ducked under the man's arm and crawled for his sword.

To my left was an open door to the outside.

In front of me I saw a dark staircase leading down.

I stumbled outside. I could hear trumpets blaring and yells and shouts from a large crowd. The joust was about to begin.

Huge stones lay on the ground. I heaved one up, finding the strength I needed, and carried it to the room. Kenway was up, sword in hand. The guard was in a corner, blood smeared on his face, his eyes blazing. His arms were out, and he rocked from foot to foot, daring Kenway to stab him.

I got up on the table, gesturing for Kenway to back him up to me.

The guard's rasping breaths filled the room, but he would not give up the fight. Kenway was sure to kill him soon.

Finally, the guard was in front of me. I lifted the rock high and hit him on the head with all my might.

He collapsed.

Kenway, sweating, his hand on his stomach, stared down at the guard's flaccid face. "You might have killed him anyway."

"He's breathing."

I took the ring of keys off the guard's belt. Kenway grabbed a lit torch. It was time to find Piers.

Chapter Thirty-Six

Kenway, with his sword in front of him, led us down the steps to the dungeon. Small torches burned, but the light was poor. I held the torch up high so he could see the steep steps. The familiar smell of mold and rot crept toward us.

At the bottom, I shone the light back and forth. The narrow passage extended both to the left and the right. All was quiet, like a tomb. I thought of Maren and the guards carrying her out, just here. I felt her disappointment in my mother and in me. Maren was dead, but her feelings lingered.

We peered inside each cell. All empty. There were no prisoners, just as during my short stay here.

My heart fell. What if Piers was not here?

At the third door down, through a small barred opening,

I saw something curled up in a ball on the floor, lit up by the weak light from the crack of a window. I rattled the bars before Kenway could stop me, calling his name, and saw movement.

Kenway took the torch from me and held it up high. By that light, I opened the door. The little form sat up.

"Piers," I whispered, afraid it would not be him.

He crawled toward me. I went to him. He wrapped himself around my waist, feeling like dusty bones. "I knew you would come back," he said in a muffled voice.

Such guilt came over me. How could I have left him?

"I'm sorry, Piers," I whispered, with stinging eyes.

He buried his head deeper into my shirt.

"I forgive you," he said.

Warmth rushed into me, for the first time in days, thawing the edges of my heart. I pulled him in tighter. He could forgive me when I could not forgive my mother. Hadn't I left him just as she'd left me?

"We must go," said Kenway. He was in the passage, holding up the torch.

"One moment," I said. "He's weak."

I dug in the small bag hanging from my waist and gave

Piers some bread. Kenway handed him the flask from his boot. Piers could eat little, but he drank the water.

"Are you all right?" I asked.

He nodded.

"We must go," said Kenway. "Help me move the guard to the cell."

It was a laborious feat getting the heavy guard down the stairs and into Piers's cell. Even if he woke, no one would hear his cries until we were gone.

"Come with me," Piers said in a raspy voice as Kenway locked the cell.

He led us down the dark passage, bending over, holding his side. I remembered the vision Kendra had shown me and knew there were bruises under his shirt. I tried to get him to lean against me, but he brushed me off and kept stumbling forward.

I thought of something else in Kendra's vision. Fyren, kicking Piers to get him to reveal the whereabouts of someone he was seeking. Hadn't it been Kenway he'd been trying to find?

But now Fyren had captured Lord Leofwine's castle, and Lord Callus's. Did he think there was no one left to oppose him, that he'd finally defeated my father? He'd tell himself that it was to avenge his mother's fate, but it wasn't that. It was a dark part of him that would never be sated. *He must not rule Deor, ever. He must not.*

Piers stopped. He leaned against the wall and pushed my hand away. "I'm all right, Shadow. My head is spinning a little, is all."

I shivered in the cold dark. I had betrayed this boy. And I had betrayed my father, too. He would be ashamed of me, just as Kenway's father was ashamed of him. I squeezed my eyes shut, trying to will the thoughts away. But they clung to me.

"Where are you taking us?" Kenway asked Piers.

"Come," he said, starting off again.

He led us into the blackness. Was this a way out? Another secret place I knew nothing of? My foot brushed against some small thing that moved. I heard it scamper away. I wondered how many rats were running with us.

Piers was moving quickly now, not so unsteady on his feet as before. Or perhaps he was just impatient to leave the dungeon. It was clear he knew this place well. I was confused by our many turns in these dark passages. I would never find my way out alone.

I felt soft earth beneath my shoes. Would he lead us back to our cave? He opened a wooden door to our left.

And there was Eldred, in long gray robes.

Tears pricked my eyes as I stared at his solemn face. He was not dead, after all. I brushed the tears away. I would not let him see me so sentimental.

"Well, come in," he said.

He looked paler. Gaunt. But still tall and intimidating. I surprised myself because I was most glad to see him. I found myself staring at him and not being able to look away.

As Piers went by, Eldred touched his head, briefly. I had never seen Eldred affectionate with Piers, never seen him affectionate with anyone. He took Kenway's torch and placed it in an iron holder. Many torches lined the walls, casting soft light about us and dispelling some of the gloom and closeness of the room.

A straw pallet lay on the floor. A chest was shoved against the wall. No books. No fire. It must be cold at night.

He pointed to the ground and the four of us sat in the dirt.

"Were you successful?" Eldred asked, looking at Kenway and me both.

Kenway gestured to me. "Your queen is here."

"Yes, yes. But what about Erce?" He looked at me. "Did you reach her?"

"We tried," I said.

He cursed. "Did you find Ingen?"

"Yes, but it didn't work," Kenway said. "Your plan failed."

"I think not. Did you see Kendra?"

"She had much to tell us." Kenway started to say more, but hesitated. Something flashed in his eyes. Was he angry at this task? At being told so very little? And not receiving any thanks? If so, being ever the loyal knight, he said nothing about it.

Eldred nodded. "Yes, but what did Kendra prophesy? Did she have any visions about this day?"

Kenway told him what Kendra saw. Eldred cursed again.

"Kenway has served Deor well," I said to Eldred.

"As he should have," Eldred replied. "Part of the reason I chose him was he had much to prove and his family had no love of Fyren. I knew he would do what I asked of him."

"Ever the dutiful knight," I said, drawing a sharp look from Kenway. "I'm sorry," I said quickly, shaking my head a little.

"And where would Deor be without such men?" Eldred snapped.

Kenway nodded at the adviser, as if they understood each other.

"You also chose him," I said to Eldred, "because he knew Ingen and her family."

"You are right," Eldred said, smiling a little. "It is a relief to have a thinking queen."

But I could not mock Devona anymore. "You are well hidden from Fyren," I said, looking around. At least his cell had no lock on the door.

"I told the regent Eldred was dead," said Piers.

A slip of smile played at Eldred's lips. "He was always a slow thinker, wasn't he, Piers?"

"I saw you stabbed, Eldred," I said. "How did you survive?"

"There was much confusion in that room. Ingrid led me out the same way you escaped."

"Ingrid?" I asked, shocked. "The queen's lady?"

"The same way we came out?" asked Kenway. "But I didn't see you."

"You were gone. We moved much slower, Ingrid and I. The hidden staircase also leads to these rooms beneath the castle."

I looked at Piers. "How did you know where Eldred was?"

He gave a weak grin, but said nothing.

"Ingrid settled me here, then brought Piers and Hilda," said Eldred.

"Hilda!" I exclaimed.

"Ingrid and Hilda nursed me back to health. I helped them, as best I could in my state, telling them which herbs worked best. Two days ago, I made them leave the castle. They were in danger as long as they stayed." His eyes were on me. "People are not always what they seem."

"Hilda and Ingrid aren't all goodness, I know that much," I said, remembering their stinging slaps.

"Who is?" He looked at me pointedly.

"But what about Piers?" asked Kenway. "How did he end up in the dungeon?"

"He wanted to continue to spy on Fyren. We didn't know Fyren already suspected him."

"You tricked me, Piers," I said. "I never guessed you to be a spy."

Piers nodded toward Kenway. "So you do like him?" he asked, smirking. "I knew it. I fooled you, but you didn't fool me."

My cheeks felt hot. The little imp. This was the Piers I remembered.

Kenway gave me a smile, but became serious when Eldred looked at him.

Piers took my hand and studied my palm. "You have troubles ahead of you, Shadow, but it will turn out in the end."

I nodded, remembering those very words.

He crawled over to the pallet. I put the pillow under his head and covered him with a blanket, as if I were his mother. Hadn't I played that role for him in a sense? I remembered, three nights ago, when Erce comforted me. Surely I had always been in her thoughts, as Piers had been in mine.

Eldred sighed. He unfolded his long body. After rummaging around in the chest, he handed me a silk dress of deep green, with a small bow.

"A gift for your birthday."

I had forgotten. On this day, I was sixteen.

"In your mother's favorite gown, you will finally look like our Queen Audrey."

"Anne's," I said, pressing my hands into the silk. She had worn this. If only I could touch her hand as easily as I touched this gown of hers. "That name Audrey does not belong to me, Eldred."

"It was the name of your father's mother, your grandmother, a strong queen, a warrior queen. Her name has always been there, waiting for you to claim it. And now you *will* claim it and repay all those who have helped you."

"I will see Fyren defeated," I said. "Kendra said I must be there, and so I will be. But *I* cannot be queen."

"This is not about you!" His face twisted. "Your duty is to Deor, your kingdom. That's not just an idea." He waved his long arm at the resting boy. "It is Piers. It's Kenway. Devona. Kendra, Ingen, Maren. Can you not see that?"

Glancing at Piers, lying in the corner, I thought of his mother's death, his father's disappearance. And then, of Kenway's guilt over not helping his sisters, his father. Of Eldred, having no life but this. Of Kendra's loss. Of Maren's face as they carried her out of the dungeon. Of Ingen and what she might sacrifice if I would not claim the throne.

I saw my own selfishness. *Shouldn't I be willing to sacrifice, too?*

"We are disconnected from nature and from each other," said Eldred. "Because of the king's death and Erce's grief. Through you, we can reconnect. Our spirits flow to you, Audrey. You are the collector, pulling in the essence of who we are, joining us together, making us more powerful. Can't you feel us?"

"I only feel your weakness," I whispered, pressing the gown to my cheek.

And then I realized why that was. It was Erce. It was her sadness. Her grief was affecting us all.

"Pain sometimes prevents us from finding our strength," said Eldred. "Let us in. Fight us no longer. Accept your fate. You will see. Our strength will awaken what has died and will make Fyren reap the whirlwind."

Let them in. Breathe in. It was what Erce told me to do. What Ingen had been trying to tell me.

Could I bear it? I remembered the pain I'd felt as I'd moved among the slain in Erce. I trembled to think of bearing the weight of all of the souls of Deor. But didn't they deserve a ruler who would be willing to take that risk for them? Wouldn't my father have done it?

"I don't understand," Kenway said to Eldred. "What whirlwind?"

"For they have sown the wind, they shall reap the whirlwind. It will all come back on Fyren. He cannot escape his own wickedness."

I closed my eyes.

"Do not fear, Your Grace."

My eyes flew open. It startled me to hear Eldred call me that.

"When you stand before him, think of us. Your people. Embrace us. Together, we will see him defeat himself."

I nodded. "Yes."

"You must hurry."

Chapter Thirty-Seven

Kenway held his sword in one hand and Eldred's dagger in the other. We had taken a secret tunnel underneath the castle and the wall. Now we stood outside the door that would lead us to Fyren.

I wore my mother's silk dress. In rich green, Eldred had said, nobles and peasants alike would know me as their queen.

The coronation was being held in the Prince's House, just outside the inner wall. It had three balconies: a single tall one, about thirty feet off the ground, flanked by two shorter ones. Thrice before, I had sat at the queen's feet while she watched jousting in the lists below.

Festivals were held more frequently during my father's time. But because of fear for the queen's life, tournaments were not held often anymore.

Most of the lords and ladies would be on the lower balconies, with Fyren on his throne at the top, close to the edge of the wall, so he could see the tournament and the people could see him crowned.

I remembered that it was a long drop. Only a short wall — perhaps two feet tall — stood between the royal spectators and the ground.

The other door onto the balcony would be heavily guarded. This one Eldred had kept hidden for his own purposes, maybe even for this moment.

Kenway looked noble, despite his dirty, torn tunic. He gripped the rusty sword in one hand and flipped the dagger handle over and over in the other. His look was fierce. We locked eyes.

"Bolt the other door when I attack the guard," he ordered.

"Yes."

"Remember what Eldred said to you."

I remembered what he said, but how could I tell Kenway I thought it a foolhardy plan? It required a faith in others and in my own fate. I didn't know if I could do what they expected of me. They were so *certain*. I wanted to have that certainty.

"Trust us, Audrey," said Kenway, as if he knew my mind.

I was seized by a sudden panic. "You must be careful."

Fear showed in his eyes, but he was resolute. We both thought he was to die.

"Audrey."

I stared back at him. Then I realized it was fear for me in his eyes.

"*You* must be careful," he told me.

I flicked my eyes to the door, thinking of what might lay behind it, and then back at him.

He shrugged a little, smiling. I did not break my gaze. *Not yet, not yet*, I thought. *Let me look at you.*

He gave me a nod. "It is time." He pushed open the door.

A guard stood not two feet from us, but he did not hear us. The crowd roared and cheered at the riders in the joust. Only one lord and his lady were on the balcony. It was Lord Llewyn, the large man with hands like paws. They stood behind Fyren, who was sitting crownless on my father's throne. He was not king yet.

A petite woman sat in a smaller chair beside him, with her white hand resting on his shoulder. I could not believe my eyes. It was Fay, the queen's lady.

Geoff was the only other guard. He was leaning over the side to watch the joust. The rapid *thump-thump* of the horses' hooves could be heard as the knights below, lances ready, raced toward each other.

Kenway plunged the dagger into the guard's back and pulled it back out. I remembered the horror of Eldred being stabbed. The guard screamed as his blood flowed. He gripped his back, arching it, then he crumpled at Kenway's feet.

Geoff turned when he heard the cry. I ran to bolt the door.

Geoff charged Kenway. Metal clanged against metal as they fought. The ladies skittered back toward the short front wall. Fyren stared at me with surprise. He was frozen in his shock. My father's murderer. He was used to secret killings.

Lord Llewyn stepped forward when he saw me as if he thought I was someone else. He had never looked at me once when I was Shadow.

Geoff had backed Kenway into a corner. He lunged, but was too slow. Kenway knocked down Geoff's blade with his sword, then reached in and stabbed him with the dagger. Geoff backed away, his hands on Kenway's knife, and fell to the stone floor. I reached down and grabbed Geoff's sword. It felt odd in my hand.

Guards banged on the bolted door.

Fyren slid out a dagger from a leather belt on his ankle, his sword already out. Kenway moved toward him. The ladies tiptoed closer to the edge, staring down. I had never seen Fay look so frightened.

"I'll kill you, Lord Llewyn, if you interfere," said Kenway. "I swear it."

I pointed the sword at the old lord. I wondered if I could kill if I needed to.

He looked at me, his face full of wonder. "This girl looks exactly like our dead Queen Anne."

"She's the daughter of Anne and King Alfrid."

Fyren stared at me, startled. "She is Shadow! She is nothing!"

Although he no longer wore a beard, Fyren looked no less sinister. How had I ever thought him kind? He now worked himself between the throne and the short balcony wall. He was not more than two feet from the edge.

The crowd yelled when they saw him. Guards were trying to climb up from the lower balconies, but the walls were too high. They helped one another up.

"She's the rightful heir, Fyren," said Kenway. "You did not murder the queen. You poisoned Kendra's child, who had been switched with Audrey for her protection."

I looked at Fay. She had a hand in it somehow. She gave me that sly smile. She thought Fyren was going to triumph here.

With a strong kick, Kenway knocked over the throne. Fyren dodged it.

Fyren leaped forward. His blade sliced the air just in front of Kenway's face. Kenway jumped back. Down came Fyren's sword again, but Kenway met it with his own. The blades slid off each other.

"You're a coward, Kenway, just like your father," yelled Fyren, his voice carrying down to the lords and ladies on the balcony below. "I always thought it was Lord Leofwine who murdered our great king." He spread his hands out, leaving himself vulnerable, as if he doubted Kenway's skill. "And now his son tries to kill me. Your family must covet the crown for itself."

Kenway lunged toward Fyren, his sword extended. Fyren brought his own down upon it.

Clink.

Clink.

Clink.

It was as if their swords were in a fierce dance.

They were close to the wall now, Fyren near the edge.

Kenway was breathing hard. His left shoulder drooped as he fought. His wound had not yet healed. Fyren must have seen it. He feinted. Kenway moved in the wrong direction. Fyren stabbed him in his old wound.

"No!" I screamed.

Kenway groaned and dropped his sword. I ran toward him, but Fyren came at me. I put up my sword, ready to fight, and heard laughter from down below.

Fyren smirked. "You always were a clever girl, Shadow, but you have overreached."

Kenway was holding his arm. He tried to stand.

"You do look like your mother," Fyren said in a low voice. "I'm surprised I never saw it. She never trusted me, that witch." He looked at me almost tenderly. "You liked me, though. As your father did. You should have seen his eyes when I killed him."

He came at me, his dagger's sharp tip all I saw.

I heard Kenway yell my name. I heard Eldred's voice inside my head. *When you stand before him, think of us. Let us in.*

Let them in, let them in. Time stretched out.

I thought of Kenway and felt his loyalty inside me, like it was my own, and of Piers and his fierce heart, and that was in me, too, and then of Eldred and his wisdom, and of Kendra and her quest for justice, and Ingen and her strong faith.

I thought of my murdered father. I felt his strength.

Mostly, I thought of my mother, dying as I took my first breath. I told her I would leave my anger behind, that she must leave her grief behind and come to me, to us. We all called to her.

My body tingled. I dropped the sword. I didn't need it.

I braced myself, but felt no pain when he hit me. I was protected by a cushion of sweet, soft air. *Erce. She is here.* Fyren bounced back, falling toward the edge of the wall, reaching for me. Instinctively, I put out my hand. He grasped my fingers, a wicked grin upon his face. A whirl of wind took him up, yanking his grip from mine. He fell backward, his dagger clanking down onto the stone. Tripping over the short wall, he plunged to the ground below.

I heard screams and shouts from the crowd. Fyren had been there in front of me and now he was gone.

I crept up to the side and looked over the edge.

Fyren's body was splayed on the ground. An ugly sight.

His blade hadn't pierced me. With the strength of the kingdom in me, he could do no harm. Erce had protected me. That was why the crowd had to see it, so they would believe.

I heard their voices. Peasants. Knights. Ladies.

Did you see it? It was a wild wind that took him down. Who is she? She looks like our dead Queen Anne, wearing her favorite green, the color of a kingdom once fertile. It was Erce. She was the wind. She protected the girl.

Lord Llewyn bowed down. "You look exactly like your mother, Your Grace. Why did I not see it before?"

Fay fell to her knees, holding her shaking fingers to her lips.

"It is the true queen," Lord Llewyn said to the lords and ladies below. "Queen Anne's daughter. Do you not see?"

I heard the chanting begin. I went to Kenway, who struggled to sit up.

"Lie still," I said.

He dropped back to the stone floor.

"Get someone to help," I ordered Fay. "Now."

"Yes, Your Grace," she said, hurrying to the bolted door.

I put my hand on Kenway's arm, listening to the people below, my people.

"Our queen. Long live our queen."

Or was it Erce's voice I heard?

Chapter Thirty-Eight

I stood at Devona's window.

Behind me, Kenway rested in a comfortable chair, out of bed for the first time in five days. He was still weak from the loss of blood, but much improved.

The ladies of the court had whispered behind white hands about the strangeness of my request. No, not request: my command.

Yes, it is the best room, the warmest, the one with the brightest light. But, still, they murmured to one another, what is she thinking? Putting him in the room of the queen who was not a queen and had tormented her so?

They feared Devona's ghost and thought the past could be locked away with a heavy door and a key. But Devona wasn't here. Only sorrow and fear and wild imaginings could keep her here. We would have none of that.

I'd discovered that life's pain must be folded into its sweetness, and that the soul would remember the sweetness, if we let it.

Like our memories of Devona, and of Fyren and his apples. Had not my own mother come to me in the sweetness of the apple, carried to me by my father's killer? Should I forget the one — the sweetness — because of the pain?

Love is worth it, Kenway had assured me. He'd been right. We could bear much, if we had the strength. I knew I had the strength.

Erce had given me that. She had taken her time about it. But, now, the cares of the people pulsed through me to her and back to us again. Like breath in and out.

Nature's green fingers pushed out of the newly fertile soil, covering the fields with hope. Empty stomachs rumbled, but they would soon be filled. We would recover. Just as Kenway would recover.

I turned from the warm breeze to look at him. His head rested against the back of the chair, and his eyes were closed. He was so still. His pale face made him look closer to the grave than to the altar.

"Queen Audrey," said Eldred, who stood behind me. He was ever at my side these days.

"Yes?" I asked, my eyes still on the patient.

It seemed that Eldred had wanted Kenway to marry me all along. I would need a loyal prince at my side, he said. I wondered if Kenway would refuse.

Eldred sighed. "A country needs an army, Your Grace." He was returning to a disagreement I thought we had put aside two days ago.

"Not the army we have. Send those home whom we have forced into conscription. Let us build an army of willing soldiers."

He nodded, with tight lips. Not pleased.

"Have you found Stillman or Piers's father?" I asked.

"Not yet."

"It must be done, Eldred."

"Yes, yes. We will keep looking."

Piers was usually on Eldred's heels, although this morning I had heard his shouts in the royal yard. From my perch at the window, I had spied him running from Cook, a large crème pie in his hands.

"And Kendra? Will she forgive and come back to live with us?"

"She has no wish to do so."

I thought of her in her windblown hut by the ocean and

felt a pang of envy. To be there, free of all these concerns, tugged at me. But a solitary life was not to be my fate, not the life I was given.

"But you will bring Ingen to me," I said. "And Tayte and her sons."

"As I said I would," Eldred replied, "Your Grace."

"We must introduce the people to Erce," I told him.

"Yes, but not too quickly," he said. "People are slow to believe."

I nodded. "Especially those in the south, who fancy themselves above faith." I sat beside Kenway. Our chairs faced the window. "Eldred, leave us, if you would."

Eldred seemed about to speak, but said nothing. His robes swished as he left the room. I knew Deor was fortunate to have such a man to advise their novice queen. It had surprised me how quickly he and I had fallen into our roles of counselor and ruler.

I put my hand on the arm of Kenway's chair, not touching him.

The first three days, he rarely spoke. Then, just yesterday morning, suddenly lucid, he had asked about his father. I had been in a chair beside his bed, reading another report by one of our spies, who had news about our enemies to the west, the Torsans. As I read, I worried. Deor had more troubles before her.

But I'd been glad to put these worries aside when Kenway had spoken. I'd propped him on a pillow and given him sips of water, back to nursing him as I had in Stillman's hut. I reassured him that his family was safe. They would be here as soon as his father recovered from the head cold he'd caught while imprisoned in his own dungeon.

And now, on this day, as I studied Kenway's face, I thought of how well I knew him and how much I didn't know. His feelings flowed through me, but were lost in the jumble of the hopes and fears of others. I barely felt that great wave of the people's emotions any more. Now, it was a gentle ripple across my heart.

His eyelids flickered and flickered. He awoke, looking at me silently.

"You are awake," I said.

"You are here." He took my hand.

I twisted the gold ring on his finger, remembering Devona doing the same.

"My mother gave me this," he said. "It was my father's."

"It is a simple design," I said, "not much like him."

"It was how he used to be. My mother told me this," he said, looking at me, "after she died."

I paused. "After?"

"She appeared to me many times, after her death, when I was just a child," he said. "Every time I was alone, she would be there, sad and reaching out for me."

I could not help but shiver. "Your ghost?" I whispered.

He nodded. "I didn't understand it. She'd been such a strong presence in my life before her death, so filled with caring. But then she was haunting me. And I didn't know what I had done to provoke it in her."

I waited, knowing this was something he had not revealed to anyone before.

"But now," he continued, "after seeing Ete, Tayte, Kendra, Erce . . . and how they love their children, I think I understand. My mother didn't want to let me go. Her love was so strong, her spirit could not leave me."

I nodded. "I see that."

Finally, he closed his eyes. Thinking he was sleeping, I stood, but his fingers found mine.

"Stay with me," he said.

"All right, but Eldred will return soon." I sat back down. "He's teaching me. There's much to know."

"There are things I can teach you."

"What things?"

"You are King Alfrid's daughter," he said. "You must hold a sword like a ruler, not like a woman."

"You try to provoke me."

"I am returning the favor, if you will remember."

He reached for me, putting his hand behind my neck and pulling me toward him. There was a question in his eyes. At that moment, we were not shadow and knight, or knight and queen. We were the same and together, joined in the space between, and that space stretched before us.

I put my hand on his cheek and leaned in for our most perfect kiss, yet.

Acknowledgments

Much thanks to:

my agent Nancy Gallt for pulling Shadow *out of slush and beginning things and letting me say "Really? Really?" a bazillion times when she called to tell me the news*

awesome editor (and author) Lisa Ann Sandell, who edits and writes beautifully, and to the committed-to-books Scholastic team

the many people who read Shadow *prepublication: Sally Barringer, Megan Crewe, Joyce Harlow, Mary Ann Hellinghausen, David McKissack, Melissa Marr, Jackson Pearce, Bettina Restrepo, Christine Suffredini, and John Suffredini my friends, online and off: the Debs; the Taylor Lake Village gang, especially Malise Fletcher, Lynda Gavin, Natalie O'Neill, and Nancy Stansfield; LJ'rs; Blueboarders; the St. Paul community, especially Heidi Clark, Norma Dempsey, and Sharon Reed; and the SCBWI-Houston folks, especially the Yellow House Writers*

belatedly, my lovely niece Miss Lilly Lauck

John and Christine, always and always and always